# A GIRL
# NAMED
# GHOST

*A Psychological Thriller by*
## S.R. WEBSTER

A GIRL NAMED GHOST

**First edition. August 1, 2024.**

Copyright © 2024 S.R. Webster.

ISBN: 979-8991163903

Written by S.R. Webster.

# Table of Contents

For the fearless, boundless storytellers and their devoted readers who devour every word with ravenous hunger.

# Chapter One

## Ghost

The private road leading up to Grandma June's was narrow and winding. Flanked by overgrown vegetation and with no sidewalk or shoulder to walk along, it was not a safe place to wander about. So when I saw a figure dart into the tree line and force its way through a cluster of tangled vines—I knew it was *him*. I had seen the man in the black fedora with the white rose enough in recent days to know he was the one lurking in the woods around Willow Lake.

When the impressive Victorian house came into view, an unfamiliar dread fell upon my shoulders. Returning to my childhood home had never been an issue before. I loved the house where I grew up, even if it looked like something out of a horror movie. And I loved my Grandma June. Bold, feisty, and weird—in all the best ways. There had never been a time when I needed any family other than her.

After parking in one of the designated spots at the end of the stone walkway, I stepped out of the car and rolled my aching shoulders. A gust of wind grabbed my hair, whipping it across my face, temporarily obstructing the view. I hesitated to pull my hair aside. Did I really want to glimpse the hatted man peering out from behind my grandmother's velvet drapes?

I had to remind myself that this was a safe space. It would always be my home. There was no reason to be afraid. I shoved my hair away and forced myself to look up.

In its heyday, the lakeside house had been vibrant and welcoming. A shining star of the Maryland Historical Society, with its steep gabled roofs, decorative woodwork, and tower accented by stained-glass windows. My grandmother had the exterior repainted after my grandfather's death and before I was born. Shades of gray and black purposely transformed the house into a "people deterrent." All that was missing—a silhouette of a mummy in an upstairs window and a flashing vacancy sign in the front yard.

"Was traffic *that* bad?" Grandma June shouted from behind the screen door. Because what other reason would I have to stand and stretch beside my car instead of coming directly inside?

"It's always bad this time of day," I said and went to retrieve the grocery bags from the back of my Infiniti.

"Did you get everything on the list?" Grandma June asked, opening the screen door as I stepped onto the wraparound porch.

Thursday evenings were our weekly dinner and my organic grocery delivery. Not because my grandmother needed it, but because she basked in the attention. Dinner and a glass or two of wine meant a sleepover. Grandma June preferred those visits, so I always packed an overnight bag.

"Everything except for the dirty chocolate herbal tea." I placed a kiss on her cheek and entered the house.

Two words described my grandmother's choice of interior design: ornamental and expensive. Walking into Grandma June's was like being transported to an extravagant antique store, minus the smell of mildew. Though I knew the only things holding up her priceless works of art were a few rusty nails.

"Darn, I haven't been able to find that tea for months," Grandma June said.

"Have you tried ordering it online?"

"Every site I've been on claims to be out of stock."

"Guess there's an ongoing shortage."

"Nah, I bet some nitwit's hoarding it. Probably Mrs. Duncan over on Kilmer Street. She's the type, you know."

I smiled and shook my head. "No, I don't know."

According to Grandma June, someone somewhere was always plotting mayhem. And once my grandmother got it in her head that *they* were up to no good, there was no convincing her otherwise. "Have you had chocolate tea at her house before?" I asked.

"She's too stingy to offer, but I bet it's her all the same."

Grandma June followed me through the lower level to the kitchen and immediately dove into the grocery bags when I placed them on the granite countertop. The industrial-sized, stainless-steel appliances looked small in the enormous kitchen. Dark quarter-sawn cabinetry was the only feature in this room that revealed the home's actual age. Everything else was modern—shiny and new.

As Grandma June unpacked and inspected groceries, I considered excusing myself to the den to watch the news. Or maybe to go out for a walk around the lake—anything to give us some distance. It would not take long for my grandmother to notice something was bothering me. The longer we were together, the harder it would be to hide the anxiety stewing in my gut.

My need to ask the forbidden question caused the acid in my stomach to rise, while apprehension heated it to a boil. How long would it take for the turmoil to burn a hole through my insides?

In the end, I dropped my overnight bag on the floor and headed for the wine rack in the dining room.

When I returned and set a glass of overpriced cabernet in front of Grandma June, she crossed her arms and leaned against the kitchen counter. For the first time, I noticed she was wearing her favorite blue dress. The one I had picked up at a thrift store years ago for a Halloween costume. The one she confiscated because she said it made her look like Janet Leigh.

"Gigi, it's a little early for wine," she said. "I haven't even put the steaks on yet."

I took a healthy sip from my glass. Today I found it more annoying than usual that my grandmother refused to call me by my given name. Instead, she used the initials of my first and middle names to create something she believed to be more suitable. She also preferred to treat me like a child instead of a twenty-six-year-old adult.

"It's never too early for wine, Gi Ju."

My grandmother sighed before lifting her glass to red-painted lips. She hated it when I referred to her as Gi Ju instead of Grandma June, or even Juniper, in the same way I loathed her use of the nickname Gigi. Unlike her, the oddity of my name—Ghost Grace White—pleased me. After all, it was the only way to honor the mother who had given me life, a name, and nothing else.

"And for the millionth time, call me Ghost."

Grandma June's hands visibly shook as she placed her glass back on the counter without taking a drink. "I will not." With a disgruntled huff, she disappeared into her custom-designed pantry.

Her hatred of my name was one of life's many obscurities.

It was not until kindergarten that I even learned my real name. A teacher's honest mistake when placing name tags on assigned desks had created the first big uproar in my life and resulted in my first argument with my grandmother. After that, I insisted on being called Ghost. Everyone obliged except Grandma June. She had warned me that the use of my legal name would cause me pain. She was right. There was no shortage of cruelty in children, and even in some adults. But I stuck it out and, over time, derived pleasure from the shock people exuded when I told them the reason for my name.

Who else can say they died on the day they were born?

I was about to pour a second glass of wine when my grandmother reappeared, arms laden with bread, potatoes, onions, and a jar of pickled beets.

"Let us enjoy a nice dinner this evening. No talk of sad things. Tell me more about that guy at work. Bishop, is that his name? It's been so long since you've been out on a date."

I watched Grandma June as she began preparing our meal, knowing full well that the conversation we were about to have would not be pleasant. For either of us.

How could I break the heart of the woman who had wiped my tears, kissed my boo-boos, and supported me in every aspect of my life?

How do I tell her that she is no longer enough?

# Chapter Two

## Juniper

Juniper White tried her best to focus on making Thursday night dinner. Her granddaughter's latest love interest was the only topic she could think of to lighten the gloomy mood descending on her otherwise fabulous home.

"Did I get that right? Is his name Bishop?" Juniper asked again, grabbing a chef's knife and a large Vidalia onion.

"Yeah."

*Chop. Chop. Chop.*

"Is he good-looking?"

*Clink.*

"Very."

*Chop. Chop. Chop.*

"Well, do you like him?"

"Mm-hmm..." The sound of slurping muffled Gigi's response.

*Clink.*

Realizing she would not get more than a one-word answer or some other noncommittal sound, Juniper let the conversation drop. But every time she heard the *clink* of Gigi's glass on the kitchen table, she turned to see how much wine remained in the bottle. This unwanted distraction led to Juniper nearly chopping off the tip of her finger, twice.

The pinched look on Gigi's face was cause for concern, as there appeared to be more to her dismay than a prickly mood or that Juniper still refused to call her by her full name. She really wished her granddaughter would let that old argument go. There was nothing wrong with the name Gigi. It was a fine name—a name that made sense! Juniper never understood why Gigi willingly tortured herself with the use of *that* name.

The way her granddaughter was drowning her sorrows in a pricey bottle of Silver Oak meant there was something darker and more pressing on Gigi's mind, though there was not much for her to be upset about. Gigi was gorgeous. Blonde and thin. A younger, prettier image of Juniper. Wherever Gigi went, men flocked, though she always kept them at arm's length. Which only confirmed how smart the girl was—and independent, too. Almost to a fault, in Juniper's opinion, with her corporate job and recent purchase of a luxury townhouse. More importantly, she was rich. They both were, thanks to Juniper's late husband, Henry White, who had been rolling in old family money at the time of his unfortunate accident.

*May God rest his soul in peace.*

The next time Juniper turned her head, Gigi was emptying the rest of the wine into her glass—a distraction that caused Juniper to embed the knife's sharp blade into her middle fingernail, ruining a perfect gel manicure. Juniper set the knife aside and dumped the finely diced onions into the oiled pan heating on the stove. Reaching for a potato to peel, she noticed a tear inching down Gigi's pale cheek. It was not like her granddaughter had been the one chopping the onions.

Juniper could no longer ignore the storm brewing at her kitchen table. She grabbed the glass of wine that Gigi had poured for her and placed it in front of her granddaughter.

"Deary, why don't we talk about it?"

"I'm not sure I can." Gigi's voice trembled. Before she had even finished draining the contents from her glass, she grasped the wine Juniper had offered with her free hand.

"You need to try, because I cannot have you sitting here crying at my kitchen table for no good reason. I've been looking forward to our dinner all week."

"I'm sorry," Gigi said, knuckling a stray tear away. "I don't want to spoil our dinner."

They sat in silence while Gigi gazed out of the bow window over the kitchen sink. The sun had set, so there was little to see on the dark lake. Then, without warning, Gigi shot up from the table, snatched her overnight bag from where she had dropped it earlier, and headed for the main staircase. As a last-minute courtesy, or so Juniper suspected, Gigi yelled down from the first landing, "I'm gonna wash this funk away. Be back in a sec."

Juniper picked up the glass of wine Gigi had abandoned and drank it in a single gulp. She had never seen her granddaughter so untethered. Gigi was all about order and control. She did not get rattled. And she certainly never cried.

MORE THAN AN HOUR HAD passed, and there was still no sign of Gigi. Their Thursday night meal—steak tenderloin with grilled onion, fried potatoes, pickled beets, and fresh bread—had been skillfully prepared, but only a single portion had been consumed.

Juniper hated eating alone. She had just placed a plate of leftovers in the refrigerator when she turned and nearly bumped into her granddaughter, who had emerged out of thin air like an apparition. Juniper cursed under her breath as she clutched her chest. "Goodness, Gigi! I'm too old to be snuck up on."

"Sorry, Grandma, I didn't mean to scare you." When Gigi looked down at the floor, Juniper knew it was not out of shame but to hide the smile pulling at the corners of her granddaughter's mouth. There was no cure for a devious child. Juniper had experienced enough "surprises" over the years to know that Gigi did not mind shocking people. If not by words, then by actions.

"No harm done, deary. Are you hungry?" Juniper said, reaching back into the refrigerator to retrieve the dinner plate.

"Starving." Gigi eyed the empty wineglasses on the table and then wisely poured herself a glass of tap water.

"Well, sit down. I'll warm up your dinner and make you a nice cup of tea."

Gigi wrinkled her nose at the mention of tea and pulled her wet, blonde hair into a ponytail. "Thanks. Are you gonna tell me a bedtime story, too?"

"Don't be a smartass." Juniper knew "smartass" was Gigi's default reaction to kindness.

"Grandma June, I really am sorry about earlier. It's been a rough day."

"Don't fret, deary. We all have them."

Juniper knew Gigi needed something to help her relax and take her mind off her problems. As a loving grandmother, she had just the thing. A unique brew of herbal tea she had developed over the years would ease her granddaughter's worries and give her the best night of sleep.

All she had to do was get Gigi to drink it.

# Chapter Three

## Ghost

"Time for some kinship care!" Grandma June announced as she approached the kitchen table with a steaming cup of tea.

The *kinship care* references started about ten years ago. My grandmother had sat me down one morning and read aloud an article from the National Institute of Health. A research study was conducted on the increasing number of grandparents caring for children. At the time, about two percent of US children were being raised by a grandparent.

They had even coined a term for it.

I will never forget the belly laugh that exploded from Grandma June the first time she said the words *kinship care*. Or how she nearly spat her coffee across the kitchen table.

"What a ridiculous name for such a wholesome, selfless act! *Kinship care* sounds so sterile and unfeeling. No matter who does the raising, family is love. And love is all a family ever needs!"

She was still chuckling under her breath, but as she continued to read, her laughter stopped. The research said that children raised by their grandparents were more prone to behavioral and emotional disturbances. When she got to the part about how those children were also more likely to be diagnosed with a psychological disorder, she balled the paper up and tossed it in the garbage.

We never discussed the article's implications because we did not need another odd stacked against us. Instead, my grandmother made jokes about the term she had deemed insulting and irrelevant, though I never found her condescension very amusing.

The cup of tea Grandma June placed on the table smelled *off.* Floral with a pungent dose of something I could only describe as metallic. She loved her strange organic brews. Swore they possessed restorative powers. Claimed that for every ailment, there was a tea mixture that could help remedy it. Not only did I not share my grandmother's strong belief in herbal healing, but I also had a solid aversion to drinking hot liquids—no coffee, no hot chocolate, and definitely not one of her steaming witch doctor cocktails.

"Grandma, you know I don't like tea."

The bottle of wine I downed had failed to encourage me to the vital task, and the lengthy shower upstairs had done little to wash away my fear. So, I ate my lukewarm dinner and avoided the cup of tea that Grandma June continued to push closer to me.

"It's not about the taste. It's about the benefits you receive from drinking it. This will relax you so you can get a good, solid night of sleep." Grandma June brandished one of her signature smirks—partially lopsided and completely smug.

"I had nearly a full bottle of cabernet, and now I'm having the scrumptious meal you cooked. I will sleep like a baby tonight," I said, knowing two of those things were untrue.

"But you'll be wide awake in a few hours once the sugar kicks in," she said with a slight shake of her head.

Grandma June was right. She usually was. Restful sleep and alcohol were never a good mix. But that did not mean I would drink her stinky tea.

Yesterday, I hit an impenetrable wall. After making the three-hour drive to Glen Haven Psychiatric Hospital, hoping to visit my mother for the first time, I discovered that Grandma June had obtained adult guardianship over her daughter. Without my grandmother's permission, I would never be allowed inside to see the one person who I knew could help me. The staff assured me, many times, that there was no getting around it.

"Any chance you're ready to tell me what's going on with you?" Grandma June asked, sliding the teacup over until it hit the edge of my plate.

The only way to get her to stop bugging me about the drink, or to get any sleep tonight, was to open Pandora's box. Rip off the Band-Aid and inflict a new wound. I did not want to hurt my grandmother, but I knew there was no other way.

I opened my mouth, prepared to say the words, and then shoveled in another piece of steak.

"You know you can talk to me about anything."

I chewed that piece of meat for a full minute before finally swallowing, then blurted out, "It's time, Grandma. I have to see her."

"What?" Grandma June asked with a tilt of her head as confusion appeared to set in. "See who?"

I saw a flash of terror in her eyes when she realized exactly what I was asking. "Oh no!" Grandma June stood up, her face pale, body trembling.

Lately, any talk of her daughter had become a painful, almost debilitating topic, which was why I had tried to take care of it on my own.

Emotions stole my voice. I had to cough to clear my throat. "I want to meet my mother."

"No, no. No!" Grandma June moved around the table to stand next to my chair and stomped her foot. "It's too dangerous. For you and for her."

I looked up at the ceiling, attempting to hold back tears. "Why?" I croaked. It was a stupid question. I already knew why.

She snatched the teacup off the table, spilling some of the contents onto the hardwood floor. "Have you forgotten that she tried to kill you?"

"Of course I haven't forgotten." How could anyone forget something like that? Though technically, I had no memory of my mother trying to strangle me as an infant. I only knew the story my grandmother told me.

"Then I don't understand why you're asking to do such a thing!" she said, downing the tea in one noisy gulp.

"I can't explain it, Grandma. But it's something I have to do. You have to trust me. I need you to say yes."

Only she did not. Grandma June took that delicate rose-painted teacup and smashed it into the cast-iron sink. Then she turned to me with a pained look and fresh venom on her lips.

"No, I will not have it! Not now, not ever. I love you too much."

My defeat was accompanied by pieces of ceramic scraping against metal as Grandma June cleaned up the mess she had made.

# Chapter Four

## Ghost

The slam of a bathroom door ended another conversation turned argument. A turn of the lock meant there would be no more said about it. Not the best way to start a Friday.

"Gigi, grab a coat!" Grandma June cried out from behind the door as I tried to slip past undetected.

"Thanks, Gi Ju," I yelled back, leaving my spare coat.

When I stepped outside of the lakeside house, a blast of frosty autumn air made me regret leaving the coat behind. If I had not been so aggravated, I would have gone back inside for that stupid coat. But the last thing I needed early in the morning was another "I told you so." An image of my grandmother rattling her head about with her all-knowing smirk was already permanently etched into my brain. Grandma June's way was the right way. The only way. I had lived by her version of the rules my entire childhood, and as promised, our life was a good one.

Slipping into the driver's seat, I started the car and turned the heat on high. It would take the engine a minute to warm up. The cold gust of air from the vents stung my already flushed cheeks. After last night's drama, Grandma June refused to talk. She said she felt sick and went upstairs to bed. This morning, I approached her from a new angle, though still not revealing the real reason for needing to see my mother, which, of course, ended in another failed attempt to get her to change her mind.

Grandma June went through phases when we could and could not talk about my mother. She always referred to her as "my

daughter" or "your mother," but she had not spoken *her* name aloud
in years. Every name had meaning, held power, so it always baffled
me that my grandmother never said either mine or my mother's
names.

I was almost eight, eavesdropping on a phone call, when I first
heard my mother's given name spoken.

"Meredith Jane." Those barely whispered words were swept away
by the air rushing through the car's vents.

I turned the fan down and drove away from my grandmother
and her creepy house, internally reciting my mother's name.
*Meredith Jane, Meredith Jane, Meredith Jane.* A mantra I often
repeated out of the fear of losing it. My grandmother told me there
was no benefit to knowing her name outside of health records. There
was no reason to hold it close. And yet I did, because I honestly
believed she was the only one who could help me.

At this hour, the traffic around Willow Lake was light. The
forty-five minutes it would take to get to the office allowed plenty of
time for reflection and, hopefully, new insight.

Over the years, I had collected many childhood stories of my
mother from Grandma June. In her youth, Meredith Jane had been a
popular, pretty girl with an abundance of friends. She also had more
than her fair share of childish drama: shoplifting from the dollar
store, egging the neighborhood bully's house, and graffiti in the girl's
locker room. Later, she had turned to darker, more sinister deeds.
Like the time Grandma June found her passed out in a circle of lit
candles with a bottle of stolen whiskey, or when she had to stop
Meredith from bludgeoning a chipmunk trapped in a shoebox. And
the terrible night my grandmother discovered her daughter dazed
and chanting nonsensical words in bloody bathwater.

That was my mother's first known suicide attempt.

The light on Kilmer Street turned yellow. A warning to stop,
but my foot did not reach the brake pedal in time. Both mind and

reflexes were muddled from a terrible night of sleep. My car barreled through the intersection as the signal turned red. An angry horn blew twice. I checked my side and rearview mirrors, saw no other vehicles, and dismissed the noise as imagined—an expected response to my reckless driving. I took the exit ramp to the highway.

Traffic on I-80 was starting to back up. Up ahead in the distance, I caught a glimpse of the pulsating blue-and-red lights of a police car...

By the age of thirteen, my mother had a lot of experience with law enforcement. Bouts of severe depression caused her behavior to decline rapidly. What once was considered typical teenage rebellion escalated into abnormally frightening episodes. Little white lies twisted into elaborate deceptions, crying fits became violent outbursts, and one by one, childhood friends transformed into mortal enemies. Medication and therapy helped to keep her quiet and complacent for a spell, but somehow she always found a way to relapse into mania. It probably did not help that each therapist she saw had a different diagnosis and corresponding medication: Hypothyroidism—Tirosint.                    Anxiety—Ativan. Depression—Lexapro.   Bipolar   disorder—carbamazepine.   And finally, schizophrenia—Clozaril.

The last analysis landed my mother in a secured wing at Glen Haven Psychiatric Hospital, where I had been told she spent most of her time alone in a padded room.

There were a multitude of medical textbooks with clinical terms and descriptions at my disposal. Infinite pages contained details on lengthy studies that led to significant scientific and medical findings. But I had not read a single one. I never thought I needed to. Besides, Grandma June had forbidden it. She could be overbearing at times, but I never went against her wishes. She had given me shelter, protection, and love when no one else could. And like Grandma

June said, those textbooks would not give you the same insight as experiencing the illness firsthand.

That morning, after going around and around on the subject of my mother, Grandma June told me it was too late. She had stood up and yelled it over the kitchen table. "Too much time has passed! There is no point in meeting her after all of these years."

I had heard similar speeches before and somehow always accepted her logic. But now I was not so sure. Things were getting more...*complicated*. And since I had been told my mother had no true concept of time, how could it ever be too late?

I used to wonder what it was like for my mother on the day they took her away—the confusion and terror of not being able to trust your mind. To have memories of your happiest and scariest moments and being told none of them were real. People talking next to you, then suddenly vanishing. Or had she been aware enough to understand what was happening?

And, of course, there was the trauma of an unplanned pregnancy. The story of my birth was both mystery and tragedy.

Cars on the highway were slowly crawling past the scene of a two-car fender bender. A young cop was speaking to a woman pointing angrily at two men. Suddenly one of the men, in a familiar double-breasted pinstriped suit and a black fedora with a white rose, locked eyes with me. I could not help but stare as I inched my car past the scene. This was the first time I had seen his face. Until now, I had only caught glimpses of him in the distance. He was a blip in my peripheral, a shadow in the fog. A shiver ripped through me when he tipped his hat and flashed a crooked grin. Then he turned his attention back to the irate woman with a dented bumper.

Once clear of the accident, I sped up to take the next exit. When I looked at the scene in my rearview mirror, the hatted man was gone. Only a police officer, the angry woman, and one other man remained.

*I do not care what Grandma June says. I* need *to see my mother.*

# Chapter Five

## Ghost

T*ap. Tap. Tap.*
    I jumped at the sound of someone rapping on my car window. I had arrived at work, parked, but left the engine running. The time on the dashboard read 8:03. I had been so tangled up in my troubles that I had made myself late for work.

Bishop Mazzeo had his face inches from the driver's side window, wielding a pair of dimples like a weapon. I gave him a stiff wave before switching off the ignition. The head of our IT department straightened and moved back as I stepped out of the car.

"Mornin', Ghost, everything okay?"

After years of casual comradery, the latest rumor around Mason, Kemper, and Witt Financial offices was that, much to the dismay of several female co-workers, Bishop had developed a crush on me. At first, I appreciated the extra attention, though there were times when I felt examined—like a bizarre fish in a pedestal tank. Of course, finding a nearly comatose co-worker in a running car might give some cause for concern.

"I'm fine, late night," I said, closing the car door and pressing the lock button on the key fob.

The corners of Bishop's generous mouth dropped. "Hot date?"

"Not unless you're into grandmothers."

Bishop had an intense laugh. "Yeah, if she looks anything like her granddaughter."

The gruff rumbling of his amusement brightened my ominous mood as a younger image of Grandma June popped into my head.

We looked alike in that we were both of average height with willowy frames and round, dark eyes. The only difference between her then and me now was the color of our hair. Hers had been golden blonde before it started turning gray. Whereas mine was such a pale blonde that it was almost white.

"Add a few wrinkles and about twenty pounds." I returned Bishop's smile and nudged his elbow. "I can make an introduction if you'd like."

"Here's my number. Make sure you give it to her." He winked and handed me a bent business card. Then we walked across the parking lot and into the five-story office building that housed the financial brokerage where we both worked.

Bishop and I parted ways when I swiped my ID card to activate the elevator. As I stepped inside and waited for the doors to shut, I watched him walk away. There was no denying his masculine physique or the allure he naturally exuded. He had the long stride of a purposeful man and wavy black hair that turned the heads of many envious females. I slipped his business card into the side pocket of my purse.

With everything I had going on, dating was the last thing I should contemplate. Yet, I continued to imagine what it would be like to hold hands with him across the table of a fancy restaurant, followed by a moonlit stroll through the park and a steamy kiss goodnight. I did not have a good track record when it came to dating. My romantic relationships always started with the promise of a love story, but usually turned into something of a nightmare.

Muzak's rendition of "Love Me Tender" sizzled through the elevator's malfunctioning speakers. A sadistic serenade while waiting for the clunky equipment to deliver me to the third floor. Time seemed to slow as the distorted static sounded less like musical instruments and more like garbled voices. Guitar strings screamed words of encouragement. *See her, meet her, learn from her.* A good reminder of where my focus needed to be. While the accompanying drums pounded out a rhythmic warning. *Stay clear, stay clear, go nowhere near.* An echo of my grandmother's sentiments.

Even pressing the heels of my hands against my ears did little to block out the constant wailing. Only the ding of the elevator doors opening released me from the audio assault.

Stress and sleep deprivation had a way of twisting one's perception.

After exiting the elevator, I went to my office, hoping my tardiness would go unnoticed. HR had never reprimanded me for being late, which happened more than I cared to admit. Mr. Sadler, my supervisor, was not a crazed clock-watcher like a couple of bosses from my past. It was my own neurosis that sparked nerves and caused my heart to race. Some days, the excitement of challenging the clock during a deadline was invigorating. Other days, like today, it caused a senseless surge of panic since nothing changed the fact that I was late.

Time was a curse and a gift. At some point, every person experiences a flip of the *time coin*. The curse happens when time steals a loved one away too soon. The gift appears when they live long enough to say goodbye.

Hope surged deep within my chest when I realized I wanted the gift of time with my mother. I had not yet said hello, so how could I ever say goodbye?

There had to be a way to convince Grandma June. Or maybe it was time to contact a family lawyer.

I signed onto my computer twenty minutes after eight and got to work answering emails and re-prioritizing my to-do list for the day. A few co-workers had walked by my open door with the usual morning salutations when Mr. Sadler arrived with a hefty financial file that needed immediate attention. Soon, the frazzled, disjointed thoughts faded as I focused on the tedious project. As an executive assistant for a financial broker, I had little time to dwell on life-amending quandaries.

A few hours later, I emerged from a pile of restructured spreadsheets and updated reports. With the correspondence on a final reconciliation sent to Mr. Sadler, it was time to stretch my legs. Usually, I took a lap or two around the third floor, hit the water cooler, and then the breakroom to participate in the daily small talk. But today, I found myself at the back stairwell door, punching in the access code and heading down to the first floor. I tried to tell myself that I was not stalking the hot IT guy who had paid me a little extra attention that morning. Except there I was, standing outside his office door, debating how to start a conversation that would lead to Bishop's face between my—

*Quack, quack, quack.*

The phone in my hand alerted me to a new text message.

*Thank God!* What had I been thinking? Temporary insanity due to a recent lack of sexual activity. I shook the raunchy images from my head. That was not like me. I did not objectify men or solicit them for midday trysts. Turning away from the IT department, I checked the text on my phone and headed back upstairs.

*Gi Ju: I'm sorry.*

I quickly typed a response to my grandmother.

*I'm sorry 2.*

When I started begging Grandma June to allow me to visit my mother in the psychiatric hospital, she pressed me for a better reason. My grandmother had always insisted that any meeting would be a mistake. She kept claiming that I could not miss what I had never known. She also worried about the risk of introducing myself to a life full of trauma, grief, and regret.

The only thing I told her was that I had been thinking about meeting the woman I had only heard stories about for some time. I felt like a part of me was missing, and she was the only one who could help me find it. Regardless of the consequences, it was something I knew I had to do.

I had not told her the whole truth, and of course, it was not enough to sway her decision. I felt like the worst person in the world when she cried out, "I've done my very best to be the mother you deserve."

*Gi Ju: I have something important to show you to help you better understand. Come back to the house. You'll see.*

Sometimes, Grandma June forgot what it was like to have a job and responsibilities. Normally, I did not mind that she relied on me more than was truly necessary. It was a blessing to still have her around with able mind and body. But not today. I was tired and distraught. I needed space.

I had reached the second landing in the stairwell when my phone *quacked* again.

*Gi Ju: Ghost, please. I've been keeping something from you.*

The phone nearly slipped from my fingers at the sight of my name—*Ghost!* To say I was shocked would be an understatement. Never, not once in my life, had she said my name aloud. How hard had it been for her to type it?

I had no clue what secret my grandmother was keeping. Until now, I was sure there were no secrets between us. She advertised herself to the world as an open book. Throughout the years, when I asked questions about my mother, she answered, though I had to time the inquiries perfectly. There were long stretches when she refused to speak of such things. But during the moments when she could, she would, no matter how painful and disturbing it might have been. Some of the stories she told were so devastating that I never doubted their integrity. I had believed her in all things, confident she held nothing back. So, why had she kept *this* hidden from me if it was so important? How long had Grandma June kept her secret: days, weeks, years?

Sitting down on the stairwell's second-floor landing, I closed my eyes. Five minutes of dark quiet should set me straight. And help me to find the right words to respond to my grandmother's text. Only no words emerged from the darkness. Instead, one of the most profoundly heartbreaking memories came forward.

As soon as I was old enough to make demands, I insisted Grandma June recount the night of my birth. I refused to go to sleep until she told me one more time. An indulgent, twisted bedtime story. Something that once fascinated me as a child was now the most unsettling event of my life.

It was the height of hurricane season in an understaffed county hospital during a flu outbreak. Ill-equipped by aging generators, the hospital's flickering power threatened to cast everyone into blinding darkness. The doctor, attending nurses, and my teenage mother were in a painful panic. A complicated, unsanctioned pregnancy followed by an increasingly complex delivery. Laboring over twelve difficult hours, my mother was crazed by raw agony. For everyone's safety, her wrists and ankles were secured to the bed rails, reducing her to a wild, spitting beast.

I arrived in the world about the time Grandma June raced into the delivery room, sweating and cursing the day. She had driven three hours from her lakeside home in a torrential downpour and gale-force winds to reach the facility. When the doctor pulled me from between my mother's bound legs, it was, as my grandmother described, the cherry topping on the horror-show cake of a day it had been. Skin a bluish-gray, head full of snowy white hair, both stained in red gore and a fleshy rope wrapped around my tiny neck. The sight of a lifeless baby was the only thing that registered with Meredith Jane. Grandma June said my mother's frantic screams stopped time. No one moved. No one spoke. Even the raging storm outside cowered in silence.

Despite being revived by doctors, my mother continued to believe I was dead. Much to the dismay of everyone, my mother had fervently insisted on naming her "deceased" child Ghost Grace White.

The other part of the story I had always wanted to hear, but my grandmother never told me, was who my father was. No one ever spoke of him, not even indirectly. In my naïve youth, I often contemplated how my parents met. If he had swept her off her feet like a knight in shining armor, or if they kept their relationship hidden like Romeo and Juliet. Because no one knew his side of the story, I created an imaginary father to fill that void so I could talk to him whenever I was down or upset. He was a kindhearted teenage boy with an infectious laugh. The only one who had looked past my mother's mental health diagnosis and saw the girl everyone wanted her to be. I always referred to him as Riggie. And he liked to call me his Lil Ghostie.

Of course, that was foolish. Later in life, I learned that their meeting had been violent and without consent. I did not like to think of myself as the product of rape, though it was the only possible scenario, since conception occurred after my teenage mother was institutionalized.

In the stairwell below, there was a squeak of a door opening, followed by the bang of it slamming shut. The sudden noise jolted me from my spot on the floor. Footsteps echoed loudly. I stood up and straightened my skirt as Bishop suddenly came into view. His head was down as he bounded up the stairs, taking them two at a time. Clearly, he was not anticipating someone standing in the middle of the landing. Rather than avoiding the collision I saw coming, I closed my eyes again and stepped directly into it.

A solid impact was made with flailing arms and legs and a shout of surprise from Bishop. I was fully prepared to be slammed against the back concrete wall. Or a bone-breaking descent to the floor before tumbling down a flight of stairs. Either one was perfectly acceptable. As a child, I could never get away with cutting or burning. Grandma June was too watchful. So, I became accident prone. Pain was a good distraction, easily managed. I needed the hurt to escape everything else, if only for a moment.

In another life, Bishop must have been a ninja. Somehow, he managed to stay on his feet, wrap me in a hug, and then turn in such a way that it slowed our fall. The debilitating crash I had been expecting was nothing more than a jarring knock into a side wall, with just enough force to steal my air and maybe leave a bruise.

I rested my head against his shoulder and focused on catching my breath.

"Holy shit!" Bishop relaxed his grip. "Ghost, I'm so sorry." Taking a step back, his eyes roamed down my body as he searched for signs of damage. "Are you hurt?"

An urgent need to disappear stripped the words from my mouth. I wanted to confess that it was my fault. Or lie and say that I should have been paying more attention. Instead, I shook my head while observing the scuff marks on his brown leather boots.

"Lose yourself again?" The softness of his voice forced me to look up. His hazel eyes bored into mine, searching for an answer. We stared long enough for his laugh lines to deepen and a frown to pull at the corners of his mouth.

I had to step away and give myself a little shake. "It hasn't been the best day." There was no point hiding what he had already witnessed.

Bishop placed an arm lightly around my shoulders. When I did not pull away, he tucked me into his side and escorted me up the stairs. "I have something that could make it a little better. How do you feel about live music?"

He smelled nice. Like fresh linen with a touch of something spicy. "Depends on the music."

"Alternative. Not the greatest, but the bass guitarist is *damn* good." Bishop sounded like he was *damn* proud of himself, too. I knew he played bass with the local band ProFusion. Flyers had been scattered around the breakroom for months, and occasionally, I would find one on my desk, not quite hidden under a stack of paperwork.

"Our first set is at nine, so can I pick you up at eight?" His hurried words were a sign of his nervous enthusiasm. I knew he had been gearing up to ask me out on a date for weeks. I did not want to disappoint him. I liked Bishop. If only the timing were better. *The freaking curse of time!*

"I don't know. Not sure I can handle two late nights in a row." Nine o'clock was not late, but there was a good chance I would not be able to stay awake through the band's first set, much less make it to their second one. The look of disappointment on his handsome face made me reconsider.

"Where are you playing? I will try to make an appearance."

# Chapter Six

## Juniper

Juniper's hands trembled as she placed the last sheet of paper on the dining room table. The entire wood surface was covered, corner to corner, multiple pages deep, with letters and drawings from her deranged daughter. Some letters had been addressed to her, while others were graphic hand-drawn images meant for her granddaughter.

Only Juniper had never allowed Gigi to see any of them.

By God, how she had hoped that her granddaughter would never know these letters existed. The plan had always been to burn them in the fire pit one night when Juniper was alone. Throughout the years, she had chosen dates of significance: birthdays, holidays, and anniversaries of the most tragic events in their lives. But she could never bring herself to do it. As much as Juniper wanted to, there was a sentimental, motherly side that would not relinquish the pages to flames. She had lost count of the number of times she had hauled the letters out of their hiding spot, only to return them a few hours later, unscathed.

Juniper had read and reread the disturbing letters in private for decades. The pages were wrinkled from repeated handling, the ink smudged from tears shed over the years. The harshly written words from a delusional, confused mind never failed to spark emotional turmoil. Some pages were not letters at all. They were sketches of gray-colored babies hanging from ropes with scratched-out eyes. Depictions of Gigi's close brush with death as a newborn. Those images were the hardest to look at.

Others were threats of physical harm that would come to Juniper and Gigi if some absurd demand was not met. Meredith had once threatened to stab a nurse in the eye if her daughter did not materialize with a scroll written in blood while wearing a yellow raincoat.

Everything about Meredith was frightening. A mother knows their child. Early on, Juniper knew her daughter was a danger to herself and, most assuredly, a threat to others. Even locked away, Meredith could be dangerous.

The history Juniper had shared with Gigi about her mother contained much of the truth, and none of it pleasant. But some details were far too disturbing to share with a child. Even so, her granddaughter had been fascinated by the stories of her mother. Juniper had feared that Gigi's interest would turn into an obsession that would eventually lead to her demanding to meet her mother in person.

When Gigi was fourteen, the team at Glen Haven had tried to unite them for a second time. It started with a phone call from a new doctor. He had surmised that a face-to-face between mother and child would relieve some of Meredith's more alarming misconceptions about her daughter. After an adamant refusal, Juniper petitioned to have the doctor removed from her daughter's medical team. The ambitious young man had not thoroughly read through Meredith's lengthy file. If he had, he would have known they had tried it already when Gigi was about three years old. A meeting that ended in disaster.

Her granddaughter might not remember how she got those scars on her back, but Juniper did. She knew all too well the trauma such an encounter would cause. Schizophrenia was genetic, and the chance of triggering an episode in Gigi was far too great a risk. Juniper had witnessed it with her daughter firsthand, and she refused to lose another child to the illness. Thankfully, her efforts had paid off, and the inexperienced new doctor was released from the medical team overseeing her daughter's care a month later.

Even though Gigi was mostly grown now, Juniper kept her from the worst of Meredith's delusions. Resurrection, demons, a devil's child, and some even darker, more sinister secrets that would remain locked away. But now that Gigi was insisting on meeting her mother, she knew these letters would be just the thing to dissuade her.

Circling the table, Juniper reached over to straighten a crooked letter and then smoothed down a creased corner on another. She checked the clock on the wall. It had been an hour since she had last texted Gigi again, asking her to return to the house. She would wait another thirty minutes for a reply before calling her directly.

In the meantime, she needed a distraction. A hot cup of tea would be nice, but that meant leaving the dining room. The letters had never been left out in the open before. It felt wrong to leave them exposed and accessible. What if something happened on the way into the kitchen? At her age, she could easily stumble, fall, and hit her head. Then, the whole world would know her shameful secrets.

The sound of someone knocking on the front door sent Juniper into a panic. She knew it was not Gigi. Her granddaughter had a key. Not once had she knocked before entering.

This was someone else. Someone who might get past her and see the full display of gruesome mania. Though she rarely saw solicitors these days. Maybe it was a brave kid selling candy. The aging gothic Victorian did not fit in with the recently renovated and newly constructed homes popping up around the lake. Her lovely house had been labeled "haunted" by the neighborhood children.

The insistent knocking grew louder, more urgent. Juniper inhaled deeply and slunk back into a dark corner. If they were nosy enough to peer in the window, the house would look empty. They had to go away if no one was home.

Heavy footsteps moved slowly from the door and along the squeaky wraparound porch, letting her know the interloper had gone to the windows. She had hoped they would leave her alone, but after a moment, they walked back to the door and began knocking again.

"Goddammit!" Juniper hissed as she quickly snatched an oversized throw blanket from a chair in the sitting room. Gently she laid it over the table, doing her best not to disturb the piles of letters and drawings. Even as she pulled, tucked, and adjusted the blanket, the knocking continued.

"What is it?" Juniper growled as she swung the front door open.

A pair of bulging green eyes doused Juniper's anger. It was not an intruder. Or some prankster kids sending their wimpy friend to her door on a dare. The man standing before her meant no harm. Daniel Garrett was a concerned friend. A friend that she had plans with this afternoon. A group was getting together to celebrate the birth of his third grandson. And she had entirely forgotten until she saw the look of shock on his chubby face.

"I-is everything okay?" Daniel stuttered as he tried to squash his apparent alarm.

Juniper reached out and gently tapped his arm. "Oh my, Dan. I am so sorry. Please excuse me. I was having a senior moment. Wait here. I will be just a second."

She headed back inside and paused at the sight of the blanketed table. She could see it now. The cover ripped away in grandiose fashion to reveal her worst nightmares, like an evil magician's trick. Except that would never happen. Dan would not come in uninvited. He was a gentleman that way. And it was four in the afternoon. If Gigi were to head over after work, which was highly unlikely now, she would not arrive until after six, and that was only if she did not stop by her own house first. She would need to change clothes or grab something to eat. There was plenty of time for Juniper to come home and prepare.

But just in case, she sent her granddaughter a text.

*Please don't be upset. Everything will make sense when we see each other. We need to talk but I forgot I have plans for dinner with friends. I will call you as soon as I get back.*

She waited as the animated bubbles popped under the message she had sent. The response was almost instantaneous.

*Gigi: Have a good time. Talk tomorrow.*

Semi-confident there was nothing to fear, Juniper slipped on a jacket and grabbed her purse. Knowing her granddaughter's stubborn temperament, she would likely make her wait until the weekend before coming over.

When Juniper opened the front door again, she met Daniel with a proper smile and greeting, then quickly turned around to lock the door behind her.

# Chapter Seven

# Ghost

It was a little after eight o'clock when I pulled into the crowded parking lot of a nearly vacant strip mall. The only business that remained open, other than Pal's Pizza, was the popular music venue, The Weather Box. Blacked-out windows were plastered with new and badly tattered band flyers. ProFusion posters were among the most noticeable. With their bright, twisting-melty colors, it looked like you were staring at a field of wildflowers while on an acid trip.

From my car, I watched as a line began to form at the club entrance.

I had tried to play it cool when I nonchalantly told Bishop I would do my best to make an appearance. But at the end of the workday, I raced home to shower, primp, and deliberate over my wardrobe. Tonight was the night to take a break. And I had every intention of seeing Bishop naked at the end of it. Since he had taken pain off the menu in the stairwell, I would have to settle for the next best thing, pleasure in the bedroom.

I stepped out of the car to the muffled sounds of a beating drum and thrumming guitar strings. It was too early for their set to have started, so the band must have been working on the soundcheck.

"Hey, looking pretty good there, Ghost." I stopped mid-stride as two co-workers emerged from the parking lot. Selina and her equally uninteresting lackey Kendall gave me a once-over as they strolled across the pavement in spiked heels and tight skirts. My outfit did not compare. My casual sweater and jeans combo was soft and demure compared to their brazen red-light fashion.

"Haven't seen you outside of work in forever," Selina said.

To an outsider, the interaction might appear conversational, even friendly. It was anything but. Selina and Kendall could barely stand sharing the spotlight with each other, much less with someone like me. But tonight, they did not seem to be interested in competing. More likely, they were ready to join forces against the office outcast who had somehow managed to catch Bishop's eye.

"Been a long week. Needed a break from the normal routine," I said, hoping to appear flattered by their attention. I knew I had failed when they began maneuvering around me. Regrouping, I smiled, showing plenty of teeth. "You both look fantastic."

Out of the corner of my eye, I saw Kendall flash a sideways grin. For an instant, she looked like a snarling beast. Then I realized she had also said something as she walked away.

When I caught up to them, they were laughing with the bouncer, bypassing the line of patrons at the door. I paused, unsure if I should follow them or head to the back of the line.

The decision was made for me when Selina reached back and grabbed my wrist. "Oh, girl, you're coming with us. Shots at the bar!"

Inside, the decor was on trend with stylized industrial minimalism. High ceilings with exposed beams, pipes, and ductwork. Brick-red flooring accented by steel bar stools and round high-top tables. A continuous series of stone-topped metal troughs snaked through the center of the vast space. Hanging above them were large iron weathervanes depicting the type of alcohol each modified bar served. Scattered sporadically around the club were also tin tubs filled with bottled water.

"What's your poison? Vodka, tequila, whiskey?" Selina said, slipping through the crowd with ease and still with a firm hold on my wrist. Kendall followed close behind.

We reached the bar, and I was quickly penned in with Selina on one side and Kendall on the other. I felt like a corralled animal. Only time would tell if I was the horse they led to drink or the pig they intended to slaughter.

Selina leaned across the counter to tug on the harried bartender's sleeve, cutting off a couple who had been patiently waiting to place a drink order. The bartender turned, clearly irritated by his sharp, narrow-eyed expression until he caught sight of Kendall bending over to giggle in Selina's ear. I stepped back so they could have center stage.

"Hey, ladies, what'll it be?"

"Three shots of tequila!" Selina announced, though I had not answered her earlier question on my alcohol preference. Not that it would have mattered. We were standing at the bar-trough that, as the above sign indicated, only served tequila drinks.

The bartender poured heavy and included one for himself. When handed a glass, I cheered them with a forced smile and downed the shot. The gulp of liquid burned furiously on its way to my empty stomach. I cleared my throat politely rather than coughing directly in their faces. Blinking back the sting of tears, I glanced behind me to where the band was still setting up.

The raised wooden stage with its levels of speakers on floor-to-ceiling scaffolding was a flurry of activity. A group of guys hurrying about with last-minute details and equipment adjustments gave the space even more of a construction vibe. From the occasional pauses and bouts of laughter, the band members were also making small talk with the crowd gathering below. Through the commotion and dim lighting, I could not tell if Bishop stood among them.

I turned my attention back to the bar when I heard Selina order a second round. I was not much for drinking and driving. If I wanted to get home safely, I needed to make myself scarce. My first thought was to excuse myself to the restroom, but these two looked like notorious bathroom buddies, which could result in unwanted company. Then again, they were focused on flirting with the bartender. Why bother announcing my departure when it would be easy to slip away into the growing crowd?

Selina and Kendall had their fingers trailing up and down the bartender's arm, inspecting a colorful dragon tattoo, when I took a couple of steps back and bumped into something hard.

"Twice in one day." I recognized Bishop's distinct laugh. I was about to turn around when two muscled arms slipped around my waist, and a chin rested on my shoulder. "I'm a lucky guy." His breath smelled of mint and hops. "Glad to see you made it out. Having fun with the girls?"

From the slight movement on my shoulder, I knew he had nodded toward our co-workers at the bar. Selina and Kendall were still trying to engage the bartender, who had to break away to serve some very annoyed customers.

I laid my hands over his and relaxed into the embrace. "Kind of feel like Carrie on prom night with these two," I said, not entirely joking.

"You think they're that petty? It looked like you were having a good time." Bishop slid his pinky finger around mine and squeezed. There was something endearing in that simple gesture.

Kendall and Selina were oblivious to everything and everyone as they continued to tease and distract the bartender. "Some people never outgrow their teenage cattiness. In case you haven't heard, there's a rumor going around the office, and they are none too pleased about it."

Bishop's lips brushed the rim of my ear. "You mean the one I started."

My jaw dropped as I pulled away and turned to face him. Bishop looked appetizing in faded jeans and a tight army-green T-shirt that brought out the flecks of gold in his hazel eyes. "Wow. Never would have suspected you of gossipmongering."

A smile stretched ear to ear, deepening his already irresistible dimples. "Had to get your attention somehow. You were not picking up on my subtle hints."

"Ha, they weren't that subtle," I said, jabbing him in the arm.

Bishop playfully rubbed his bicep while I stood pondering his confession. He was either a smooth player with perfected techniques or he had real feelings. Surprisingly, I began to hope it was the latter.

There was a clamoring behind me and then a high-pitched shout. "Bishop!"

Selina and Kendall, having finally noticed him, rushed over. I watched Bishop's smile fade as they brushed me aside to drape themselves around him, all the while gushing over his appearance and musical skills. Kendall was even bold enough to run her fingers through his tousled black hair, which she did while casting a snide look in my direction.

He nodded and accepted their praise as he sidled closer to me. His attempt to avoid their greedy hands was in vain. "Huh, guess you weren't wrong about them," he mumbled, looking down at his watch.

Kendall reached behind Selina and then thrust a shot glass at my chest, splashing tequila on my cashmere sweater. "You forgot this."

Bishop did not miss a beat. Stepping forward, he knocked past them to grab a handful of napkins off the bar. Then, quickly placing his hands on my shoulders, he steered me away. "Sorry, ladies, I must steal Ghost for a bit."

We did not wait for a response, just left them by the bar with Kendall holding a half-empty shot glass.

The venue was packed as he guided me toward a back hallway. Bypassing the bathrooms, he pushed through a side door labeled Employees Only. There was a closed door with an emblazoned Manager sign to the left. On the right was a lounge with various sitting areas and a wall of tall lockers. Bishop handed over the napkins and stalked over to the large center table, where he picked up a beer and took a swig.

He seemed angry, though there was not much reason to be. It was nothing a trip to the dry cleaner could not fix. "What's wrong?" I said, dabbing the wet spot on my sweater with a paper napkin.

"There's something I've been dying to do for months. But with those two out there, I have a feeling you might not be here that long."

I was still attending to the stain when Bishop stepped over and kissed me. It was sudden, rough, and probably not how he intended.

The kiss was a surprise. I pulled back to take a breath and saw his look of defeat. He shook his head and opened his mouth. I saw the apology coming but did not give him a chance to say it. I was rusty but knew we could do better than a sloppy spur-of-the-moment spit-swap.

"Come here." I grabbed the front of his shirt and hopped up to sit on the table. Opening my legs, I made room for him to move into my space.

He said nothing, but there was a hint of a smile on his full lips as he pressed against me. Placing my palms on his chest, I felt the rise and fall when he took a deep breath and released it. Then his skilled fingers were pushing under the hem of my sweater. Big hands sprawled over my back and up to my neck, leaving a trail of goosebumps wherever he touched.

Every nerve ending ignited. I licked my lips, anticipating his next move. He could not take it too far as we were short on time, but at that moment, I had never wanted the distraction of a man more. Cupping his face, I slid my thumb over his bottom lip, but before I could press my mouth to his, Bishop kissed me again. That kiss, his real kiss, was firm, confident, and seductive. He took everything I offered and then some.

Now, there was zero chance of me leaving the bar alone tonight.

# Chapter Eight

## Ghost

The evening was flying by, and I had thoroughly enjoyed it ever since Bishop and I entered and exited the bar's employee lounge. There, we had decided that he would drive me home so I could partake in as much fun as I wanted without concern. He had also insisted that he would be a perfect gentleman, claiming he would say goodnight at the door or crash on the couch.

Bishop had no idea I had decided hours ago that he would be spending the night in my bed.

It was not until the beginning of ProFusion's second set that I ran into my co-workers in the bathroom. They had a new girl with them. A petite redhead who made a complementary addition to Selina's dark hair and Kendall's light. They were a striking trio as they approached while I washed my hands in the sink.

"Ghost, we thought you left," Selina said, turning on the faucet beside me. "Have you met Ava?"

I turned from the sink to pull a paper towel from the dispenser. "Hi, Ava, nice to meet you."

Kendall was waiting for a stall to open, her legs jiggling with the urge to pee. "Yeah, she's Bishop's girlfriend. Well, she was until *very* recently."

And there I had it. The reason they had reacted badly to Bishop's office rumor. They were friends with his ex.

*So, I am the pig going to slaughter.*

"Ghost, is it?" Ava attempted to fling her hair back but ended up smacking herself in the face. "What a s-stupid name." She mumbled something under her breath before speaking more clearly. "You need to be careful. Bis-shop's a bad guy. An asshole looking for more asses."

Selina laughed, relishing the girl's drunken misery a little too much.

I moved to throw my paper towel in the trash when Ava stumbled in front of me.

"I'm s-serious, Ghost! S-stay away from him. I'm telling you, he's a s-scary, horrible person. A total monster!" She closed her eyes as she swayed forward but managed to keep herself upright.

"Thanks for the warning," I said. Ava sounded like a drunk, bitter ex-girlfriend.

A curvy woman came out of a stall, making a tight situation more constricting, especially when Kendall darted to the empty stall, bumping Ava into me as she went.

"Bitch!" Ava spat.

Selina nodded her agreement and glared. The curvy woman did her best to mind her own business. While Kendall had uttered something from inside the bathroom stall, all I heard was a stream of piss. I was in the sixth grade the last time I had been confronted with a physical altercation. And like then, I had no intention of fighting now. Especially with someone who could barely stand.

"So, you're saying Bishop is a scary monster and I should be wary?"

Ava sloppily wiped a drop of saliva from her chin. "Yeah, that's what I'm sayin'."

"Perfect. After all, I'm a spooky Ghost," I said as I pushed past Ava, dropped my towel in the trash, and exited the bathroom.

I had not gotten but a few steps from the bathroom when I felt a hand on my back. I thought it might be Ava insisting we come to blows. Instead that hand gave me a congratulatory pat. Boisterous laughter followed.

"Oh my god, that was brilliant. You guppy-faced them!" The curvy woman from the bathroom started laughing again. I was unfamiliar with the term "guppy-faced," but her laugh was so infectious I joined in.

"I'm Mina," she said. "Did I hear those girls right? Your name's Ghost?"

I stopped laughing. "You heard them correctly."

Mina laughed again. "That's freaking awesome! My friends have a table near the vodka bar. You should join us." She was unapologetically loud, and I immediately liked her.

"Sure. Can we stop by the whiskey bar first? I'll buy you a drink."

"As long as we make a toast to stupid bitches."

"You got it."

It turned out that Mina and her wife Jessa were celebrating their second wedding anniversary with a group of close friends. They were silly, noisy, and, as far as human beings go, absolutely perfect. I had so much fun with them that I missed "last call" and failed to notice the band packing up.

It was not until Mina tapped my shoulder that I realized Bishop was standing beside the table. "Is this your monster?" She had a grin like the Cheshire cat.

I pointed to Bishop, knowing it was time to go home. "Yup, he's a real beast."

Mina howled, literally howled. "You're a cute bass player, just not sure you're worthy, man. That Ava girl was a grade-A bitch. But we can see that Ghost likes you."

"Ava? What happened?" Bishop suddenly looked concerned. He moved around Mina, placing an arm around my shoulder. I would be lying if I said I did not need his support. As in physical support. I was not falling down drunk, but I still felt like I might topple over. It had been a fucking long week.

"Her and a couple of friends fluffed their feathers at Ghost in the ladies' room. But know this, our girl never backed down. She left them to stew in their stupidity."

"Thanks, Mina. I knew you had my back the whole time." I broke away from Bishop and fell forward to wrap Mina and her wife Jessa in a group hug. "Love ya, gals."

"Remember, Tuesday, Jimmie's for happy hour," Jessa said.

"I'll be there!" My words were muffled by the abundance of boob in my face.

Bishop gently pulled me out of the embrace. "We'll be there," he announced, even though he had not been invited. I appreciated his boldness. Maybe it was the alcohol, but it felt like our shift into coupledom had already transpired.

KEEPING TO HIS GENTLEMANLY promise, Bishop opened his Jeep door for me. He also handed me a bottle of water and asked that I let him know if I felt sick so he could pull over. He was beyond patient with my inebriation on the ride to my house. There was not a song on the radio that I did not know the words to.

When he pulled into the driveway of my townhouse, I honestly thought he would drop me off and bail. To my delight, he walked me to the door and asked if he could come inside.

"Sorry if I turned into a handful tonight," I said, flipping on the light and punching in the alarm code.

Bishop perused the entryway and open living space before heading to an island barstool where he sat. "No need to apologize. It was nice to see you let loose."

I walked into the kitchen to check the contents of my fridge. Eggs and toast seemed like the best option for a late-night snack. "Hungry?"

"I could eat," he said, looking around the open space. Last year, I bought the three-story townhouse for its open floor plan, white oak floors, and luxury en suite.

"Eggs and toast okay?" I said, placing the necessary ingredients on the counter. It was weird having Bishop sitting at my kitchen island. Weird in a good way.

"Sounds good. Need any help?" I heard the stool creak as Bishop got up and moved around to stand behind me. He was so close I could feel the heat radiating off his body. I passed him a loaf of wheat bread and a tub of margarine.

While I scrambled the eggs, Bishop manned the toaster. There was a moment of awkward silence, and then he turned to me. His glistening eyes appeared sorrowful, or maybe he was just tired. "I'm sorry Ava sought you out. Just so you know, we had five or six dates, and that was some time ago."

"It's okay. I can handle Ava and any other jealous exes you have out there." I dumped the eggs onto two plates and placed them on the island counter with two glasses of orange juice.

Bishop remained quiet as he finished buttering the toast and then joined me. We did not say too much as we ate our meal. Bishop commented casually about the band's upcoming schedule and a few excerpts of the rowdy episodes he viewed from his spot on the stage. I did not offer details on the minor incident with Ava, but I did compliment the band and thanked him for a fun night.

He was helping with the dishes when he nudged my side and then pulled me into an embrace. I practically melted, reveling in the strength and warmth of his body encasing mine. "Ghost, I—"

"Spend the night with me." I could not help but interrupt; I was afraid he would say he had to leave.

He squeezed me tighter and kissed me on the top of my head. "I will lay beside you, but I'd rather sleep with you when you're fully sober."

"Fair enough, but I sleep naked," I said, pressing against his chest. The rumble of his laughter sent flutters straight to my lower region.

"So do I," he said. And then I led him upstairs.

# Chapter Nine

# Juniper

Juniper gave Daniel Garrett a friendly hug when they parted company on her porch. The dinner had been a fantastic celebration. Nothing was more special than the promise of a new life in the world, especially when the party happened on half-price senior night at the best Mexican restaurant in town.

For a couple of hours, Juniper had laughed with friends and forgotten about the paper horrors she had left piled up beneath a cashmere throw blanket. They were lucky. People like them had only ever known healthy, happy, and sane families. She hoped that her friends would never have to experience the unending challenges that accompanied mental illness.

When Juniper entered her home, she could tell something was wrong. The air was different—heavier, thicker somehow, dense, like a storm approaching in the height of summer. She found it hard to breathe. The only sound her ears detected was a methodical ticking from the grandfather clock in the library.

There had been nothing more from her granddaughter—no call, no text, not that she had expected to hear from her. Gigi had messaged Juniper that they would talk tomorrow. But what if someone had gotten inside? Or what if Gigi had changed her mind and come over?

Juniper dropped her purse and rushed into the dining room. A flick of a light switch illuminated the blanketed rosewood table, which appeared lumpy but otherwise undisturbed. Not a single wrinkle in the fabric, which did not seem possible. She was in a hurry when she had covered the letters. Frantic to hide her secret and rid herself of the intrusive knocker. How was it so neat and tidy? So perfectly contained? Or was she just being paranoid?

Determined to shake the uneasy feeling, Juniper searched every inch of her four-story home but found nothing odd or out of place. Her worries should have been put to rest, but the unsettling wrongness she felt only increased.

Returning to the first floor, Juniper surveyed the dining room again. Why did everything feel so wrong? She moved through the lower level to look out each window and then went about unlocking and relocking the front and back doors.

While inspecting the lower level for a third time, Juniper was drawn back to the dining room table. She continued to check and double check the letters, lifting each edge of the blanket to assure herself that the letters had not moved. She had to be sure not a single page had shifted. Each time, she found everything exactly as she had left it. The lack of disturbance only escalated her concern.

Glancing into the living room, Juniper noted the time. The antique clock on the mantel indicated that it was close to midnight. She had been roaming her house for hours in a state of distress, and she still could not find the cause for the hairs on the back of her neck to stand up on alert.

Juniper had spent the last twenty-six years protecting Gigi from her mother's madness. She had already lost her daughter. She could not risk losing her granddaughter, too.

That was the reason she had kept the letters hidden all those years. It was why she had done everything in her power to keep the two of them apart.

Then it dawned on her.

The reason the sickness had come over her as soon as she walked through the door.

It was the letters.

The horrible feelings she was experiencing had everything to do with the exposed pages presented neatly on the table for any wandering eyes to see. Though logically, Juniper knew there were no eyes other than her own in the house. The whole idea of showing the letters to Gigi was a mistake. She had witnessed the fragile state her granddaughter was in. It did not take a genius to see how troubled Gigi had been lately. Now would be the worst time to reveal a damaging, life-altering secret.

Juniper loomed over the dining room table, visualizing the vulgar writings hidden beneath the plush fabric she fisted in her hand. With a jerk of her arm, she whipped the blanket from the table and then frantically went about gathering the papers as they scattered to the floor. Once she had compiled the letters back into stacks, sorted by date, addressee, and level of content, she retrieved her jumbo-sized Samsonite suitcase. The one she kept hidden. All her darkest secrets were stowed under a king-sized bed. The case contained both a key and a combination lock. No one was getting it open without the key and correct numbers unless they had a saw and hammer. The letters and drawings would remain locked away.

Gigi was more of a daughter to her than Meredith had ever been. She would not risk losing that. Not ever.

When her secrets were once again safe and secure, and the anxiety had faded, she decided to ring her granddaughter. It was just after two in the morning. The call went straight to voicemail.

"Gigi love, sorry about today. And sorry it's so late. We can no longer deny that I am a ridiculous old woman. When you get this, give me a call. Anytime, doesn't matter."

She would not have anything to show Gigi when she finally came to the house. Juniper did not know what she would tell her granddaughter when they spoke, but she had time to figure it out. If she had to play the feeble-minded old lady card to keep her little family intact, then by All the Gods in the Universe, she would do it.

Iced tea had been her choice of drink at dinner, but now she needed something stronger. Juniper changed into her pajamas before pouring herself a glass of Old Rip Van Winkle whiskey. The first gulp was smooth liquid fire. She added an oversized ice cube and settled into her favorite chair in front of the TV.

RELAXING IN HER BALMORAL recliner, Juniper fell into a fitful sleep. The stress of the day had come back to her in dreams, along with ancient memories she had hoped one day to forget.

The dream started with her standing at the end of the pier, watching her husband, Henry White. He was standing in the lake, wearing his dark blue suit. The one he wore to weddings and funerals. He looked younger than she remembered as he walked toward her. The brackish water was up to his waist. Raising his hand in a friendly wave, he smiled.

At that moment, Juniper remembered what it felt like to be in love.

As Henry moved closer, she saw blood dripping down the left side of his face. The trickle soon turned into a gush, and then the whole side of his head caved in. She screamed as he fell sideways and disappeared beneath the darkening water.

Another scream followed hers, this one small and high-pitched. The cry of a child. When Juniper turned around, she saw her daughter. A young, teenage Meredith was pointing and shouting, "You killed Daddy!"

But that could not be right. She had not done anything.

Juniper went to look for the person who had done this awful, terrible thing. She was about to jump into the water when she noticed the blood on her hands and the wooden oar she was holding. The tip had a long, jagged crack. It was soaked red. Matted with blood and a fleshy clump of brown hair that had once belonged to her husband.

She went to comfort her daughter, who was still shouting and pointing from the other end of the dock when Gigi arrived. Her granddaughter looked fierce. Gigi was dressed all in black, her lush platinum hair blowing in the breeze and dark eyes glistening from the sharp winds. Gigi reached over and took Meredith's hand. They smiled at each other and spoke words that Juniper was unable to hear. Then they started walking away.

Juniper yelled for them to come back. She shouted for them to stop, to wait. But they never acknowledged her. Either they could not hear her, or they were ignoring her. She tried to go after them, but her legs would not move. It was as if her feet had been anchored to the pier.

Then, the lake water turned to blood and began to rise.

Terror jolted Juniper awake. The sound of breaking glass rang out as her flailing hands knocked something from the side table. Juniper jumped to her feet and began pacing the living room, ignoring the spilled whiskey and broken crystal. She had had this nightmare before. A warped, twisted version of the boat accident that stole her husband's life.

The grief support group she had attended at her community church told her it was survivor's guilt. Which she knew to be true. Both her and her daughter were in the small rowboat when it capsized.

Life was delicate, but the people who lived it were clumsy. Juniper had failed to check the weather report that fateful morning and lost her husband because of it. She lost her daughter the next year. Meredith's already weak mind shattered into disrepair after having witnessed and survived that tragic day on the water. Juniper could not—no—*would* not risk losing Gigi. She was the only person in this whole screwed up world that meant anything to her. Whatever it took, Juniper would keep Gigi safe and sane.

# Chapter Ten

# Ghost

The morning sun woke me before I was ready. As it crept its way through a partially opened blind, a burst of pain exploded behind my eyes. I was in for a well-deserved hangover. At least it was Saturday, and there was no semblance of a plan other than heading over to Grandma June's house. I rubbed my head, knowing it was not the time to get sucked down that rabbit hole. My grandmother had kept her secret this long—what would it hurt if she kept it a little while longer?

Bishop was still asleep, lying on his back, one arm tucked behind his head and the other draped over his waist. Before climbing into bed last night, he had taken off his clothes but left his boxers on while I had stripped down to nothing before turning off the lights. I was daring him to break his promise of no sex. Unfortunately, he had stayed true to his word on that. It was a peck goodnight and then he moved to the far edge of the mattress, hitting the pillow and cursing under his breath.

I gently slipped out of bed so as not to wake him and made my way to the bathroom. After relieving myself, I brushed my teeth and pulled my hair into a sloppy bun. Turning in the mirror, I could see the bruise on my back, where I had bashed into the stairwell wall. It had turned a dark shade of bluish purple that would blacken more before it lightened to a greenish yellow. Neither color combination complemented my fair skin. Thankfully, it would not be too long before it faded out of sight. Eyeing the fluffy robe hanging by the door, I chased a couple of ibuprofens with a full glass of tap water.

When I came out of the bathroom, wearing the robe, Bishop was propped up in bed, smiling. "Good morning, sunshine."

I could not help admiring his chiseled chest and sculpted abs. "Ugh, don't tell me you're a morning person?"

He ran his fingers through his bed-ragged hair, then patted a spot next to him on the bed. "I am."

Before joining him, I returned to grab the bottle of Advil and another glass of water. He did not look any worse for wear, but looks could be deceiving. I placed the pills and drink on the nightstand and then sat down on the edge of the bed.

"Just in case," I said, nodding to part one of my hangover remedy. Part two consisted of a relaxing afternoon on the couch with plenty of caffeine and a greasy pizza. I was hoping he would hang around and join me.

"Thanks." He reached for the water and drank deeply.

Setting the empty glass down, he placed his hand on mine and gave a slight tug, indicating that he wanted me to move closer. To oblige, I moved up on the bed next to him. He sat unmoving for a bit, and then I noticed his heavy-lidded eyes focused on my cleavage that was now visible through the loosely tied robe.

I held my breath when he slid his hand inside my robe to cup my breast. Resisting the urge to touch him back, I allowed him the opportunity to explore. With his head nuzzled against my neck, I watched as he parted the fluffy material, his hand leisurely trailing down my side and across my lower stomach. I gasped when he suddenly moved to take my hard nipple into his mouth.

I ran my fingers through his thick hair and pulled him up for a kiss when my cell phone rang. The alarm clock on the bedside table read 8:30 a.m. There was only one person it could be, and I was not about to let her ruin this moment. Ignoring the call, I pulled him on top of me and kissed him hard. He responded eagerly, slipping his tongue between my parted lips as he moved his hands up to my face.

The friction of skin-to-skin contact ramped up my desire. I arched my back, loving the feel of my breasts against his bare chest.

My cell phone rang again.

I paused. Bishop eased back with raised brows.

The phone quieted, and we resumed kissing and touching. I had my hand down the front of his boxers when the ringing sounded a third time.

"Sorry," I said, rolling away and grabbing my cell phone from the nightstand. Bishop got up and headed into the bathroom.

"What is it, Gi Ju?" I growled, literally *growled* at my grandmother.

"Did I wake you?"

"Yes." It was better than telling her she had interrupted what was sure to be hot, dirty sex.

"Sorry, deary. I just had to call and tell you how terrible I feel about yesterday. I might have overreacted, made it out to be a bigger deal than it actually might be. You know how sensitive I am about *her*. Your mother's so ill, and I've always wanted to spare you from seeing her like that. Please forgive me."

"What about the secret you've been keeping? A secret that you waited until now to tell me." I could not help asking, even with a half-naked man less than twenty feet away. I also could not hide the disdain in my voice. I had trouble discerning the source of my anger. Was it over her refusal to grant permission for me to see my mother, the *big* secret she had been keeping, or her untimely interruption? There were so many to choose from.

"I hate to admit this, but I lied. I just wanted you to come to the house. I'm sorry for the things I said. And I'm sorry for keeping you from your mother all these years. I still feel that it's best if you two never meet. The day you were born, it was so difficult for her that she didn't speak for a whole year. Her delusions are horrible, and her aggression is extremely frightening. I'm even scared of her, and I gave birth to her. For you, I fear it will be so much worse."

Of course, Grandma June always considered my feelings first. Forever fearful that my mother's long-lasting hatred would ruin me if I experienced it firsthand.

And who knows, maybe it would. My mother never wanted me. I was forced on her.

Grandma June coughed into the phone, started to speak, and then cleared her throat.

"Are you okay?"

"Yes, deary. Sorry. I'm a bit emotional right now. Give me some time. I'm not saying I'll grant your request, but I will think on it some more."

It was not a no, which was major progress for Grandma June. I was not sure what had made her reconsider, but I was not about to question it.

The toilet flushed, and then I heard the sink faucet turn on. It was time to end our very private conversation. "Thanks, I appreciate that. I've got some things to do this morning, so I'll give you a call back a little later, okay?"

"Wait, are you still upset with me?"

"No, I'm not. Now I gotta go," I said as the bathroom door opened, and an incredibly sexy man stepped out.

"I love you."

"Love you, too." I hung up the phone as Bishop walked around the bed and plucked his T-shirt off the back of the checkered armchair.

"Everything all right?" he asked. And much to my dismay he continued to get dressed.

"Yeah, Grandma June's just anxious to get your number."

"Ah, can't wait to meet her." He sat down on the chair. While he pulled on his boots, I tightly secured my robe.

"As much as I want to spend the morning in bed with you, I have some obligations today." Bishop's frown reminded me of a pouting child. Was it disappointment? Or was he intentionally blowing me off?

"Okay," I said, then added a shrug, attempting to show indifference rather than the defeat I truly felt.

I got off the bed and went over to the dresser. The need to put on something more substantial was growing by the second. Not wanting to come across as frantic or crazy, I tried to slow my movements as I opened and closed drawers.

Suddenly, Bishop was peering over my shoulder into my underwear drawer with his hand on the back of my neck when his fingers brushed against one of my old scars. He must have noticed a line of raised skin, because he tugged the collar of the robe down far enough to expose my neck and shoulders, along with the darkening bruise on my back. "That's a nasty bruise. Is that from yesterday?"

I nodded.

"I'm so sorry." Cool fingertips moved around to caress the older damaged skin. "How did you get these scars?"

The marks he surveyed were faint and slightly raised. Three jagged lines ran from my left shoulder almost to the center of my back and ended at a puckered divot, where a small chunk of flesh had been torn away near the base of my neck. I did not think I was particularly self-conscious, but I almost always wore my hair down. I did not like that he touched the scars now.

Shutting the drawer, I turned around and bumped against him, almost dropping the athleisure wear I had pulled out. "I was attacked by a dog when I was a toddler."

"That must have been traumatizing."

"Not really, I don't remember it, only the story Grandma June told."

One thick eyebrow rose over a squinty eye. "My brother was bitten on the hand by a dog when he was little. A very minor incident compared to yours, and he's still terrified of dogs to this day."

Not knowing what else to say, I shrugged. His concern seemed to fade as he rubbed his hands down my robe-covered arms. "Can I give you a ride back to your car?"

"Oh, right. I completely forgot."

"Feel like stopping for coffee and donuts on the way?"

He flashed a dimpled smile, and before I could stop myself, I kissed his five o'clock shadow. "Sure. Meet you downstairs in three minutes."

WE WERE SEATED IN HIS Jeep, heading down the highway, when he nudged my arm with his elbow. "Tell me more about yourself."

I fidgeted in my seat.

"Hmm, we're doing this now. You first, though. I want to hear what I'm going up against."

Bishop rumbled with laughter as he changed lanes, preparing to take the next exit ramp.

"I have two siblings—younger sister, Florina, and younger brother, Navid. My mother's originally from Ireland, and my father's Persian and Italian. We have a touch of Romanian and some English mixed in, which makes us a pack of mutts. We're very close. We have family weekends at our ocean house every few months."

The tires let out a squeal when he took the exit ramp a little too fast.

"Let's see, I started playing guitar when I was thirteen. I needed a cool hobby to make up for the fact that I was a total computer nerd. Studied computer science at Johns Hopkins, where I also played lacrosse. As for work, you already know. And...I'm hoping I've just started a long, sensual relationship with the coolest woman I know."

I was smiling when he turned into the parking lot of a Dunkin' Donuts and switched off the engine. "Now it's your turn. I'm withholding caffeine and sugar until you tell me more about yourself."

This was the part that I had been dreading. He had described the perfect family, though I was sure they had their fair share of ups and downs. It was nothing like my disaster of a life. But I was not about to lie. It was always best to tell the truth, even if it meant our relationship ended here.

Steadying my twiddling fingers, I took a deep breath and released it slowly.

"It's just me and my grandma. She's English-Dutch, married a Scotsman. But I'm not sure of my full heritage because I never knew my father..." *Nor should I want to.* "My mother's been institutionalized with schizophrenia since she was a teenager. My birth is a mystery or mistake, depending on who you are and how you look at it. I—"

My mouth clamped shut so hard it sent a sharp pain through my back molars. Usually, I skirted around any subject regarding my mother. Why had I revealed those intimate details to him?

Bishop's eyes were burning into me. But I refused to meet his gaze and see his pity by scanning the almost empty parking lot. I would let him come to his own conclusions about how I was conceived. I could not bring myself to tell him I was a product of rape or that nature had tried to correct the error on the day I was born. However naïve it was, I chose to cling to the fantasy that my parents had a loving and consensual relationship.

"I-I refused my grandmother's money and worked odd jobs to pay my way while studying business finance at the community college." Because I thought that without her money, she would have less control over my life. I was dead wrong about that.

"Ended up taking the first real job I was offered. Which is probably why I'm still an executive assistant and not a financial analyst. Let's see, I bought my townhouse a little over a year ago. Other than some traveling, I mostly work and look after Grandma June."

He patted my hand and then jumped out of the Jeep. "Not anymore. Now, you have to make time for date nights with me."

"Is that so?" I said, opening the door, even though he had walked around the front of the Jeep to open it for me.

He smiled. "Yes, I insist on many nights and days, too."

"Wow, so greedy." I started to relax when he took my hand in his.

"Only when it comes to you."

We were almost at the door of the donut shop when something moved off to the left, catching my eye. I turned as Bishop reached over to pull the front door of the donut shop open.

*He* was back. The man from the roadside accident was in the parking lot. And as always, he wore the black fedora with the white rose and a theatrical pinstriped suit. When he saw that I had noticed him, he tipped his hat with a toothy smile and got into a beat-up Honda.

A chill flittered around my shoulders.

The hatted man was backing out of the parking space when Bishop nudged me. "Going in, or have you changed your mind?"

I was half tempted to ask Bishop if he had seen the oddly dressed man in the green car but then wisely held my tongue. I did not need Bishop to confirm my deepest, darkest fears were coming true.

"Going in. Thank you."

# Chapter Eleven

# Ghost

Bishop and I enjoyed a simple breakfast of coffee and donuts. An iced coffee for me. It was just the distraction I needed. We continued to talk about ourselves, him more than me. His playful flirting lasted until he announced that he was going to be late, though he never specified what obligation he risked being late for. I had gotten over the brief moment of vulnerable exposure from earlier and accepted him as honest and having good intentions. We had also made a dinner date for Sunday at a new upscale restaurant in Harbor Point Marina.

I was determined to make this a great weekend. Saturday afternoon would be spent nursing a mild hangover with junk food and bad TV, while looking forward to a romantic dinner with a man who was quickly becoming one of my favorite people.

I had my car and was heading home when I took a detour into the mall parking lot. Sunday's date called for a new dress.

The shopping mall was quiet as the stores were beginning to open. The only people around were a group of elderly walkers who preferred to get their daily exercise safely indoors. As I passed them by, they issued a joyful greeting in unison. I smiled and wished them a "Good morning" in return.

THE THREE-WAY MIRROR in the back of my preferred boutique revealed the sexy, sophisticated style I had been aiming for.

The dark gray slip dress had a tight-fitting bodice with half sleeves and a long skirt with a slit that showed just the right amount of leg when I moved. As I stood there admiring the reflection, I thought of the shoe store next door. There had been a pair of yellow heels in the window. Together they would make a bold fashion statement. I ducked back into the dressing room to change and then headed for the other store to grab the shoes and maybe a new clutch.

Another hour later, I was exiting the mall with a garment bag slung over my shoulder, my purse under one arm, and a shopping bag in each hand. It was time to zip through a drive-thru and head for home.

I had taken a few steps outside when I saw a green Honda idling at the curb. It looked a lot like the car from the donut shop. The distance made it impossible to make out any facial features, but I could see a silhouette of the person sitting inside. The driver wore a hat.

A fedora-shaped hat.

The hatted man usually appeared when I was overly stressed or tired. I saw him twice today. It did not make sense. I was happy with Bishop this morning and had been perfectly content taking my time to shop for a dress and other indulgences. These were pleasant diversions from my worries. So, why was I still seeing him?

The only answer to my question was a jittery feeling in my gut. This was bad—really, really bad.

I turned around and went back inside. The mall was busier than before. People bustling about, everyone in a hurry. Kids were screaming and darting around the play area, trying to outrun their annoyed parents. It was complete mayhem. The kind of chaos I could get lost in.

Hurrying past one of the big-box stores, I headed toward the food court. The crowds were even thicker in this section as it neared the lunchtime hour. I looked for an exit close enough to where I had parked so I could slip out, hopefully without seeing the hatted man.

*How do you escape a delusion?*

*I bet my mother knows.*

Juggling my bags, I dug my phone out of my purse on the off chance that the hatted man was a real person. How would the police react to a report of a man sitting in his car outside the mall? He could simply be waiting for someone. I would not want to come off as paranoid or worse. He had not done anything other than acknowledge me with a crooked smile and the tip of his hat. *Wait, that's not true!*

I had been catching glimpses of the strange man for days, which meant that if he was real, he had been following—stalking—me for over a week.

Despite my attempt to calm my nerves with half-assed rationalizations, there was no escaping the terror I felt whenever I saw the man in the bad suit.

Through a set of glass doors on my right, the edge of the orange-flagged parking lot emerged. It would be an exposed walk through the aisles of cars to get where I had parked, but from this angle, it was unlikely that I would be visible from the front entrance. I was moving for the doors when something crashed into my shins. I heard a squeal just before I stumbled and lost my balance. One hand flew out to brace myself, while the other kept a firm hold on my purchases.

Only there was no fall. It felt as if someone had latched on to the back of my sweatshirt to steady me. Whoever it was, they had saved me from the embarrassment of sprawling face-first onto the floor.

"Donovan, what are you doing?" A frazzled woman appeared and reached below my knees to pick up a boy with a plastic skateboard. "Miss, I'm so sorry," she said, hauling the kid to his feet.

They left the scene in a flurry of activity, flailing arms, and angry words. I was in the process of collecting myself when I felt a lingering presence behind me. The scent of mothballs and outdated cologne was a dead giveaway to the person standing too close.

*Do delusions smell, too?*

I could not look. It was not physically possible for the man in the black fedora to stop my fall. Though the shiver running across my shoulders tried to tell me otherwise.

*Ignore it.*

I took a deep breath and moved toward the exit.

"Excuse me, I think you dropped your phone." The voice had a hint of an accent I could not place. An authoritative tone that reminded me a lot of Grandma June's pastor.

A sigh of relief. It was not the hatted stranger after all.

I turned around to thank the kind man for his assistance—

A black curtain dropped over my eyes. For a second, I could not see anything but darkness. Then a speck of light and a faceless blob emerged. The remaining haze cleared at an agonizingly slow pace.

Two bright blue orbs were the first details to sharpen fully. I had to lock my screams behind clenched teeth as the rest of the details came into focus. Black hat. White rose. Striped suit. Crooked grin.

The imaginary man had a smile plastered across his face as he pointed to a spot on the floor between us.

When his fat-knuckled finger started wiggling about, I finally looked down.

A cell phone in a red polka-dot case. Apparently, I had dropped my phone.

I knelt to pick it up. "Thank you." My voice was a mousey squeak. The sound of a weak and frightened woman. Or the voice of someone who did not want to get caught talking to herself in the middle of a crowded mall.

I stood up. The man moved back a couple of steps and ran his fingers across the brim of his hat. He seemed to be waiting for something.

I looked around, hoping someone would notice us, but no one appeared to. The woman who had grabbed her kid off the floor had not acknowledged him, but she had been distracted and in a hurry—like everyone nowadays.

With a sharp tilt of his head, eyes narrowed, he said, "I'm Terrence. Terrence Riggie."

*Riggie!*

I slapped my hand over my mouth to keep the anguish from spilling out. But I could not stop the tears from brewing. It had been so long since I heard that name. It was my special made-up name for an imaginary father that no one else knew about. We would play behind the boat shed with a little red truck I had found partially buried near Grandma June's rose garden.

Suddenly it was too hot. Sweat was beading around my temples. I swiped it away with trembling fingers. I had to get away from this—

*Wake up! Run!*

As I turned and ran for the exit, pushing and knocking against people as I fled, I heard a man shout—

"Lil Ghostie!"

I stopped mid-stride. Had the hatted man shouted that name, or was it only in my head? No, of course, he had not said it. *He's not real!* The name *Riggie* sparked memories of my internal conversations during difficult times in my life. The ones where I pretended that my adoring father called me his "Lil Ghostie."

The conversations I only ever had with myself.

A chill of terror washed over me, but still, I looked back.

I saw Terrence Riggie standing next to a hunched elderly man. The group of seniors I saw walking earlier were there too. They were chatting and laughing, though I could not tell if they were interacting with the hatted man or if he was lurking beside them.

By the time I reached the car, I felt less woozy but still a little out of breath. Tossing my bags in the trunk, I slipped inside and locked the doors before starting the engine. I had to take a minute to calm myself and slow my heart rate, but I also had to be able to drive away quickly if the need arose. I closed my eyes and took a couple of deep breaths—slow and controlled inhales followed by long, deliberate exhales.

Reaching for the radio, I switched it on. A soothing voice sang of new love and promises. The lyrics sparked an image of Bishop and where I hoped we would eventually find ourselves. Happy and in love. Because I refused to end up alone and locked away.

When I opened my eyes, there was no stalker. No creepy man named Terrence in a black fedora with a white rose. There was only a lively parking lot full of family and friends out for lunch and running errands. I was safe.

And then I saw it.

The beat-up green Honda inched past the aisle where I was parked.

# Chapter Twelve

# Juniper

Strong western winds blew ripples across Willow Lake, not an actual lake but rather a large inlet off the Siren River. Juniper sat on the top of a low piling. Bending over slightly, she began pulling at the damp rope she kept knotted to a cleat on the end of the pier.

The autumn months were the best time of year to catch blue crabs in Maryland. The crustaceans that commercial fishermen did not snatch up over the summer flourished in the connecting rivers, lakes, and estuaries until it was time for their winter migration to the bottom of the nearby Chesapeake Bay. With dozens of blue-ribbon wins at the county fair for her crab cakes, dips, and soups, she religiously baited her traps with seasoned clams and fresh chicken necks. The steamed crabs that were not eaten right away were picked clean of their succulent backfin meat and frozen for special events and holidays.

Juniper was in the process of moving six large male crabs to the live box when she heard the clacking of footsteps on the dock. Recalling her nightmare, she froze. Part of her expected to hear her daughter's screams for a dead father. Though her husband's remains had been recovered long ago, there were days when Juniper found herself scanning the placid waters, anticipating his return.

Physically shaking the horridness from her mind, she stood, knees popping. The damp fall air brought out the worst in her bones and joints. Every year the pain increased with the changing of the seasons. And every year Juniper dreamed of relocating to a beach down south.

But that would never happen. Not as long as her daughter was alive. Juniper might not be able to be with Meredith, but she would never abandon her.

Juniper turned to see who had paid her an unwelcome visit, her hands instantly lending support to the crick in her lower back. *Damn arthritis!*

Gigi was a sight to behold. She was a natural beauty, even wearing an outfit the youngsters referred to as athleisure wear. Juniper called it what it was: pajamas. Gigi did not need makeup, but Juniper still noticed that her granddaughter was barefaced and disheveled. If Gigi had come to the lake house without at least some mascara on her lashes, Juniper knew it was a turmoil-driven drop-in.

"Grandma, how many did you catch today?" Gigi came in close to peer over the side into the live box. Juniper recognized the faint scent of alcohol and sweat. Her sweet, responsible granddaughter had been drowning her burdens and had likely come to announce some reckless decision. Juniper's heart sank.

"Six, just now. Caught seven earlier this morning. Plus, I already had a few in there from yesterday."

Gigi wrapped an arm around her grandmother's shoulders and placed a kiss on her icy cheek. "Steaming them up for dinner tonight?"

Juniper leaned into her fragile granddaughter as Gigi guided her back to the house. Even with the deep chill reaching into her bones and causing her to tremble, she was reluctant to go inside. Indoors, they would talk. Inside, she would hear more of Gigi's pleas and likely some new ultimatum.

"Depends, dear. Are you staying for dinner?"

"Probably not. But I thought we'd have lunch together. Want to veg out in front of the TV for a bit? I brought pizza." Gigi sounded sad but hopeful as they stepped off the dock and onto the path leading up to the house.

"Of course." Juniper stood up straighter. Her aging body and deteriorating joints felt a million times better with no other aid than a few simple words from Gigi. It was not the visit she had feared. Maybe her granddaughter would grant her the time she needed. She would not be pressured. It was not a decision to be made lightly. "Oh my, what a pleasant surprise this is. I did not expect to see you today. You said you had things to do."

Gigi turned her big doe eyes to the shoreline as she wrapped herself in a hug, rubbing her hands briskly up and down her fleece-covered arms. "My plans changed."

It was obvious Gigi was in a state of duress. So, perhaps Juniper had not escaped *that* day after all. "What's the matter, deary?"

Postponing her answer, Gigi walked across the grass and grabbed the pizza from the back of the car before joining her grandmother on the porch. "Feeling a little overwhelmed. I thought we should talk in person about some things. But now I'm not sure."

Gigi explained that after grabbing a pizza from a local spot near the mall, she had turned right instead of left to go home and kept driving with no intentional destination until she arrived at the lake house.

Juniper knew there had to be more to that story. Opening the front door, she stepped into the warmth of her dimly lit house. "It's okay if you changed your mind about wanting to see your mother."

"I haven't changed my mind," Gigi said through clenched teeth, then slammed the door behind her.

Juniper flinched at the sudden outburst but did not turn around. Instead, she continued through the house to the kitchen, where she retrieved a pair of Lenox plates and cloth napkins from the pantry. Calm and easy was the way to accomplish her goal. There was no need to upset her granddaughter further. But, if necessary, she would not hesitate to pull out her old calming remedy. It had always worked so well on Meredith.

"Of course not. This is a big deal, and there is nothing wrong with taking some more time to process it fully." Juniper already knew it would be a cold day in Hell before she changed her mind and allowed the two to meet.

Gigi tossed the pizza box on the kitchen table and flopped into a chair. "Yeah, maybe you're right."

Juniper looked over at her granddaughter and smiled. "When am I ever wrong, deary?"

# Chapter Thirteen

# Ghost

The afternoon had turned out mostly as planned. Rest and plenty of grease and caffeine in the form of a pepperoni-and-onion pizza and two diet sodas. Binge-watching romantic comedies at the lake house was a welcome distraction. Four hours later, Grandma June was asleep on the sofa, curled up and lightly snoring beneath an oversized cashmere blanket.

It would be dark soon, and I wanted to get on the road. I needed a hot shower and a good night of sleep at home in my own bed.

Switching off the TV, I went to the kitchen to do a quick cleanup. I wiped down the kitchen surfaces, wrapped the leftovers in tinfoil, and placed them in the fridge. I was going to toss the pizza box in the garbage when my movement caused something to flutter along the floor. Moving in for a closer look, I spotted a piece of trash that lay barely noticeable beneath the oak hutch in the dining room.

The timeworn floorboards creaked as I crawled under to retrieve the discarded paper. At first, I suspected a sales flyer or a billing statement. Then I noticed the deep creases as if it had been folded and unfolded many times over. The ruled paper was discolored with age. A spot of dark brown stained the bottom left corner.

The page appeared blank. I stood and flipped the paper over.

Staggering, I grabbed hold of a dining room chair to prevent myself from tumbling over. My vision blurred as I read the penciled cursive scrawl. While I focused on the faded letters that were slowly turning into words, my brain struggled to comprehend their meaning. By the time I reached the end of the letter, my heart was beating erratically in the back of my throat.

It was a letter from my mother. Written nearly fifteen years ago.

A squeak of springs from the Baxter T-Arm sofa, followed by a rustling, alerted me to my grandmother's wakefulness. Quickly pocketing the letter, I snatched the pizza box from the dining room table and tossed it on the outside garbage bin as I exited the house. I was in my car and putting it in reverse when my grandmother appeared on the wraparound porch. Grandma June was rubbing sleep from her eyes and looking somewhat perplexed.

I should have stormed up to her, waved the letter in her face, and demanded answers. And I would have if not for the short hairs on the back of my neck that flagged an unusual warning. I knew I had nothing to fear from my grandmother, and yet I could not bring myself to get out of the car. It could have been out of fear. Or maybe it was anger. With hands shaking, I pressed the button to roll down the car window and bid Grandma June goodnight before backing up and speeding off.

A few minutes later, I found myself in a convenience store parking lot with the car's interior light on. After silencing another call from Grandma June, I took out my mother's old letter and read it with tears streaming down my face.

*Dearest Ghost,*

*I don't know if you are receiving my letters. Or if you can even read them. Can empty eye sockets see? Is decomposing flesh able to open an envelope and unfold the paper inside? All I know is that you exist in that house beside a tricky demon who ruined the world with its lies.*

*When my beloved came and wrapped me in his arms, he gave me a gift. You and the promise of freedom. I loved you both so much. But then he went away, and he took you with him. He's gone, but somehow, you're still there. You can erase the wrongs. Even with unseeing eyes, you are capable of revealing the truth. Only then can we be together.*

*A happy family reunited in Hell where we belong.*

*Love,*

*Merry-Mom*

# Chapter Fourteen

# Ghost

I sat in my car in that store parking lot, screaming and pounding my hands against the steering wheel. Then I used my fists to punch the driver's side door until I heard the crack of plastic. I kicked my feet and pulled at my hair. But no matter how hard I tugged or hit, there was no release from the agony of my grandmother's betrayal.

For the first time in my life, I truly had no one. The only person I could always count on had proven to be untrustworthy. I clutched the evidence of decades of deceit tightly in my bloodied, swollen fist. My mother had been writing to me for years. Grandma June had kept that from me.

I glanced down and smoothed out the page that contained my mother's words "—*are you receiving my letters?—can you read them?*" She had been writing to me for years! *Why would Grandma June keep that from me?*

The letter did not match what I had been told. There was no hatred in what my mother wrote. No threats. The writing seemed hopeful. As if I had the power to fix something for her. Instead of listening to stories about my mother, I should have found a way to meet her. Had I received this letter when it was sent, I would have written back. All these years, we could have been communicating. I would have gotten to know her. My mother could have given me answers or possible clues on how to cope with a faulty mind.

Instead of giving us a chance at having some semblance of a relationship, my grandmother told me scary stories and kept us apart.

I was physically beaten and emotionally drained. My skin itched. I was a broken honey jar lying in the desert sun beside a giant anthill.

Frayed nerves were nothing new. Lately, I found myself stressed and often bewildered by a plethora of pressing issues. But never had I experienced anything like this.

I could forgive my grandmother if she had held the letters—I knew there were more—until I was old enough to understand. But not now. It was too late for her to continue with that kind of farce. And what about all the other things she told me about my mother?

*"Your mother hates you!"*

*"She prayed and wished for your death before you were born."*

*"She put her hands around your tiny throat and squeezed. If it wasn't for the nurses..."*

*"It will be the death of her if she ever sees you again!"*

How much of that was true? And how often had Grandma June exaggerated or flat-out lied?

I folded the crumpled letter, placed it in the center console, and looked into the eyes of the man sitting next to me. The hatted man had perched himself in my passenger seat. The black hat with the white rose dangled from the end of his pinstriped knee. It was the first time I had seen him without his hat on. I could not help but notice the blunt, square shape of his head.

He reached over and lightly placed his hand over mine. A compassionate gesture over the loss of my sanity. But I never felt his touch. And in that moment, I knew I was exactly like my mother.

"Why are you here?" My voice croaked, and I covered my mouth as I coughed through the strain. "How did you get here?"

He ran his long fingers over the brim of his hat before placing it back on his head. "Because you need me."

I fought off the new assault of tears and swallowed the pain. "No, I don't. You're not even real."

"I'm as real as you want me to be. Don't worry, everything is going to be okay."

Only it was not. Nothing was okay. A few hours ago, Grandma June had told me, "It's okay." And now an imaginary man in a stupid hat and a flashy, ill-fitted suit was repeating the same words.

Trauma, stress, or whatever I had been experiencing had forced my subconscious to make sense of the day's events. Not so different from dreaming at night. I closed my eyes and wished the hatted man away, just like when I willed the monsters in my nightmares to disappear.

When I opened my eyes, the hatted man remained. A sloppy lopsided grin had transformed his appearance into something more sinister.

I started the engine and put the car in drive. "I think it's best if you go away."

"I think it'd be better if we talked." He continued to speak as I shook my head. "Why are you so distraught? And why are you sitting out here alone, crying in the parking lot of a 7-Eleven?"

Leaning closer, he tilted his head as if to examine me. "It's been my experience that talking helps. Most people share their feelings with a close friend or family member. But sometimes speaking to an unknown helps, too. Since I'm here, you might as well tell me what's troubling you."

It seemed like the only way to rid myself of his presence was to talk. I had just been thinking that I needed to speak to someone. *Is that why he appeared?*

"If I tell you what happened, then will you go away?"

"Yes." His answer came quickly, like an eager puppy under a dangling bone.

I took a deep breath, released it with a sigh, and then put the car back in park. "And after I tell you, I'll never see you again, right?"

"I cannot promise that." He reached out, almost touching my hand, before tucking his arm back to his side. "Ghost Grace White, what do you have to lose?"

*What did I have to lose...other than my mind?*

"Come on, out with it," he pried. The grin I mistook as sinister a second ago appeared genuine. Now his crooked smile ignited something different in me.

The floodgates opened.

I told him everything.

AN HOUR HAD PASSED, and the hatted man was still sitting in my car.

"Reading that letter, it was like having my guts ripped out. Nothing in my past feels tangible now. Everything was a lie, and I stupidly went along with it. Never once had I thought to question my grandmother. I blindly accepted everything she said as truth. Perhaps the letter is complete insane bullshit. I dunno. But it's left me feeling empty inside. Like a shell of a person."

"Like a ghost," he said, chuckling.

I nodded politely. "Yeah, like a ghost."

Only what I said was not entirely true. Speaking the words aloud, sharing my real feelings had given me a spark of hope. The brittle shell already felt as if it was thickening around the edges, and maybe, over time, it would fill in again.

"I can assure you of one thing, you are not a ghost. You are a lovely woman who deserves better. My advice would be to take charge of your life. Do not sit back and let another dictate it for you. Find a way to meet the mother you've only ever heard stories about. Find your truth and fill that void. And if I may be so bold as to say, I believe it'd be wise to put some distance between you and that grandmother of yours. Sometimes people with the best intentions end up causing the most damage."

I nodded. The hatted man gave solid advice.

Flicking the brim of his hat, he opened the passenger door. "Be sure you put some ice on those knuckles."

Oddly, I thanked him for his company as he exited the car. I was no longer worried that an imaginary man had given the guidance. The fact was, I felt better. And as strange as it might sound after experiencing a full-on hallucination, I felt more in control of my future. I had a semblance of a plan that I was going to execute.

By the time I pulled into the driveway of my townhouse, I was confident of my decision. No more relying on Grandma June's stories. No longer would I follow her advice. Or ask for her permission. I was going to find a way to create my own stories. A new chapter in my life was about to begin, and I alone would be the author.

# Chapter Fifteen

# Juniper

Juniper rubbed her temples and placed her face closer to the steaming mug of dark roast coffee. Caffeine and pills were usually the winning combination whenever she had too much to drink or not enough sleep. But this was not a typical headache. The sharp hammering in her skull began the moment her granddaughter sped away with an expression of sheer terror on her face. What could have spooked Gigi so badly that she would flee without saying a word?

*My house isn't haunted.*

Contrary to popular belief, though people whispered about Juniper's home when she had it repainted just weeks after her husband's death, the real rumors started after Juniper overheard Gigi inform a neighborhood kid that they painted the house black and gray to attract demonic spirits. Her granddaughter also claimed there were chalked pentagrams all over the walls. Juniper watched as her sneering granddaughter opened the creaky cellar door and dared the obnoxious boy to go down and take a look for himself. From Juniper's spot at the window above, she thought the tough kid would accept the challenge. But when Gigi growled—a deep gut-wrenching sound—the punk kid sprinted away into the nearby woods.

Thankfully, that *boy* never came around again.

It was the first time Juniper had witnessed any unstable behavior. Fearful that Meredith's madness had been passed down to her daughter, Juniper watched Gigi more closely after that. At night, she prayed to the deities of this world and the next to spare her precious granddaughter. During the day, she began perfecting the art of snooping.

Nobody knew the dangers of keeping secrets better than Juniper White.

A few days later when nothing had been discovered, she had snuck into her granddaughter's preteen bedroom and nosed through her journal. She was not proud of her actions. A person's privacy should be protected except in this case. Had she not stooped to the level of an undesirable, she never would have found out about the indignities her granddaughter suffered.

The latest journal entries were mostly about neighborhood kids, classmates, and the bullying Gigi had been experiencing at their hands. As Juniper continued to read with gritted teeth, she discovered the secret Gigi had been keeping. Her granddaughter was the recipient of unwanted male attention. A more recent entry told Juniper everything she needed to know.

*"Dear Diary, Brad Evans won't leave me alone. I don't want to kiss him. He needs to stop touching me. I've tried everything, but he won't stop. I bet he'll stop if he thinks I'm crazy like my mom. That's what I'll do. I'll scare the crap out of him!"*

According to the diary, the abuse had been going on for three weeks. For three whole weeks, Gigi had been touched, kissed, hit, and ridiculed by this *Brad Evans* and others. And not once had Gigi come to her grandmother for help!

The only thing that eventually calmed Juniper's fury was that Gigi had not come up with the idea of threats and demons on her own. Her odd behavior and daring words were a result of the stories Juniper told. The ones Juniper continued to tell in order to keep her granddaughter from ever wanting to connect with her mother.

In part, Juniper was relieved. Thankful that her granddaughter stood up for herself in a creative yet effective way. But she was still angry. Disappointed in Gigi for choosing to keep it from her, and enraged that her granddaughter had been dealt yet another undeserved blow.

Now they both had secrets. While Juniper kept her secrets for the greater good, to shield and protect, she could not fathom the reason Gigi had felt the need to keep the abuse she had suffered hidden.

*It didn't make sense then, and it doesn't make sense now.*

Juniper sat back in her chair and grabbed the lukewarm cup of coffee. She had called and texted Gigi a dozen times already. But her granddaughter still had not responded. If it was not so late, and she did not have this unshakable headache, she would have driven to her granddaughter's house and demanded answers. For now, she was sidelined, torturing herself with old memories and the ever-dreaded fear of what-ifs.

For years Juniper wrestled with the shame of having a mentally ill daughter. The criticism and judgments people cast upon the White family were primarily out of fear and ignorance. But even so, their harsh words and dirty looks left gaping wounds on Juniper's psyche and sometimes on her physical being and property as well. Meredith had done some terrible things, and there had been a short stint of vandalism just before she was committed to Glen Haven. The social injustice and malicious attacks nearly ruined Juniper's reputation. Social pariah was not a label Juniper wore well or for long. Refusing to endure the humiliation, she used the only thing she had plenty of—money. Armed with an innocent newborn and gobs and gobs of charity, Juniper bought her way back into the good graces of her community.

Since the day her granddaughter was born, Juniper had done whatever was necessary to keep Gigi content with a stress-free life. Juniper believed a child raised without fear or worry would grow into a sound and stable adult. She had failed to protect her daughter that way. Juniper refused to make the same mistake twice.

In the beginning, she had no desire to take care of her daughter's daughter. The day Meredith went away, Juniper celebrated her freedom—for months. She was finally free from the violence, the anger, and the hatred. No more late-night emergency room visits. No more screaming, breaking, crying, or meds.

For a while, Juniper lived a quiet, normal life. Then the day came when she learned of her daughter's rape, which was followed by even more unfortunate news.

Meredith was pregnant.

The day Meredith gave birth, the gods opened the skies and let their anger rain down on earth. Juniper barely made it to the hospital in one piece. Soon after she arrived, the baby died. Initially, Juniper viewed the death as a kindness. Nature's way of correcting a mistake. But then medical science intervened, and Juniper cursed the doctors for reviving the poor thing. A child created by violence, incubated in insanity, would only grow to become a monster.

Juniper had always believed that bad people were born that way. She never thought to question her belief until she held her daughter's baby in her arms. When Juniper looked into Gigi's big doe eyes, she did not see a monster. She saw a miniature version of herself. Ten tiny toes, ten tiny fingers, and a cupid's bow mouth. Gigi was perfect in every way. Well, almost perfect. The name her daughter had insisted on giving the baby was less than desirable. Hell, it did not make a lick of sense. But it was the one stipulation Meredith had clung to. Any adoptee of her daughter would have to keep her given birth name.

A social worker barged in just as Juniper was about to hand the baby off to a nurse. Brash and loud, the old bat started barking about needing a decision and signing papers. It turned out that if Juniper did not take custody, the baby would become a ward of the state.

Juniper's beliefs wavered the moment she recalled a news broadcast on the neglect and abuse foster children often faced. If Gigi was not born a monster, then surely she would become one after being reduced to a form of currency for a callous moneygrubber or turned into a pervert's plaything. No, Juniper would not allow her blood—her kin—to suffer that way. She had almost smacked herself in the head for being so stubborn and stupid. Instead, she took the baby home. She was determined to nurture *this* child into something loving and wholesome.

Four months later, Juniper legally adopted Gigi.

It had not taken very long for a special bond to forge. One that went far beyond the typical grandmother and granddaughter relationship. Juniper was Gigi's everything, her always and forever. A nurturing mother, a proud father, and an indulgent grandparent.

Already life with her grandchild was a much different experience than the life she had with her daughter. Provide, protect, and confide. That was her mantra when it came to raising Gigi. Of course, Juniper was most proud of the fact that, over the years, they had become best friends.

*Though what kind of friend takes off without a word and then refuses to answer your calls?*

Juniper sipped her coffee and immediately spit it back into the mug. It was ice cold. She had spent too much time pondering ancient history in the kitchen when she should be getting to the bottom of Gigi's current troubles. It was not like it was something she had never done before. Juniper had resolved plenty of issues without her granddaughter's knowledge. This would just be another one of those times.

# Chapter Sixteen

# Ghost

If Grandma June had anything to say about it, my mother would die without ever again laying eyes on me.

Except it was not up to her.

As soon as I found out about the guardianship, I should have contacted a lawyer. Asking for permission had been a mistake. I would have to threaten Grandma June. And if that did not work, I would take it to the streets. The only things Grandma June loved more than me were her money and her reputation.

Once I arrived home, I numbed my swollen hands with ice packs and took some ibuprofen. I was exhausted, but the chaos in my mind would not allow me to fall asleep. I continued to pull my mother's letter from the nightstand drawer to read. Each time, I promised myself it would be the last. I would put it away and lie back, determined to get the rest I needed, only to sit up and pull the letter out again. I kept reminding myself that tomorrow I would seize the day with a phone call or an email. Then I would enjoy my date with Bishop—the only thing I had felt excited about in a long time.

Turning off the bedside lamp, I fluffed my pillow and laid my head down for the umpteenth time. Only to be bombarded by another scary realization.

I had become my mother.

My episodes might have been considered tame and positive compared to Grandma June's crazy tales, but what about the next one?

Would I soon lose myself in in-between worlds, never knowing what was real and what was fake? Or would I be able to manage it and live a productive life outside of an institution?

Then again, what if my grandmother's stories were untrue?

Chills like frozen fingertips ran the length of my spine as I imagined all the things I could become.

Already knowing sleep would be impossible to find, I grabbed my laptop and dove into the turbulent waters of mental illness. For the first time, I searched the spectrums of schizophrenia and all their related disorders.

While reading, I learned schizophrenia and something called schizoaffective shared some symptoms and treatments, but that schizophrenia involved more psychosis-like hallucinations, delusions, and bizarre thoughts, which I had recently experienced firsthand.

Schizoaffective was more related to mood disturbances like mania and depression. And though I was not wholly lacking in those highs and lows, I did not feel the disorder met my current criteria. However, only a doctor would know for sure.

My final diagnosis, the one that seemed to check all the boxes, was schizophreniform. A temporary psychosis brought on by stress and trauma that only lasted a short period of time. If I freed myself from external stressors, then maybe I could rid myself of the hatted man. With schizophreniform, I would not suffer my mother's fate. It gave me a spark of hope to hold on to.

SUNDAY WAS A DAY FUELED by a never-ending stream of caffeine. Somehow, I had managed to get a helpful legal assistant on the phone who could schedule a Tuesday evening appointment with Mr. Rutledge. According to my online search, Paul Rutledge was a highly sought-after, no-nonsense family lawyer with a near-perfect track record.

Last night, Grandma June called several times to find out why I had left the house in a hurry and without a proper goodbye. I wanted to call her out on the years of deception but resisted the urge. While I listened to her voicemails, I purposefully left her text messages unread, just so she would feel the dismissive sting. The depth and width of the well of lies she had dug would remain a mystery for the time being.

Tuesday could not come soon enough.

I was daydreaming about walking up to Grandma June with the news that I was hiring a lawyer when the doorbell rang.

Bishop arrived at 6:05 p.m. Respectfully five minutes late. When I opened the door, his brows shot up and his jaw dropped. His dark hazel eyes surveyed my body. I could feel him taking everything in from my silky straight strands down to my bold yellow heels. While he absorbed the masterpiece created for him, I admired his handsome ensemble of pressed black jeans, a white dress shirt, and a tweed sports jacket.

Bishop released a gruff breath. "Now I feel like the one going to prom."

"The name's Ghost, not Carrie." If so much as a drop of wine touched my dress, I would lose my mind. More than I already had.

"Oh, this is no horror movie." Bishop leaned in and a waft of linen and spice ignited my senses. "You are a vision of joyous perfection," he whispered before pressing his lips to mine.

We held that kiss a touch too long. I pulled away before it went any further and we missed our dinner reservation.

"You look pretty amazing yourself," I said, stepping out on the front steps with him. After I locked the front door, he took my elbow and escorted me to his vehicle. The rugged Jeep had been replaced by a tan Mercedes.

Always a gentleman, Bishop stood aside as he held the passenger door open.

"Pulling out all the stops." I slid past him and down into the buttery leather seat.

"Just keeping up with you and that dress," he said with a brilliant flash of dimples.

I could not help the grin that came to my lips every time Bishop glanced over. Or when he ran his fingers through his hair, purposely nonchalant, each time I caught him staring in my direction. He was so distracted by the slit in my dress, exposing a bare leg, that he never seemed to notice the red scrapes on my knuckles and almost missed the turn into the restaurant parking lot.

We linked arms as we walked into Harbor Point. Leaning into each other, we chuckled conspiratorially while eyeing a nervous teen and her sweaty date accompanied by a set of parents. A chaperoned first date for a pair of sixteen-year-olds, we guessed. And then it dawned on me that Bishop and I were on our official first date. One with all the exuberance and none of the awkwardness.

Despite having reservations at the exceedingly sought-after upscale establishment, it was a ten-minute wait. Bishop grabbed a martini and a glass of Sauvignon Blanc at the bar. He handed me the wine and then clinked the rim of his glass against mine.

"Cheers to young love," he said with a wink and loud enough to gain the attention of the timid teens. They stood behind the parents, close enough for their arms to touch, but neither was brave enough to take the other's hand. I smiled at them, took hold of Bishop's hand, and held it up for them to witness.

Suddenly, a look of determination passed over the young man's face, and he zealously reached for his date's hand. He was rewarded by a sheepish smile from the girl, who did not pull away. The teens cast beaming smiles our way as they followed the parents proudly through the restaurant to their table.

I continued to watch as they were seated. The young man had been taught manners and proceeded to pull out the chair for his date. Both still had bright smiles etched into their tender faces.

There's something special about first loves. I might be older and more experienced, but tonight, with Bishop, I was as giddy as those teenagers. This was already the best date I had been on in years, and we had not even made it to our table. And whereas that young man would likely end his night with a PG-rated kiss goodnight, I hoped to receive a bit more attention from my date.

"How old were you when you went on your first date?" Bishop asked before taking a sip of his martini.

"Fourteen, I think. And it was nothing as nice as this. His name was Trevor. And his mom drove us to McDonald's for milkshakes and then dropped us off at a matinee."

He set his drink down and rested his elbows on the high-top bar table, leaning in close enough for me to smell his gin-coated breath when it hit my cheek. "Did you make out in the back row of the theater?"

I turned my head, briefly brushing my lips against his. "We most certainly did not. I was overly excited about the *Transformers* movie back then."

"Poor Trevor." Bishop's voice was raw and edgy. "I would have tried to do a lot more than kiss you in that theater."

"Too bad we're not in a dark theater now."

A few sexually charged minutes passed, and I thought we might skip dinner altogether when a tuxedoed waiter arrived and escorted us to a plush corner booth. Once seated, Bishop ordered a rare vintage bottle of cabernet and requested the cucumber canape appetizer. With his non-use of the menu, it was obvious that he had been here before. Possibly with his ex-girlfriend Ava.

As quickly as that thought roared, I silenced it. I was not about to ruin a great night with thoughts of another woman.

Bishop ordered the Chilean sea bass that I sampled at his insistence. He also received a taste of my meal, a hand-fed piece of sesame-crusted ahi tuna. The entire dinner was scrumptious. We were anxiously awaiting our dessert when he switched the topic from workplace antics to something I had completely forgotten about.

Bishop leaned forward in his seat and stretched his hands out so that his fingers touched mine. "I apologize if I overstepped by inviting myself the other night. But if it's okay with you, I'd like to join you and your new friends at Jimmie's Tuesday?"

The new friends he referred to were Mina and Jessa. The lovely couple I met Friday night at The Weather Box when I had gone to hear his band play. We had made plans to meet for happy hour to see their favorite girl group and have a drink or two at a dive bar on the outskirts of town.

Only those plans were not going to happen. Now I was meeting with the family lawyer on Tuesday evening. Hopefully, Paul Rutledge would put the fear of God into Juniper so that I could get into Glen Haven and finally meet my mother.

After what I had just been through with Grandma June, I knew I could not lie to him, even in the early stages of dating. *Always better to tell the truth.* Especially after discovering that the most important person in my life had been lying to me for the entirety of it.

I pulled my hand back and ran a finger around the rim of my wineglass. "Of course, I wouldn't mind if you came. I think it'd be a fun night out. The only problem is my plans recently changed. I have an important meeting Tuesday evening."

The waiter returned, placing a slice of cheesecake between us with two forks. Bishop sat back in his chair, removing his hands from the table. "Um, okay."

He looked so dejected that once the waiter was out of earshot, I continued with details I should have kept close to the chest. "I'm going to see a family lawyer. My grandmother has adult guardianship over my mother. She's refusing to let me see her and I'm fighting back. My mother and I are long overdue for our first meeting."

"Wait, you have never gone to see your mother before?" His hands were back on the table but not close enough to touch. "Not once, ever?"

He seemed surprised even though I had told him yesterday that I had never met my mother in person. I did, of course, appreciate that he had not reiterated the fact that she had been locked up her entire adult life as a paranoid schizophrenic with bouts of depression and anxiety. Not that he knew any of the particulars. And now that I thought about it, he had not been affected by that news, which was odd. Despite society's recent push for more understanding, most people cringed before changing the subject.

"I'm sure you realize it's a long story and not the best one to tell during a lovely dinner such as this—my grandmother kept us apart for reasons I'm sure she thought were for the best. But now it's time. I've waited too long." I was angry at Grandma June, but I was not an idiot. I knew she had reasons for lying about my mother. Not that I would forgive her anytime soon.

"I'll go with you." It was not a question.

"What?" I coughed and grabbed a napkin to cover my mouth. No way he was serious. This was a big deal, and it was personal. Much too personal to share with someone I had not even had sex with yet.

"This is important to you. I want to support you without being too involved. I can sit in the waiting room. I know I might be overstepping again, but you should have someone close by for after. You might need a shoulder to cry on or a sounding board to scream at. I have some experience with the system and how it handles mental illness. My sister, Florina, has battled depression for years. She's been hospitalized a few times."

So, his younger sister was the reason he had not turned and run away when he heard about my mother's illness. I sighed and picked up my fork, broke off a bite of cake, and savored the creamy, sweet goodness.

It must have been food euphoria, his rational thinking, or perhaps his extraordinarily good looks. Whatever the case, over wine and a piece of chocolate cheesecake, I had somehow agreed to let him accompany me to the meeting with Mr. Rutledge.

THROUGHOUT DINNER AND the ride home, I made certain that my phone had remained silent. Now that we were pulling into my driveway, and I would be inviting Bishop inside for an evening of uninhibited sexual encounters, I checked my phone. Grandma June had texted and left more voicemails. She was relentless and I would not have a repeat of the other morning. So, after making Bishop a whiskey nightcap, I excused myself upstairs to strip down into something more comfortable and then answered my impatient grandmother. I pulled out my mother's old letter from my nightstand drawer, snapped a picture, and sent it off in a text.

*My lawyer will contact you when I'm ready to talk!*

Relief, they say, feels like a weight being lifted off your shoulders. Confronting Grandma June was better than that. It felt like I had surpassed the farthest mark in a race. Climbed the tallest mountain and swam the widest ocean. I had achieved the unachievable. I felt victorious.

Even though technically I was not a step closer to meeting my mother.

Refusing to let the good feeling fade, I changed into my naughtiest lingerie. And then added a red silk robe as the finishing touch. Before I left the bedroom, I paused in front of the mirror and saw a confident woman staring back at me.

When I returned downstairs, Bishop had removed his jacket and was sipping on a heavy pour of whiskey. I sidled up next to him, removed the glass from his hand, and opened my robe. He swallowed hard as he inspected my lacy undergarments.

Then his hands were on me. His lips pressed tightly to mine before his tongue slipped inside for a taste. I made quick work of the buttons on his shirt. I was undoing his belt when my robe fell from my shoulders. My naked lower back was pressed against the cold kitchen island when his pants dropped to the floor.

Bishop took a step back. He stood eerily still as he appeared to savor the moment. When he groaned and closed his eyes, I knew he had committed my body to memory. I shivered at the thought of what he would do when he recalled the image later.

And then suddenly, I could not stop trembling.

The night at the club, Bishop was the distraction I desperately needed. Now, somehow real emotions were involved. I could not quite put my finger on it, but I was sure this was more than physical lust. I wanted Bishop in every sense of the word. And nearly squealed when he opened his eyes and hoisted me onto the marble counter.

A dimpled, devious grin was the only warning I received before he pushed me back and climbed on top of me. I could barely breathe. Excitement had robbed me of my ability to think. Pleasure was the only thing my brain processed. Strong hands on my body, soft lips on my skin, and the pleasure of him moving deep inside me.

# Chapter Seventeen

## Juniper

Juniper slapped her face again. Harder this time than the last. She was sure a red mark had formed and risked leaving a bruise on her left cheek if she did not stop.

Though why should she? Juniper knew the punishment was deserved.

After reading Gigi's text message, Juniper had sat in a state of suspended animation for hours. Now it was time to be reprimanded for being so careless. How in the hell could Juniper have missed a letter? And how had she gone an entire day without noticing it?

Wherever it was that her granddaughter had found it, the only saving grace was that the letter was not one of the many addressed to Juniper. One of those would have been much harder to explain.

At first, Juniper wanted to apologize and beg for an audience. But wisdom steadied her hand. She had to consciously refrain from making yet another mistake.

Maybe she was getting senile in her old age. If only she was five years younger, an incident like this never would have occurred. A feeble, weak-minded idiot, that's what she had become. There was only one way to fix the damage she had caused. It was the same actions she had taken in her youth.

The decisions and choices Juniper made were never easy. But she always managed to make the right call. For better or for worse. This was just another one of those times. Her hand had been forced. No use in fighting it.

Unfortunately, once Gigi made the request to see her mother, she knew the end result would be tragic.

Gigi's astounding text had pinged her phone at 9:45. Hours later, Juniper's excruciating decision was made. Thick clouds created a black moonless night as she made her way down to the dock.

She always kept the special arrangement of ingredients close at hand. The recipe was simple. Lumps of backfin crab meat mixed with breadcrumbs and crushed oyster crackers. Parsley, Worcestershire sauce, lemon, salt, and Old Bay for added flavor. Mayonnaise, Dijon mustard, and egg to bind it all together. And then just a touch of that extra special ingredient. She had everything she needed, including the live crabs down at the pier.

No one could resist her famous crab cakes. They were Meredith's favorite when she was a little girl.

It was eerie going down to the dock late in the evening. Even on a clear night, the light never quite reached the end of the pier. Normally, Juniper took cautiously light steps on the uneven boards so as not to trip or make herself heard. It was a habit she adopted after the death of her husband. If his spirit remained out there on the water, she thought it wrong to disturb it.

On this night, she wore boots with wooden heels and rang a tarnished cowbell that had no purpose other than collecting dust in the old boat shed. Tonight, she would speak to her dead husband as if he were listening to her every word.

"Henry, you old ass, our little family is in shambles. But your bad genes will not rule the day," she bellowed as she swung the bell and stomped her way down the pier.

Plopping down on a piling, she pulled the live box to the surface, the swimming blue crabs darting to and fro in their efforts to escape the confines of the wire cage. Juniper made quick work of removing them from the live box and placing them in a lidded basket. Then she kicked the cowbell into the black water.

The crabs would be steamed alive. Something she would like to have happen to all despicable human beings who caused too much havoc in the world. To hell with prisons. That was a crummy hotel stay compared to what she would do. Show someone what it meant to be cooked alive, and surely the crime rate would falter.

It would also help with the food shortage in America. Good meat was good meat; it did not matter much where it came from. She doubted any starving soul would turn down a steaming bowl of stew. They cared little about the origins of the meat that garnished it as long as the food tasted good.

And she could make anything taste great. That's what good cooks did. They strived their entire careers to create edible masterpieces. And Juniper was no different, though she had never received training as a chef.

"The world's a different place now, Henry," she mumbled as she hoisted the basket of clicking crabs onto her hip. "I don't think you'd recognize it at all."

Juniper paused and turned toward a faint noise she heard in the distance. A whisper carried by the wind over the water. Perhaps Henry was attempting a response from beyond the grave. "Damn it, you old fool, there's nothing for you to say about nothing anymore," she said with a huff and then made her way back up to the house.

She was stepping off the dock and moving around to where the grill and propane tanks were kept when she shrieked and started waving her hands about. Almost as if someone had startled her, only no one was there. The crab basket she had been carrying toppled to the ground. With the top flipped open, the crabs scurried out, seizing their chance at freedom.

Days of frustration fell upon her like a stack of bricks. Bending at the waist, she screamed at the grass until her lungs gave out. She had to find a way to keep the inevitable from happening.

When she straightened back up, she adjusted her clothes, smoothing her hair back and ultimately regaining her composure. Determination set in again as she went about collecting the scurrying crabs she could find. Several had vanished into the darkness and would eventually make their way back to the water.

As Juniper prepared the steamer pot, she nodded her head until her hair fell in disarray around her face. Losing those crabs was a minor sacrifice. But she refused to lose any more of her family.

"I still know how to make things better. My way is the right way...the only way. And a peace offering works best."

Pulling a dented tin of Old Bay from her jacket pocket, she doused the snapping crabs with the potent spice, purposely blinding their beady, black eyes. All the while wishing she could blind the world from seeing the terrible things that were never meant to happen.

Juniper pushed her hair away from her tear-streaked face. "Henry, I can't lose her. She's all I have left... Yes, yes, I will see that everything is made right again," she muttered as she dropped the crabs into the scalding steam pot.

# Chapter Eighteen

# Ghost

A damp ponytail, no makeup, and slightly wrinkled slacks were signs that I had left home in a hurry this morning. Not to mention that I had nearly tripped over a container my grandmother had left at my front door.

A batch of her famous crab cakes was a blatant apology. I pocketed the note that was taped to the lid. And to ensure I made it to work on time, I scooped up the insulated container and took it with me. Her guilt could sit in the office community refrigerator until someone came around and ate it.

Mondays in the office were almost always hectic, but today everyone was frenzied, close to the point of mania. Needless to say, my post-sex smile faltered rather quickly when I heard the news. Our firm was at risk of losing one of our biggest clients, due to a long-running oversight on the account. That kind of loss came with publicity and could potentially have a landslide effect on our customer base. All hands were needed for damage control and to get things rolling in the right direction.

I had spent all morning reworking the figures from a previous year's report. My eyes were practically crossing from comparing hundreds of lines of printed data to online reports, searching for that troublesome repeated error. Those unable to help with the crisis knew how to keep their heads down. So, it was surprising to hear laughter coming from the cubicles down the hall.

A few minutes after the giggles quieted, I happened to notice a head of wavy, red hair passing by my office. Curious if it was one of the executives from the botched account, I got up and peeked around the glass door. Bishop's ex casually strolled through the cubicles where Kendall and Selina shared a workspace. Ava threw a last-minute glance over her shoulder that had me ducking back into my office.

I had not expected to see *her* again. And here she was conversing jovially with my co-workers. No doubt she was planning to run into Bishop during her visit.

Bringing outside drama into the workplace was not a smart move, even by Kendall and Selina's standards. Especially on a day when upper management and board members were locked in a volatile meeting with repercussions that could lead to firings within the company. Not to mention lawsuits.

Back at my computer, I was trying to focus on the tedious, time-sensitive project when I heard footsteps approaching. The cackling trio paused outside my office. A waft of odiferous perfume assaulted my nose as they crowded around the doorway.

"Want to join us for lunch? It's a nice day out, so we're walking over to Dot's Bistro." A dramatic eye roll from Ava watered down Selina's sugary sweet invitation. The last thing they wanted to do was to sit across a table from me and break bread.

"We're also grabbing the carry-out orders for the board meeting," Kendall added, cheapening the invite even more. What they really wanted was an extra pair of hands to do the heavy lifting.

"As tempting as that offer is, I'm in the middle of a project," I said, turning my attention to the stack of spreadsheets on my desk. "Enjoy." I did not care if they enjoyed their lunch outing or not. I just wanted them to leave my office.

"Are you sure? Bishop will be joining us."

The mention of his name from Ava's lips caused my neck and shoulders to stiffen. I hoped they had not noticed my cringe or how my hands were now fisted over my keyboard. With a calming breath,

I forcibly straightened my fingers and swiveled around in my chair with a bright smile. "No thanks. I'll see him later," I said in my best singsong voice that sounded more like a strangled ostrich.

Ava stepped forward, capturing my attention with a deadpan stare. She had a slight smear of black mascara under her left eye. "I wouldn't do that if I were you." Her voice was low, almost a whisper. "He's devious and you're a *nice* girl. It's worse than being a notch on the proverbial bedpost with him. Especially one that's been carved to the size of a toothpick." The way she pursed her pink lips reminded me of the cracked mannequin in the second-hand shop window on 9th Avenue.

I did not want to jump to conclusions about Bishop, nor did I want to give Ava the satisfaction of rattling me, even though she had done exactly that. I tried to remind myself that she was in a bad emotional headspace and possibly a little unhinged.

Not all that different from myself.

Desperate times, desperate measures. I understood that well enough. There would be no giving into the temptation of letting her know exactly how much I had enjoyed Bishop over the weekend. *No catfights in the office today.*

"Okay. Have a nice lunch." I turned back to my work and opened a new email. It did not matter what letters or numbers I typed. The message would never be sent. I only had to appear busy so they would take the hint and get the hell out.

What started as one of the better days I had in weeks was not going to end well. The damage was done. I could feel it in my jittering legs and hot cheeks. I was mad, anxious. They had achieved their goal and gotten under my skin. It was no secret among women. When it came to men, we knew which buttons to push. They did not know Bishop and I had sex last night, but I was sure they assumed we did the night we left the bar together. But regardless of when it happened, who's to say it would happen again?

Bishop had made plans to go with me tomorrow to meet with the lawyer before we had sex. Would it be that big of a surprise if he called and canceled at the last minute? Probably not. The thought of going alone, without a shoulder to cry on or a sounding board—the shoulder and sounding board that I did not know I wanted or needed until he suggested it—had me seeing red.

*Fuck! I need a walk.*

CIRCLING THE BLOCK at a brisk pace should have settled my nerves and soothed those prickly emotions. A little fresh air and movement usually did the trick, but flaming curiosity got the better of me. Suddenly my legs were taking me west, past the parking lot, across the street. As much as I wanted to turn around, an equal part of me wanted to witness the truth for myself. Good or bad, I had to know. Bishop and I had not seen each other since he had rushed out of my house this morning, sporting a sizable boner. Could last night truly be all there would ever be between us? Had Bishop been honest about their relationship being nothing more than a few subpar dates?

Ava did not seem to think so. The repeated attempts to scare me off were proof of that.

Dot's Bistro was a quaint deli less than a ten-minute walk from the office. A green-and-white canopy shaded the sidewalk where a pair of wooden settees framed the doorway. It only took a glance through the glass storefront to spot the menacing trio. Selina, Kendall, and Ava were eating sandwiches and conversing at a four-top table. There was an empty chair beside Ava. Pausing behind a telephone pole, I breathed a sigh of relief. They had lied about Bishop joining them for lunch. I should have known better. Why did I continue to believe every word that spilled out of anyone's mouth?

Satisfied and with a renewed sense of positivity, I started to head back to the office when I glimpsed a familiar movement. There was no mistaking his striking physique or that powerful stride. Bishop was there, weaving through the restaurant from the back bathrooms. He stopped behind their table, ate some fries he snagged from one of the plates, and then placed both hands on Ava's shoulders. Feeling the sting of stupidity, I closed my eyes.

*I am such an imbecile!*

When I opened my eyes again, Ava looked up at Bishop, her eyes brimming with indiscernible emotion. Then she turned with a tight smile and stared directly at me.

Initially, I wanted to storm into the restaurant. Yell, scream, rip out clumps of red hair. But for what reason? I had no claim on Bishop. We worked together, liked each other, made each other laugh. We even had one near-perfect date followed by an amazing night of sex. But that did not mean we were an item, much less exclusive.

In fact, at that moment, I decided that Bishop did not mean anything at all.

Pulling the strap of my purse tightly over my shoulder, I did my best to *stroll* away from Dot's Bistro. The best thing I could do for myself was to bury my head under a pile of work, go home, lick my wounds, and try to forget the disaster of a day it had turned out to be.

*There's always tomorrow.*

When I reentered the office building, the downstairs lobby was empty, which was not surprising given the hour. The front desk was always vacant between noon and one thirty. Visitors who arrived during that time would have to wait or use one of the three touchscreen monitors to gain an access code for the elevators.

What did surprise me was the imaginary man who had tucked himself in the far corner, ironically next to a fake Ficus tree.

The hatted man waved me over when he saw me heading for the elevators. I did not want to get caught talking to a tree in the lobby, so I ignored his presence. Reaching the elevator, I scanned my ID and repeatedly pushed the button as I waited.

When I failed to acknowledge the hatted man, he got up and made his way through the cavernous lobby to the elevators. His dress shoes clacking on the marble tile echoed the whole way. "I've been waiting for you. There's an urgent matter we need to discuss."

I shook my head and kept my voice low. "Not now, I have too much going on today." At any moment, someone would walk into the building and see me talking to myself. This could not continue. I had to get a handle on my mental state. *No time for delusions today.* Not that there was ever a suitable time for one of those.

"I don't mean to impose. But we must speak."

The ding of the elevator sounded behind me. I took a step back as the doors opened, keeping my body in the middle to block the hatted man from entering. Though how do you really stop a figment of your imagination?

"You cannot come upstairs," I said as I reached over to press the button to close the doors. It was an uncomfortable, drawn-out moment while a staticky rendition of "Only the Lonely" played on the overhead speaker. We stared at each other for a couple of seconds before the sight unfolding behind him grabbed my attention.

Grandma June was outside the lobby door, one hand reaching for the handle while awkwardly balancing a cell phone to her ear. If I were to guess, she was ringing my cell phone in an attempt to find neutral territory to state her case. Or she was coming to scold me for not thanking her for the crab cakes she left this morning. Regardless, she had to know she was the last person I wanted to see. Which was why she had chosen to show up at my office. Pragmatic and calculating, she knew I would not make a scene in front of my co-workers.

But I needed to get back to work and distract myself from the fact that I was losing my mind—and that Bishop could play me for a fool as easily as Grandma June.

Noticing my distracted gaze, the hatted man glanced over his shoulder. Then the elevator doors closed, and thankfully, both he and Grandma June disappeared.

# Chapter Nineteen

## Juniper

The semi-opulent lobby of Mason, Kemper, and Witt Financial was surprisingly empty. Juniper walked over to one of the long, cushioned benches adjacent to the front entrance and waited. She had hoped that Gigi would have phoned her by now. But then again, Juniper had no idea what her granddaughter's workday was like. Gigi could be pressed for time, hustling to get things done in order to leave early.

Her granddaughter had been working as an executive assistant for a few years and not once had Juniper been inside her office. The only reason she knew the location of the building was because Gigi had made a stop here one day when they were out running errands together. If Juniper had arrived under normal circumstances, she would have gone to the touchscreen monitors stationed by the vacant reception desk or called Gigi's cell phone. She had already placed one call. And she was not sure if there was another way to get upstairs in a secured building.

Searching five floors housing dozens of offices would not have been a viable option. Besides, the note Juniper left with this morning's peace offering, an extra spicy batch of broiled crab cakes, told Gigi to meet her in the lobby at one o'clock.

Juniper had stayed up late into the night cooking her specialty and delivered it to Gigi's home before the crack of dawn. Both of them would deliver the second batch to Glen Haven. There was no need for lawyers. Juniper knew she could work this out with Gigi the old-fashioned way. A sensible talk, some tasty food, and perhaps a bit of trickery.

Juniper could feel the mountain of guilt she had been carrying finally start to crumble. She was basking in the quiet, picturing how the rest of the day would pan out, when a man and two women bustled into the lobby, each carrying white, long-handled bags. The aroma of fresh deli meat, garlic, and pesto permeated around them as they paused, continuing an argument that apparently had begun outside.

"That was unnecessary. She's still out there crying. You need to go back and talk to her," said a dark-haired girl in high heels and skintight pants. The man she addressed wore a menacing scowl that marred his otherwise handsome face. Even at her age, Juniper appreciated the beauty of a stormy man.

Abruptly the man pushed forward. He might have thrown his hands up in the air with noticeable frustration if he was not carrying so much. "She's not as innocent as she appears. Besides, I tried to be nice. Ava refuses to listen. We are not a couple. You two shouldn't have encouraged her the way you did. It only made things worse."

Juniper loved nothing more than juicy gossip and relationship drama. She pretended to type out a message on her phone and watched with keen interest. It was like viewing an episode of sloppy reality TV.

"How was I supposed to know? I honestly thought it was just an office rumor," a light-haired girl chimed in with an explanation that even Juniper doubted to be true.

The dark-haired girl nodded in agreement. "Yeah, me too."

The man practically growled. "Well, it's not a rumor. Never was. If I have anything to say about it, Ghost and I will be together for a long time."

Juniper's lips tightened at the mention of her granddaughter's birth name, but a man interested in her sweet Gigi was someone she had to meet. This must be Bishop, the IT guy Gigi talked about. Checking the time on her watch, she stood up and approached the tense trio.

"Excuse me. Um, sorry to interrupt. I couldn't help but overhear," Juniper said, batting her eyelashes. An old habit from her youth whenever she was in the presence of a fine-looking man. "You know Miss White? I'm Juniper White, her grandmother."

The man put his back to his two hare-brained companions and addressed Juniper with a pair of dimples that almost made her weak in the knees. "You must be Grandma June. I've heard a lot about you."

"Oh my, all good, I hope." She held back the urge to flutter a hand over her heart. There was no need to flirt with a man half her age.

"Of course, it's only been good," he said with a subtle rumble of laughter. "I'm Bishop Mazzeo."

"It's so nice to meet you, Mr. Mazzeo. I don't mean to be a bother, but I'm in a pickle. I'm here to meet Gigi, but she's not answering her phone, and I don't want us to be late for our appointment."

She made a point of grimacing as she glanced over at the elevators.

"I have arthritic knees, so walking up and down stairs takes forever. And I have a terrible fear of elevators ever since I got stuck in one as a child. Would you be so kind as to go up and ask her to come down? I'm sure she's just busy and lost track of the time."

Juniper believed she had played her part of a helpless old lady well. Bishop looked like he would be more than happy to assist. He had to think that buttering up to her would be an excellent way to gain more favor with her granddaughter. Not to mention, she doubted Gigi would deny any request from this man.

The dark-haired girl, who appeared to be carrying the lightest load, stepped in front of Bishop with a wide smile. Right away Juniper did not like this one. She was overly made-up, almost to the point of fake, which might have been appealing to some. But a wise person would see her for what she truly was—spiteful and insecure.

"It's been a crazy day here, but we're heading up to the board meeting with lunch now. We'll let *Gigi* know you're waiting," the dark-haired girl exclaimed. "I'm Selina, by the way. This is Kendall. We both work with your granddaughter."

"Aren't you two the sweetest dears. Thank you."

As the overly posturing pair moved past her on their way to the elevator, Juniper held out an arm to hold Bishop back. "My hearing's not what it used to be, but did you say something about *dating* my granddaughter?" she asked with a conspicuous smile.

"We just started dating, but I've been interested in Ghost for a long time."

*That awful name!* Juniper rarely heard it spoken—and twice now from this man's lips. It felt as if he had flung a curse on her.

"Not to interfere, but I'm afraid my granddaughter is dealing with some unfortunate family troubles. She's very fragile, so please tread kindly and carefully. I don't want her upset and wouldn't want to see you get hurt." Because if this too-handsome of a man ever caused her sweet granddaughter pain, she would pluck those dimples right out of his scruff-covered cheeks.

With a tilt of his head, Bishop's hazel eyes narrowed in response, but his friendly smile never faltered. Perhaps he perceived Juniper's advice as a threat. "Yes, ma'am. I understand. I have only the best intentions when it comes to Ghost."

Juniper gritted her teeth and patted his arm, noting the sizable hardness of his bicep that bulged from holding the heavy bags laden with lunchtime meals. "That's wonderful to hear, Mr. Mazzeo. I won't keep you any longer. It was so nice to meet you. I hope to see you again soon."

From the angle of her head when she made eye contact, she gauged that he was slightly over six feet tall. Well-built, athletic. Most likely between one hundred ninety and two hundred pounds. He would be a formidable opponent should he ever need to quarrel.

"It was a pleasure meeting you, too. We should all have dinner sometime," he said as he headed for the elevators.

"That would be lovely."

She watched as he swiped a card at the elevator and waited. He must have felt her eyes on his back because he turned and gave a slight nod as the elevator doors began to open. Once inside, the sharp rise and fall of his shoulders was a sure sign that she had unnerved him.

Juniper went back to sit on the padded bench near the window. She angled herself so she had an unobstructed view of the elevator doors and patiently waited for Gigi to arrive.

When the time on her watch reached 1:15 p.m., she decided to give her granddaughter another call.

Straight to voicemail.

The elevator dinged and the doors opened. Juniper stood, expecting to see Gigi emerge with an apology for her tardiness. Instead, a disheveled man in a brown suit with a red, sweaty face rushed by her. Barreling through the front doors, he ran to a gray luxury sedan parked near the entrance and sped off.

"Five more minutes," Juniper mumbled, smoothing down the front of her pink polyester dress.

While waiting, Juniper tried not to think the worst of her granddaughter. There had to be a reasonable explanation for why Gigi would make her wait. But what if there was no good reason? What if Gigi was doing it out of spite?

Five minutes turned into ten. And there was still no sign of her granddaughter.

Why would Gigi intentionally make her suffer? Was her granddaughter so angry over the discovery of her mother's letter that she no longer cared about the only person who ever cared about her? Juniper had not even been given a chance to explain. It was not fair. After everything Juniper had been through and everything she had protected Gigi from, Juniper deserved better than this.

Snatching her purse off the bench, she knuckled a falling tear and exited the building.

# Chapter Twenty

# Ghost

In the last thirty minutes, I had spent more time looking over my shoulder than doing actual work. Between catching Bishop with Ava and knowing that my grandmother was lurking in the building, I was not accomplishing anything. Not that it mattered much. The board meeting was running long.

At this point, it did not appear as if the damage could be undone. Any second now, Grandma June would come waltzing down the hall and into my office, forcing an interaction in a place where it was inappropriate and a conversation I was not prepared to have.

Of course, I had also been keeping an eye out for Bishop. Not that I wanted to see him or had something to say to him if I did.

Then again, the thing I truly feared most, and had to bury, was the fact that another hallucination could make an appearance in my heightened state of anxiety.

"Hey there, mind if I come in?"

I jumped at the sudden intrusion even though there was no mistaking his voice. A low, charming rumble that felt like velvet along my skin. It was as if I had conjured Bishop just by thinking of him. The same way my overstressed mind had crafted the hatted man.

"I'm kind of busy," I said, staring at the floating bubbles on the computer screensaver.

I felt the heat of his presence behind me. "Is that why you didn't go with your grandmother?"

"What?" I turned around and sighed as an unexpected image of his naked body flashed through my mind's eye. Then those perfect dimples appeared, and I almost forgot how angry I was supposed to be.

"Are you okay? Your grandmother said you were supposed to meet her in the lobby. Do you two have an appointment or something? Kendall and Selina were supposed to let you know she was waiting."

*Appointment? Oh, no!* Had she contacted her lawyer? *Shit!* I snatched my phone off my desk. With all the chaos this morning, I had put it on silent. There were seven missed calls. All from Grandma June.

"I haven't seen them." *Well, not since the bistro...*

Bishop stepped forward, knelt, and then placed his hands on my knees.

I suddenly remembered the note as I set my phone back on the desk. It was the one Grandma June dropped off on my front steps with a container of crab cakes. *Where did I put it?*

"That's odd. But it has been a crazy day, and you know how those two get. Probably saw something shiny. I would have come myself, but you know, kind of insane around here."

*Oh, you have no idea.*

I had turned to open the bottom drawer of my desk when Bishop leaned into my line of sight. "So, dinner tonight? Italian or Chinese?"

I really did not have time for him. But looking at all of his gorgeously portrayed innocence, my heart rate skyrocketed. I closed my eyes to help refuel the fury, reminding myself of what he had done. How he had likely lied about his relationship with Ava. How he touched and laughed with her...which was only a few hours after Bishop and I had spent the night together. *Am I just another notch on a carved-up bedpost?*

"I don't know. We might need to take a rain check." A familiar saying played in my ear: Fool me once, shame on you, fool me twice, shame on me, fool me three times...

Grandma June had fooled me my entire life. Why should he be any different?

"Can I ask why?" The light circles his fingers drew around my kneecaps made my skin tingle.

"Ava." Her name slipped out before I thought better of it. I should have told him I was tired or had to work late. Because now I was the one who sounded jealous and petty.

"What does Ava have to do with anything?"

Ava had everything to do with how I felt toward Bishop: regret, disappointment, indecision.

"I saw you with her. Laughing, your hands on her shoulders—which was only minutes after she came in here and told me—"

"Hold on." Bishop's hands disappeared from my knees as he sat back on his heels. A scowl had deepened the lines on his forehead. His voice turned vicious as he spat his words. "Ava and I are nothing! We never were. I only stopped into Dot's to help them with the lunch orders for the board meeting." After a deep breath, his tone softened. "But there is something between you and me. We could be great if only you would trust me a little."

There was an involuntary shake of my head. "Trust is earned, not given."

"And that takes time. The only way to prove it is for you to give us more time. I haven't done anything or said anything that would make you not trust me."

I could hardly believe his wide-eyed look of innocence. Or that he had thrown the logic of *time* in my face.

"Ava has issues. I tried to let her down easy again and again. It hasn't gone well. I don't like hurting people, and I wasn't thrilled with her screaming and crying out in the parking lot. But that's how I spent part of my lunch hour today. Honestly, I had no idea she would be with Selina and Kendall at the restaurant."

Leaning forward, his eyes pleaded for me to believe him. "Can you give me the benefit of the doubt here? Don't shut this down because of some mean girl stunt. Not to sound like a lovesick puppy, but I really, *really* like you."

I was a yo-yo in his hands. There was no point in denying my feelings, not to him or myself. "I like you, too. But—"

"No buts." He shook his head, then moved close enough for our lips to almost touch.

I hated the constant waffling. Torturing myself for days, even weeks while I debated a choice. My mind had been so troubled over decisions I could and could not make that it conjured a hatted man in an ill-fitting suit to haunt me into action. Why was I so afraid of making a decision?

Probably because Grandma June had made them all for me.

If ever there was a time for an error in judgment, it was here and now with him.

"No pressure, then." Our chemistry was undeniable. However, our fate was likely doomed. If Ava's jealousy did not ruin it, my insanity surely would.

Bishop rose to his feet and offered me a hand.

As soon as he pulled me from my chair, he wrapped me in a tight embrace. My entire body seemed to relax. It was a rare moment of tenderness on an otherwise shitty afternoon.

"So, you met Grandma June?"

"I did. She was sweet until she found out we were dating, then I don't know."

Could he already be wise to her deceitful ways after a single encounter? "What did she say?"

"It's not so much what she said but how she said it." He slightly shrugged his shoulders as if attempting to brush off his suspicion. He was wise to be suspicious of Grandma June.

"She can be intense and a tad overprotective. Plus, we're not in the best place right now." I nearly cringed at my own words. How could I speak in her defense after everything she had done?

"Want to talk about it over dinner?"

I nodded. If we were to survive as a couple, I would have to open up and share some of my worries and fears. Not all at once, but some background might be necessary if he was going to accompany me to the lawyer's office tomorrow. "Shrimp with garlic sauce and fried rice."

"Chinese it is."

AS SOON AS BISHOP LEFT my office, I dove for my purse and dug out my grandmother's crumpled note.

*Dear Gigi,*

*There's nothing I can say that will change what I did. But try to understand that keeping those letters a secret was and still is for the best. I am sorry you found out the way you did. We have much to discuss. How can we do that if you refuse to pick up the phone or return my calls? I have never been more hurt or confused by your behavior, which is why we have an appointment at Glen Haven today. The two of us will sit down with your mother's doctors and have a proper conversation. I'll pick you up. Meet me in your office lobby at one o'clock. Please be on time.*

*Love forever and always,*
*Grandma June*

# Chapter Twenty-One

# Juniper

Juniper did not enjoy the three-hour drive, even though the sun was shining and traffic was light. She turned on her favorite compilation of jazz songs to brighten her dark mood, but her head refused to bop along to the music. The passage of time moved differently in periods of joy than in times of sorrow. Joyous hours passed you like a speeding freight train, whereas stretches of turmoil moved like a three-legged lizard creeping uphill in a blizzard.

It was a real surprise to Juniper when she pulled up to the gates of the Glen Haven Psychiatric Hospital a few minutes ahead of schedule.

Larry Little had been operating the guard station for nearly ten years and would recognize Juniper's red Challenger as soon as she turned off the highway onto the single-lane road. She was a familiar elderly face that arrived weekly for visits with her daughter. He no longer bothered to check her ID or the visitor's logbook. As she pulled up, he gave a quick wave before punching the button to open the tall metal gates. Juniper rarely waved back. Today would be an exception. On the drive over, she had tried to convince herself that this would be one of her last trips to this godforsaken place.

Larry smiled like he had won the lottery when she raised her hand and flashed a set of straight, white teeth.

Driving up to the third municipal building on the manicured grounds, she found the only guest parking left was a prime spot, a wide space close to the front entrance and without a handicap stamp on the pavement. Juniper could not recall a single time in all her visits when a front-row spot was open. A bark of laughter escaped her lips as she retrieved the second batch of crab cakes from the cooler in the backseat of her car. It was almost as if the universe was taunting her.

How could the rest of the world be perfectly in order when her life was in shambles?

She longed for the day when her life would be free of unwanted obligations and tedious planning. No more worrying, no more looking over her shoulder. During her ride, as her tears dried, she fantasized about selling the grand Victorian lake house and moving to Florida. She just wanted to be the kindly old lady who lived next door. The one everyone loved and looked out for.

"Happy days lie ahead," Juniper announced as she strolled through the front doors of Glen Haven.

Cream-painted walls with colorful framed landscapes, cushioned armchairs, and sleek sofas accented by faux antique side tables piled high with outdated magazines made up the cozy waiting area. While the initial entrance appeared wholesome and welcoming, the true horrors that occurred in this place remained hidden behind a thick security door.

"What was that, Mrs. White?" a stern voice echoed from the ether.

Juniper shook her head as the intercom outside the locked ward alerted her to the person behind the reception desk. It was none other than that meddling nurse, Zelda Watson. Another stain on an overall putrid day.

"Just talking to myself," Juniper said, approaching the Georgian-wired glass window. A metal door and that window were all that separated her world from theirs.

The middle-aged woman with flawless brown skin and a dome of curly black hair looked up from her seat behind the window. "I thought Ghost was coming with you this afternoon. I was looking forward to seeing her again."

Juniper's knuckles turned white as she tried to squeeze all her bad emotions into the plastic container she held. Zelda was neither a doctor nor a mother. She was utterly clueless as to the proper management of a child diagnosed with mental illness. The nurse preferred to treat Meredith as a friend, reading to her at night and putting silly ideas into her head that she would someday have a life outside of Glen Haven. Juniper felt the woman should have been fired years ago. If not for negligence, then for the sheer fact that she was completely ridiculous.

"*Gigi* isn't coming. Not today." *Not ever.*

The left corner of Zelda's mouth lifted into a devilish smirk. "You're going to deny Ghost access to her *own* mother?"

"Gigi appears to have changed her—"

"The whole staff is excited for the meeting." Zelda interrupted as she rose to her feet. "Meredith has been calm and even a bit upbeat since learning that her daughter wants to meet her."

Which was knowledge her daughter never should have been privy to. Giving a woman with mental illness false hope would only lead to distrust and outbreaks of violence. Even an imbecile could figure that out.

A set of keys attached to Zelda's wrist jingled as she moved the short distance to the security door. With a click of the lock, the door opened. Standing aside, she welcomed Juniper into the ward.

"You know what happened the last time *she* saw her daughter?"

"Yes, I do. It was an unfortunate incident, but a lot has changed for Meredith in the last twenty-three years. My goodness, it's been such a long time. Too long for a mother and daughter to be apart."

Zelda had no idea what she was talking about. Forever was the right amount of time for Juniper's daughter and granddaughter to be apart. The event Zelda had only read about in a report years later,

Juniper had actually lived through. She had been the one to rush her screaming grandbaby out of the room, blood streaming down her tiny back after a violent attack.

At the time, her daughter was delirious with grief over an imaginary boyfriend that she believed to be Gigi's father. She had insisted something bad had happened to him. When really something terrible had happened to Meredith. An orderly raped her after a group therapy session when she was merely seventeen years old. Her warped mind could not process the painful event, so a series of elaborate delusions took its place. Distraught over the fact that no one would answer her questions as to the boy's whereabouts, she turned on the toddler sitting on her lap.

Slapping Gigi's face, Meredith demanded that her child reveal the truth about it.

Before Juniper or the attending orderlies could get the terrified child to safety, Meredith had torn Gigi's little shirt, raked her jagged nails through her tender flesh, and bit into her plump back. No one could forget such a thing.

"So, what contraband do we have today?" Zelda asked as she pulled the container from Juniper's viselike grip to inspect the contents.

The fact that Juniper was allowed extra privileges never sat well with Nurse Zelda, which was the fermenting root of their mutual dislike. Juniper knew her benefits were earned. After all, it was her money that had funded the entire west wing expansion.

Juniper was escorted into the common room, where she found her daughter rocking in a wooden chair facing a window that was too high for her to see out. Not that Meredith would have wanted to view the comings and goings of the outside world. Everyone knew the world inside, the one she had created for herself, was always plenty busy.

Zelda handed the container back to Juniper. "If you need anything, I'll be right over there."

Juniper knew that Zelda had pointed to a spot near the exit. It was the same spiel she heard each visit. An orderly was in attendance, constantly surveying the room, while the attending nurse sat back, observed, and sometimes took notes.

Meredith never greeted her mother upon arrival. It was almost as if she went out of her way to ignore her mother's presence. Juniper did not mind. They both had tentative ways of dealing with one another's existence. The violent girl of flesh and bone that once ruled over Juniper's life had been reduced to a woman of twigs and paper—slight, brittle, and pale.

Over the years, Juniper realized that she preferred her daughter this way.

A screech echoed through the large room as Juniper dragged a chair over from a nearby game table. She placed the padded folding chair beside her aging daughter, sat, and waited.

Meredith was focused on a collection of tongue depressors fisted in her hand like a bouquet of flowers. Each wooden stick was brightly colored in varying shades of wax crayon. With twitching fingers, Meredith removed a flat stick from her right hand and balanced it delicately along her narrow thigh. Parched lips slowly formed numbers as she counted. The process was repeated until all the sticks lay flat—one on top of the other—balanced precariously upon her lap.

"Hello, deary," Juniper whispered so as not to startle her daughter. "I've brought your favorite crab cakes." She raised the plastic container for Meredith to see. "Tonight, you get to skip the group meal. Isn't that exciting?"

The first thing Juniper noticed when Meredith turned her head slowly, like a ventriloquist's puppet, was the brightness in her daughter's eyes. It was not the usual dull, vacant stare.

Juniper twisted around in her chair. "When did she receive her last dose of medication?"

Zelda responded without looking up from her notepad, "Meredith has been receiving a reduced dosage over the last week. She's making incredible improvements."

"Under whose authorization?"

Zelda delayed her answer by placing the blue cap back on her pen, sliding it into the front pocket of her lab coat, and snapping the notepad closed. Juniper was about to say something nasty when she felt a firm tug on the container she was holding. A second later, her award-winning crab cakes were ripped out of her hands.

Juniper spun around. Meredith was grinning when she cracked open the Tupperware and peeked inside. As she inhaled the spicy aroma wafting up to her nose, Meredith's smile grew. "Thank you, Momma."

Juniper gasped and clutched at her heart. Her daughter's voice was deeper and raspier since the last time she had heard it. But in all her years, there had never been a sweeter sound than the word *Momma*.

In the time it took Nurse Zelda to cross the common room, Meredith had gobbled down an entire crab cake.

"I know they're delicious, but it's not dinnertime. You have to save the rest for later," Zelda said, removing the plastic container from Meredith's greedy hands.

A stunned Juniper watched as Meredith calmly went about licking her fingers in search of whatever tasty crumb or spec of spice might remain.

No resistance. No violent outburst. But she was humming a familiar tune that Juniper could not quite name. She could hardly believe what she was witnessing.

"And to answer your earlier question, Dr. Lawrence has issued a new treatment regime for Meredith. Please address any concerns to him directly."

If Juniper had not been in such disbelief over her daughter's progress, she might have retaliated against Nurse Zelda's condescending tone.

# Chapter Twenty-Two

# Ghost

A few uneventful hours had passed before a loud commotion pulled me from my chair. I moved to the corner of the office and checked my phone for my building's emergency alert message while also listening for the sound of gunfire. When no message appeared and nothing else occurred, I poked my head out of my office just as others started to ease into the hallway. More shouts and screams sent people ducking into corners and behind desks as whatever was transpiring in the main conference room seemed to escalate. Looks of interest and fear ricocheted over the faces of many anxious co-workers. Everyone appeared to be concerned and clueless as to what was happening.

Emotions had been running high before the meeting even started. Could an argument between board members have caused someone to snap?

Almost as suddenly as the noise began, it stopped. Bewildering glances were exchanged in the grave silence that followed. Before anyone could act, the quiet was shattered by pounding footsteps. Two board members, whose names I could not recall, ran out of the conference room quickly. Seconds later, others came tumbling out. Some had blank expressions, while other board members were red-faced and gasping. I exited my office as one middle-aged exec bent at the waist and vomited her lunch on the carpet.

I jumped when someone's hand dropped on my left shoulder. With a slight squeal, I spun around to face my boss. A sullen-looking Mr. Sadler was in a chaotic state. Brown suit rumpled, graying hair sticking up in odd places as if he had repeatedly run his hands over his head. He had walked up behind me, which meant he had not come directly from the conference room.

"The paramedics are on their way." Mr. Sadler paused to clear his throat as he stepped around me. "There's been a terrible accident. We need all of you to go back to your desks and wait. Please try to be patient."

"What happened? Is everyone okay?" a nondescript voice bellowed from somewhere in the office.

"Mr. Witt appears to have had a heart attack and passed away. Mr. Kemper was injured in the ensuing panic, but it looks like he'll be okay."

There was a combination of gasps and chatter as people slowly dispersed.

Mr. Witt lay on the conference room floor for another twenty minutes before the police and medics arrived. By the time they placed his body on the gurney, details of the events that left one company founder dead and another wounded were circulating throughout the building. Several co-workers popped into my office to share what they had heard. Some of the particulars between the stories were conflicting. However, the end result remained the same.

Apparently, not long after the lunch break, Mr. Witt had started showing signs of duress. In his late sixties, with known heart issues, everyone was alarmed when his head bobbed, and he began to mumble. Saliva dripped from his chin, creating a puddle on the table where he sat. When Mr. Kemper approached to make sure he was okay, Mr. Witt unexpectedly lashed out. He screamed a series of nonsensical words and then began punching and pulling on Mr. Kemper. Scratched at his face. Bit down on his hand until he hit bone and almost severed the pinky finger when Mr. Kemper pulled away. Then Mr. Witt turned and spat the fingernail he had torn from Mr. Kemper's hand into his face as he announced his superiority before running headfirst into a wall. The impact knocked him unconscious. He lay on his back unmoving until Mr. Mason knelt to check for a pulse. As soon as his fingers pressed into Mr. Witt's thick neck, the man came to and spewed more profanities. Claimed the room was full of cheats and liars. "All devils" he was said to have declared before clutching at his chest. Shortly after that, he took his last breath.

When most of us were allowed to go home, it was close to seven o'clock. Interviews were still being conducted for those who had been present in the boardroom during the incident. Thankfully, I was not among them. I had reached my car when a familiar voice called my name.

Bishop darted over with one arm slung into his jacket as the rest of it flopped shapelessly against his back. "Crazy fucking day, huh? How are you doing?"

I could not have agreed more. The entire day had been one clusterfuck after another. Instead of expressing the shared sentiment, I said, "I'm okay."

Bishop finished putting his coat on with a huff. I reached over to straighten the jacket collar that had gone askew. The corner of his mouth twitched up and grew into a full smile.

"Are you still up for dinner tonight?" he asked, wrapping a muscled arm around my shoulders and tucking me to his side.

"Yeah, I think so." I nuzzled into his chest, breathing in his signature scent of linen and spice.

He kissed the top of my head, then lifted his arm to check his watch. "See you at your place in an hour, maybe an hour and a half."

"Sounds good." And it was. With the horrible finale that ended the workday, it was nice to have something to look forward to.

A SCALDING HOT SHOWER helped wash away the residual negative thoughts from the day. Dressed in cotton pajamas, I sat on the couch and turned on the TV to catch up on the news. An exuberant game show host appeared on the screen, shouting at contestants to "spin the wheel." I clicked the remote to change the channel. A pack of hungry lions roamed the Serengeti stalking a lame gazelle. I switched the channel again, and it was there. Breaking news of the death that had occurred at the offices of Mason, Kemper, and Witt. The reporter stated the deceased's name and age: Carl Wallace Witt, sixty-eight years old. Noted his status as a financial mogul and a loving family man. The cause of death was listed as a suspected heart attack but officially undetermined, pending a full autopsy report.

I had not really known Mr. Witt. We only ever saw each other in passing, with no more than a greeting of good morning or good afternoon. Although there had been one memorable exchange, two years ago, during a holiday party. That night, he had talked in depth about his mother's recent passing and the importance of spending time with loved ones. I wondered if he ever reached the goal he had spoken so passionately about. Did he find peace of mind in finally putting family before business?

If he managed to do that, then perhaps his time had not been wasted.

It was half past eight when Bishop rang my doorbell. Prying myself from the comfy spot on the couch, I went over and opened the door. My mouth was already watering at the prospect of a warm meal.

Bishop barreled through the door in navy blue sweats. He had a delicious-smelling bag in one hand and a backpack slung over his shoulder. "Did you get the email from Mr. Mason?" He was practically vibrating with anxiety.

I shut the door and joined him at the kitchen island counter. "I've been trying to veg out. Haven't looked at my phone or laptop since I left the office."

Slipping off his backpack, he placed it on the floor and ripped open the soggy-bottomed paper bag. "Office will be closed until further notice. A couple of people were sick and taken to the hospital. Several others were acting strangely during their interviews, so investigators are having them drug tested. Rumor has it that the eleven o'clock news will broadcast employee interviews despite Mr. Mason's warning not to talk to the media. They could be looking at possible foul play."

Dumbfounded, I watched Bishop finish unpacking our Chinese dinner while my brain stuttered to catch up. Did Mr. Witt's death have anything to do with the botched account? Or was there something more sinister afloat?

*This kind of thing does not happen here*, says everyone on every episode of every real crime program. No one believed it could happen in their neighborhood, to someone they knew, or to them until it did.

Finally, moving into action, I grabbed a couple of plates from an upper cabinet and utensils from the drawer underneath. "Wow, that escalated quickly. It all seemed pretty cut and dry when we left. Mr. Witt had a heart condition. The meeting was intense. A heart attack kind of made sense." I had not planned on drinking tonight, but if ever an occasion called for it.

"Wine or whiskey?" I said, heading toward the bar cart in the corner.

"Whichever you prefer." Behind me, a breath of relief sounded, followed by the clacking of dishes and silverware.

With a bottle of Cabernet in one hand and a bottle of Sauvignon Blanc in the other, I returned to the island to find my plate already prepared. A heap of fried rice smothered in shrimp and garlic sauce. "Decided on wine, but I'll leave the flavor up to you."

Bishop looked up wide-eyed, his mouth overflowing with noodles. One noisy slurp and the dangling ribbons disappeared. "Sorry, I'm starving," he mumbled as he chewed, and then a sly grin emerged.

I went about the kitchen, retrieving two stemless glasses and the corkscrew. "No apology necessary. Red or white?"

"Let's start with white and go from there."

After popping the cork and pouring our wine, I sat on the stool next to him and took a healthy bite from my plate. No reason to be shy when he was practically inhaling his food.

"So, have you heard any of the conspiracy theories going around? By now, I'm sure somebody's saying something." Gulping the wine and diving back in for another forkful, I waited for him to clear his mouth and give an answer.

"No one's pointing any fingers yet, or not that I've heard. A couple of stockholders were acting sketchy before the meeting, but given the reason they were there..."

"It would make sense."

"Yeah, it made sense. Then Kenny, you know my partner in IT crime, well, just after lunch he found a corrupted file on the main server that someone went through a lot of trouble to try and bury."

"That sounds fishy."

Purposely corrupted data, an ongoing account error intentionally hidden, and a meeting turned deadly. None of it seemed like a coincidence anymore. The first person that came to mind was my boss. Mr. Sadler was not in the meeting when the tragedy occurred. He had come from another part of the building when he told us the news. I had not thought too much of it then, but now it was cause for suspicion. What if my boss had something to do with it?

I would not have suspected him of murder, but what if...

Could he have falsified the financial data, panicked over the meeting, and taken extreme measures?

Shit. I'd worked on that account recently. Could anything come back to me? Or could I be in danger?

"It is very fishy. I had Kenny extract the file. He took it home with him to see if any of the data could be salvaged. We'll know sooner or later if he does. Of course, it might not have anything to do with what's going on. Could be some poor schmuck wiping porn."

"Not your porn though, right?" I nudged his elbow so he would not see my hands trembling. Irrational fear of the unknown chilled my insides as various scenarios, most involving police investigators and lawyers, whizzed through my mind like speeding flashcards.

"A man needs no porn when he's got a woman like you." Chuckling, Bishop leaned in with his deep dimples displayed and placed a kiss on my cheek. Then he went about making a second plate for himself.

I took a deep breath and then a long sip of wine. There was no reason to worry or speculate. The fear creeping around my gut was unwarranted. I had done nothing wrong. There was no need to freak out and conjure the hatted man, or something worse, for a chat.

# Chapter Twenty-Three

## Juniper

The secured ward at Glen Haven was on full lockdown. Each patient that had been in the west wing common room was restrained, sedated, and tucked away for the night behind impenetrable doors. There would be no dinner with Meredith, no goodbye, and Juniper would gain no peace of mind.

All because of one inept doctor and a bleeding-heart nurse.

Juniper was certain Dr. Lawrence had made a mistake when he reduced her daughter's medication. And with only one orderly on duty to oversee the nuttiest of the nuts.

What in blazing hellfire had the administrators been thinking, putting someone like Zelda Watson in charge?

*Why must they always prove me right?*

If ever there was a time when Juniper wanted to be wrong about her daughter's mental state, it would have been today. The joy she felt hearing her daughter call her "Momma" and the obvious pleasure her daughter experienced eating her favorite meal. It had been a rare treat for both of them. Smiles and laughter were seldom a part of their lives together.

Meredith had been perfectly content to sit in her chair and sing to herself. "There's a devil in my teacup, hear him shout, tip it over and pour him out." Though Juniper found the rhyme disturbing, she appreciated the lyrical sound of her daughter's voice.

But that all ended the moment an agitated patient slipped through the fingers of the orderly. The wild escapee tried to knock Zelda over as he rushed for the exit. The nurse stood her ground and fended him off. Together, the nurse and the orderly worked to corral the frenzied man. All the while, they were speaking calmly to keep from arousing the other patients in the room who had not yet been affected by the surge of activity. That was until the man darted past Meredith, scattering the colorful stack of tongue depressors from her lap.

When Meredith pounced, hands flailing over the tile floor, it was like a siren had gone off. Lightning struck every half-witted nervous system in the room. The spell was broken. Patients came alive, slowly at first, with a groan or a twitch. But soon their movements got quicker, their voices louder. As chaos erupted, Juniper hurried to the back wall and punched the red emergency button.

And then the real terror had begun.

STORMING FROM THE BUILDING, Juniper cursed the heavens and the hells and every deity that reigned in between. She slipped the special poem she had written, the one she had planned to read to her daughter at the end of their visit, into her purse. Then coming upon a trash can, Juniper broke the lid off the plastic container of crab cakes and dumped the remaining contents. Tossing the rest of a perfectly crafted meal fueled a roaring fire. She threw the empty container down on the cement sidewalk and proceeded to stomp and jump until she had turned her favorite Tupperware into a hundred tiny pieces of useless plastic.

In need of a moment of serenity, Juniper walked over to a lone bench nestled in a grouping of pale dogwood trees near the front corner of the building. There she sat, hoping to collect her thoughts.

Juniper was not a violent person, but at times like this, when life spun out of her control, there was no combating the darkness that flooded her mind.

First, she imagined sitting on the bench long enough to follow Zelda to her car when she left for the night. Using the tire iron from the trunk of the Challenger, she would bash the nurse's skull in. Juniper tried to repress the smile that tugged at the corners of her mouth as she pictured the life draining from Zelda's eyes. Like a red-hot match gradually cooling and then blowing to ash in the wind.

Several minutes clicked by as she was assaulted with another death setting for the troublesome nurse. Zelda beaten and bloody by the abuse administered from Juniper's fists. The silver-handled paring knife she used to pick crabs stabbed through Zelda's bruised and swollen right eye. Each corner of her mouth pulled into a gruesome smile with rusted hooks and fishing line. What better use for her late husband's fishing tackle? Zelda gutted like a catfish. Her innards stuffed in the bait box of the crab trap. So little would go to waste.

Infuriated over the day's events, needing an outlet for the rage coursing through her veins, Juniper spent several minutes relishing the scenarios and then shook the evil, unthinkable acts from her head. Anger brought out the darkest, most grotesque thoughts, but Juniper would never succumb to them.

"Mrs. White, are you okay? Visiting hours ended a while ago."

Larry Little, who was not so little, approached with a suave kind of waddle and a black flashlight swinging in one meaty hand. It was a perfect weapon to wield, and his fingerprints were all over it. Unable to resist, Juniper imagined using that heavy light to beat Zelda senseless, ultimately framing the kindly guard for the crime.

Juniper fussed with the buttons on her jacket, her shaking fingers practically useless. "I didn't realize. I just needed a minute to collect myself. It was utter chaos in there today." Eyes wide with fear, she gasped and knuckled away an unexpected tear.

"My poor daughter and several other patients were wrangled, sedated, and locked away." With lips trembling, she continued.

"Such a horror to witness my child manhandled so viciously. A mother never gets used to seeing such things." After a sniffle and a hiccup, she raised her voice. "Damn near gave me a heart attack."

Larry plopped down next to her on the bench. "Do you need me to call someone? A glass of water might help."

"Oh, no, that's sweet of you to offer," she blurted out. "I think I'm calm enough now to make the drive home."

"Are you sure? It's no trouble," he asked, rubbing a hand over his bald head with a sigh. Tending to an old lady's hysteria was probably the last thing he wanted to deal with at the end of the workday. Still, Juniper suspected he was a decent enough human being and would do whatever needed to be done.

"You're far too kind, Larry Little. I'll be okay."

Juniper started to stand. Larry hopped to his feet as if on cue and offered a thick arm. Taking hold of his elbow and still eyeing the flashlight he held in his other hand, Juniper allowed the guard to escort her the short distance to her vehicle.

Much to her surprise, Glen Haven had at least one competent employee.

Once she was tucked safely inside her vehicle, Larry said goodnight. He was about to close her car door when the front doors to Glen Haven burst open.

Zelda ran out, frantically waving her arms about and screaming, "Mrs. White! Wait, Mrs. White!"

Juniper did not bother getting out of the car as Zelda rushed around Larry Little and rested both hands on the roof. Leaning in through the door that the guard still held on to, Zelda forcibly swallowed what Juniper thought to be a thick lump of emotion. "Mrs. White, I'm so sorry—"

Juniper held up a hand, signaling Zelda to be quiet. She already knew what had happened—she did not need to hear the words spoken aloud. The truth of the matter was evident in the deep lines carved into the nurse's normally flawless features.

Meredith was dead.

# Chapter Twenty-Four

# Ghost

The sound of rustling pulled me from my restless slumber. The bang that followed had me scrambling to my feet. Bishop remained undisturbed, sleeping peacefully on the couch. A pair of half-empty wineglasses stood abandoned on the coffee table. After polishing off almost two bottles of wine and a filling meal, we had fallen asleep waiting for the late-night news broadcast. We hoped to gain more insight into the tragic events of the day and see which employees had the balls to go up against Mr. Mason's gag order. But neither of us had made it to the eleven o'clock hour.

As I moved through the kitchen, past the laundry room to the back door, the flickering light of the TV faded away. It should have been completely dark in the narrow hallway. The overhead light was off, the outside motion detector had not been turned on... and yet a bright, eerie glow illuminated the edges of the door as if the sun had perched itself upon my back steps.

I stood there trying to make sense of it when the back door began to...*breathe?*

Over and over the center pushed out, bowing like a fat round belly, only to get sucked back in again.

What phenomena would cause a solid wood door to move like that?

A tornado?

The weather had been clear, with no chance of rain in the forecast. It was also quiet as a graveyard. If a twister had touched down in the area, the rumbling and sirens would have alerted us to the danger long before it reached my back door.

*Fire!*

Could another townhome have caught fire and the blaze spread to my little patch of a backyard? Or was my mind burning up with increasing insanity?

My grip on reality had been strained over the last few days. Now I wondered if I had lost hold of it. Fear should have consumed me as I stepped closer and pressed my palms to the door. The wood was cool to the touch. I knew opening a closed door during a suspected fire was the last thing anyone should do. But I did not believe that was happening here. With a constant warning nipping at my ear, I was torn between opening the door and walking away. So instead, I leaned against it and immediately felt the door move beneath me. Gently pushing forward and then pulling back. A soothing sensation, like an infant nestled on her mother's chest.

*Knock. Knock! Knock!*

Jarring thumps on the outside of the door caused me to jump away. After a brief second of stillness, the knocking sounded again. Louder, harder, faster. The constant pounding rattled the door with such force I thought the hinges might break. Then as abruptly as it had started, the knocking stopped. I hesitated a moment, then turned the deadbolt to unlock the door. When no one came bursting through from the other side, I cautiously opened it. The light that had been pouring in around the door frame vanished. It had been snuffed out by a night so black I could barely see my hand in front of my face. Chills collected around the back of my neck and proceeded to claw their way down my spine.

Whatever this was, it was not natural.

I tried to close the door, but it would not budge. I pushed with both hands, smashed my shoulder against the wood, shoved with all my might, and still the door would not move. I screamed at the door, threw my fists against it, but no matter what I did, the door remained open to the blackness that lay beyond. Then I noticed *it*. The *something* that was emanating in the darkness. I could not see it, but I knew it was there. And I could feel it inching closer. So close that the whispers it sputtered were now audible. I held my breath while trying to make sense of the strange noise. Only the sounds never formed a coherent word. Until, between the hisses and grunts, one word became clear... A shout in my face—*Ghost!*

"Ghost!"

My body was being shaken by a pair of vise grips that were painfully latched onto my arms. I woke with a shout. My heart pounded as my eyes searched for the source of the threat. That was when I saw Bishop's startled expression. A few silent seconds passed before I finally noticed the familiar sights and smells that confirmed I was in my living room.

I was sitting on my oversized sectional. Bishop had a white-knuckled grip on both of my forearms.

It was a dream. The door, the blackness, the voice. None of it had been real.

Well, Bishop had been real, as he had called my name and shook me awake.

I leaned forward and pressed my forehead to his. "Wow, that was some nightmare."

"Yeah, you're telling me... Are you okay?"

"I'm good. Crazy day, crazy dream." *Or just crazy me.*

"For a second there, I thought I was going to have to slap you," he said, releasing his deathlike grip on my arms.

"Not advisable, I might have hit back," I said, kissing the end of his nose.

He leaned over and plucked one of the wineglasses from the table. "Want to tell me about it?"

We had drained the bottle of white wine during dinner and had been sipping on a Cabernet while watching TV. Much like in the dream, we had fallen asleep before the late-night news broadcast.

"Not much to say. I walked to my back door and there was this weird light, but when I opened the door, it was complete darkness, and then I heard a whisper—"

I shook my head. That was not a memory I wanted to recall.

"It was more how the dream made me feel."

Bishop swallowed a gulp of wine. "Which was?"

"Hunted. Threatened." I grabbed the other glass of wine and drained its contents.

There was a long pause of quiet, and then Bishop's hands were on me. Warming a path over my back, he gave my shoulders a firm, comforting squeeze. "I think we missed the news. I fell asleep."

"Lucky for us, I hit record on the DVR," I said as I reached for the remote, clicking the buttons to pull up the digital news recording.

Bishop grinned wickedly before snatching the remote from my hand and pressing the pause button. "Great, then we can watch it anytime." His usually deep voice had been reduced to a gruff murmur.

I lay back down, smiling as Bishop maneuvered himself on the couch, lining his body up to mine, but did not make full contact. As he hovered over me with wine-coated breath, the desire in his half-lidded eyes was undeniable. Anxious to fully erase the memory of my nightmare, I grabbed the bottom of his sweatshirt, pulled it over his head, and tossed it aside. By the time his lips found mine, we were completely naked on my living room couch.

# Chapter Twenty-Five

# Juniper

The clock read half past midnight when Juniper arrived at Gigi's house. When she used her key to gain entry, she had expected to find her granddaughter tucked contently in her bed. Instead, Juniper was greeted with a pungent odor. A combination of sex and stale Chinese food. For a second, she wondered if her famous crab cakes had been part of that meal.

Juniper was guided into the living room by the dim glow of a TV. When she reached the couch, she squeezed her eyes shut at the sight of naked bodies intertwined. Bad enough she had to see her granddaughter looking somewhat battered in post-coitus, but the sight of Bishop's flaccid member nearly sent her over the edge.

Where was Larry Little's flashlight when she needed it?

Juniper was about to retreat and slip out undetected, the same as she had entered, when she noticed the frozen image on the television above the fireplace. A paused news broadcast. It had not been the anchor's comically skewed face, caught mid-sentence, that grabbed her attention. Moving around the end of the couch, she closed in on the disturbing headline on the suspended ticker below. The story that had been about to air was an update on a reported death at Mason, Kemper, and Witt. New information had become known with shocking eyewitness interviews.

*Bejabbers!* What else could have possibly gone wrong today? *By St. Booger and all the saints at the backdoor of Purgatory!* Was this the reason Gigi had stood her up?

Sitting on the edge of the couch, inches from Bishop's hobbit-sized feet, she reached for the remote and was about to hit the play button when a shrill scream broke the silence.

"What the hell, Gi Ju! What are you doing here?" Gigi quickly grabbed the clothing that had been discarded on the floor. "You know you're not welcome right now." Gigi slipped a thin cotton shirt over her head, covering a dark bruise on her back and red handprints on her arms, before throwing a pair of thick sweatpants on Bishop's lap.

Juniper raised a brow, wondering what kind of kinky sex her granddaughter was into.

"I know. I am sorry," Juniper said, knowing the news she had to deliver was more important than any irate tantrum her granddaughter was about to throw. With a stiffened spine, Juniper set the remote down. "Why didn't you meet me? I thought you..." She nodded to Bishop. "Is *he* the reason you missed going to see your mother today?"

"No, he's not!" Gigi had worked herself into quite a frenzy. She had already put her top on inside out and was fighting the bunched-up legs on a pair of striped pajama bottoms. "There was too much going on at the office today. Besides, your note said we were meeting her doctors, not *her.*"

Unlike her granddaughter, Bishop appeared calm and collected. He seemed neither surprised nor embarrassed by the strange predicament he found himself in. Juniper decided to address him directly. "Bishop, I need to speak to my granddaughter. Would you please excuse us for a moment?"

Without warning, Gigi rushed her grandmother, yanked her up by the arm, and boldly pushed her toward the door like she was a bothersome salesman. "Gi Ju, it's late... You need to go!"

"Please stop calling me that." Juniper kept her fists clenched at her sides, holding back the urge to strike the imbecilic child. She had never hit her granddaughter in anger and hoped to keep it that way.

"I'll stop calling you Gi Ju when you start calling me Ghost!" A drop of spittle landed on Juniper's face. Gigi was practically foaming at the mouth and exuding a level of hostility that regrettably reminded Juniper of her daughter. Correction, *dead* daughter.

Taking a deep breath, Juniper tried to cool the wicked blaze threatening to ignite. She would not lose everyone she loved over the course of one horrifically bad day.

"My sincere apologies to both of you for arriving unannounced. It's been a very trying and tragic day." Then she turned to Bishop again. In the softest, kindest voice, she implored him to obey. "Gigi and I have an urgent family matter to discuss."

Though his eyes narrowed, he dipped his head ever so slightly. "Ghost." The sweet, drawn-out way he said it was no doubt meant to offend Juniper for refusing to call her granddaughter by her given name. "I'll be upstairs if you need me."

A subtle expression passed over Bishop's face as he tilted his head to Ghost and slid a protective hand around her waist. Juniper had been around long enough to identify such a look. He was a man in love. Foolishly in love with her granddaughter.

"No!" Gigi stood her ground by holding Bishop to her side, showcasing them as a united front. "He stays. You leave. We're not doing this tonight."

Juniper knew she would not be able to talk herself out of this mess. Best to retreat and fight another day than press on and lose the entire war. She still had cards in her deck to play, and Bishop had unknowingly slipped her an extra ace. Mentally, she had already begun compiling a list of things she needed to do. But first, she had to deliver a devastating blow to an irrational girl.

"I didn't want to tell you like this, but...your mother died today."

A rush of righteousness flooded Juniper's veins as she watched the color drain from her granddaughter's face. Gigi visibly struggled to find her words and failed.

"Just imagine if you had been there to see it. Your stubbornness and anger saved you from that, so I guess that's one thing we should all be thankful for." Juniper could be as mean as a bullying child when the moment called for it.

"How did it happen?" Gigi squeaked out as Bishop tightened his hold, helping to keep her upright.

Juniper felt a slight quiver in her chin. Taking a deep breath, she shook her head. "The doctors screwed up. Changed her meds, which caused seizures and then death."

"Ghost, I'm so sorry." Bishop kissed her forehead as he attempted to steer her back to the couch.

"I never even got the chance to say hello," Gigi whispered. "I'll never hear her voice."

Juniper watched in shock as her granddaughter grieved a woman she had never known—the same person who tried to kill her twice. Gigi should save those tears for the one that truly mattered.

"Oh, but you have said hello and you have heard your mother's voice."

Gigi's eyes widened as she halted and stumbled away from Bishop.

"You and your mother are not the strangers you thought you were. One of the biggest mistakes in my life was placing you on your mother's lap."

A single gasp sounded before the room fell into an uneasy silence.

"Of course, you don't remember. You were so young and so small. But the scars on your back are a permanent reminder of exactly what I've been protecting you from. Oh, that ghastly day when your mother tore your shirt from your body, dug her jagged nails into your soft skin, and took a big, bloody bite out of your tender flesh."

Gigi's tears came faster. Silently they fell as her fingers inched behind her neck and over her shoulder to touch the familiar scars. "T-that was a dog, you told me—"

"It shouldn't be a surprise that I lied on many occasions. Every despicable thing I've ever done has been to keep you safe! But thankfully, we have nothing left to fuss about. She's gone."

"You almost sound happy about it," Bishop mumbled.

Juniper refused to respond to the barely audible challenge from an idiot man. But she did watch carefully as Bishop's shaking hands moved cautiously up Gigi's back. He had seen Gigi's scars, too. When their hands met, he laced his fingers with hers and held on tight. A man instinctually defends and shelters those he loves.

With nothing more to say, Juniper opened the front door but then paused to take one last look at the horror-stricken couple.

She had turned around and was about to step outside when someone grabbed her arm, forcing her to stop.

Gigi's expression was deadpan, her voice cold and empty when she said, "I need my house key back."

"Is that necessary?" Juniper was surprised by the quaking in her own voice. Fumbling through her purse for her keys, she coughed, attempting to clear an unfamiliar lump of emotion stuck in the back of her throat.

Gigi did not speak, only nodded, eyes firmly locked on the keyring Juniper now held in her hand.

"Be mad at me if you want. It doesn't change who your mother *was*. And it won't fix the damage she's done." Juniper slid a silver key from the ring and tossed it at Gigi.

There was a series of clinks as it hit the hardwood floor and bounced.

"I'm the *only* family you have left now," Juniper hissed through clenched teeth. "Shutting me out will not change a thing!" she yelled over her shoulder as she walked out and slammed the door behind her.

# Chapter Twenty-Six

# Ghost

As Grandma June stormed out of the house, a framed picture of a surfboard leaning against a palm tree jumped from its nail and crashed to the floor. My world had just imploded between the foyer and the living room, and Bishop was there to witness every humiliating second of it. I stared at the floor. A wadded piece of paper that had fallen from my grandmother's purse and a single house key lay among the glistening glass shards.

*My mother's gone! And she's taken the answers I need with her.*

As I stood there, replaying my grandmother's cruel words, I tried to recall the biting incident but could not. All that came to mind was my grandmother's stupid story about a dog. How much could a three-year-old remember anyway?

Except our meeting ended in trauma that left physical scars. Even at a young age, it was something I *should* remember.

I was physically shaking from the effort it took to remain standing, to not collapse in a ball of hysterics at Bishop's feet.

Unsure of how much longer I could hold myself together, I bent over and started scooping up the glass, purposely fisting the broken pieces in one hand.

Bishop interrupted my efforts by pulling me up. After carefully picking bits of glass from my bloody palm, he wrapped my hand in a damp dishtowel. "Why don't we get a broom for that?"

Without a word, I headed for the kitchen pantry. I had to do something. Anything to get past this moment and on to the next. Whatever that might be.

When I returned with a broom to clean up the mess my grandmother had made, I found the front door ajar. For a second, I thought Bishop made a quick exit. I would not have blamed him if he fled. *God only knows what the man thinks of me now.* But then I saw him, half-in, half-out of the house, fiddling with the locks on the door.

"Shit!" He stepped back inside and slammed the door closed, flicking the deadbolt with extra force. "It's not the right key."

"What?"

"This isn't your house key. She left the wrong one. Do you think she did it on purpose?" Bishop held out the key.

The silver Kwikset looked like every other house key. It would be impossible for anyone to tell one apart from another. Unless you tried it, which I never would have thought to do.

"She was upset. It must have been an accident." Then again, how well did I know my grandmother? I never expected her to show up the way she did, to keep the number of secrets she had, or to blurt out something so hurtful it nearly fossilized my heart.

Bishop tossed the key over to the counter and ran his hands roughly through his hair. "Just in case, you should get your locks changed. Not a bad idea to consider changing your alarm codes, too."

"After tonight, I seriously doubt she'll come back."

"You never know. There was something a little off about your grandmother. And not just because she barged in 'uninvited and unannounced.'" His impersonation of my Grandma June was pretty spot on.

Bishop took the broom from my hand and pulled me over to the couch. "I don't know her like you do, but something struck me as odd when I talked to her in the lobby today."

Flopping down on the same cushion my grandmother had recently vacated, I plucked a half-empty glass from the coffee table.

"You think she's crazy?" I asked, drinking what was left of Bishop's wine.

I feared Bishop's answer because, at that moment, my mind had conjured an image of the hatted man lurking in the shadows. He was not in the room yet but would certainly make an appearance soon. Which would also be "uninvited and unannounced."

Bishop nestled next to me, one arm over the back of the couch, his fingertips resting lightly on my left shoulder. "She wasn't exactly acting *normal*. The way she cringes anytime someone says your name. It's...strange."

"She just lost her daughter, you know. But maybe she is crazy. Maybe my entire family's insane." I closed my eyes, refusing to shed another tear in his presence. That was my biggest fear, and I had just voiced it out loud. I was barely able to admit the possibility to myself. Even after having experienced several hallucinations.

"No, no way. You can be a little eccentric at times, but you're not crazy." He was now gripping my shoulder as he leaned in closer to peek under the red dotted towel that I was still holding around my hand.

The puncture wounds were not nearly as deep as I had hoped they would be.

"You don't know me well enough to say that."

When I tried to pull away, he collected me into his lap.

"Sure I do," he said, nuzzling his nose into my hair. "We've worked for the same company for years and hung out for work and socially on numerous occasions. And now we're together. I'm pretty good at reading people. Besides, I don't date crazy."

"Really? You dated Ava."

"Ha-ha, Ava's clingy, manipulative, with severe self-esteem issues, and very close to becoming a full-blown alcoholic. Which can make her appear nuts at times, but she's not crazy."

Though the subject matter was dark, I appreciated that he purposely tried to keep the conversation positive. But I also knew the growing darkness would suffocate even the tiniest flicker of optimism.

"But what if I am? What if I end up exactly like my mother?"

"You think you'll develop schizophrenia overnight?" Bishop squeezed tighter as if he alone could protect me from that future.

"It's possible. Doctors say it's genetic." It sure seemed like I had become schizophrenic overnight.

The other night, I had researched all forms of illness that involved hallucinations. Since my symptoms were triggered while facing a wide range of emotions and high levels of stress, I had come up with a probable diagnosis: schizophreniform. Unlike schizophrenia, which lasts a lifetime, schizophreniform was a type of temporary psychosis and was often genetic. My break with reality could last for one month or six months. Only time would tell if I had gotten it right. If the hatted man who had called himself Terrence Riggie continued to appear after six months, then as far as I was concerned, they could lock me up and toss the key away.

We sat on the couch in silence for a long while. I thought for sure Bishop had fallen asleep when he suddenly moved. Grabbing the remote, he turned off the TV. I was about to get up and take our wineglasses to the kitchen when he scooped me into his arms and proceeded to carry me upstairs. I would have protested the manly, knight-in-shining-armor routine had I not been such a wounded bird. The strength and support he exuded was needed more than I cared to admit. Laying my head on his shoulder, I resigned myself to the fact that we would have a loving but short-lived relationship.

Bishop was everything I had ever wanted or hoped for in a man, and I did not deserve him.

# Chapter Twenty-Seven

# Juniper

In the early morning hours, Juniper entered her Victorian lakeside house with the vengeance of a screeching wraith. Her tight-knit plan had nearly unraveled. Though she clenched a few remaining strands in her fist, she knew those threads could disintegrate and slip through her fingers at any moment.

Red-faced and sobbing, she screamed at the kitchen tile. Beat her hands on the dining room table. Smashed her most valuable china vase against the wall. Shouted at the living room TV as she switched it on, and then raucously made her way up the intricately carved staircase.

The first stop upstairs was the main bedroom. Dropping to her knees with bone-crushing force, she scrambled to maneuver the oversized Samsonite from beneath the king-sized bed. Hands shaking, she entered a series of numbers on the coded lock and failed. Tried again and failed. *Why is it not working?*

Forsaking the suitcase in the middle of the floor, she used the oak bedpost to get back on her feet and then headed for the bedroom she used as an office. There, she sat down and booted up the desktop computer that she rarely turned on anymore. Once the screen loaded, an update began, preventing her from conducting the necessary business at hand. Business that should have been taken care of hours ago.

Slapping her palms on the roll-top desk, Juniper tilted her head back and howled until her lungs gave out. When she regained her breath, she voiced her concerns to a world that had suddenly turned against her. "Why?" she asked. "What have I done to deserve this?"

When no response came, she continued to question the empty room. "How can so many things go wrong all at once?" She had lost her daughter today and quite possibly her granddaughter, and not a single person seemed to care.

Who or what out there hated her so much that they would wish her to suffer so unjustly?

In the silence of the room, she plucked an answer out of midair. *No one.* Not a single soul hated Juniper White. Well, there might have been someone once, but he was gone. Dead and buried for many years.

An image of a decomposed body in tattered, soiled clothes emerged in her mind. She stood up and shook the image from her head. That was complete hogwash. No one was returning from the grave to exact their revenge.

Juniper sat back down. The computer update had reached fifty percent. That was when a single name came to mind. Gigi's new love interest, Bishop Mazzeo. Every unsettling, bad thing that occurred happened after he became a part of her granddaughter's life. Not to mention the challenge he had thrown when he questioned her grief. Juniper's perfect world was off its axis and about to careen out of orbit.

If Bishop thought he could steal her granddaughter away with his good looks and manly charms, he had another *think* coming.

Juniper did not spend the early morning hours searching for a funeral home, contacting friends, or writing the obituary for her daughter as she had set out to do. Instead, she used the rest of her waking hours looking for information on a newly suspected foe.

Bishop Mazzeo might be a beautiful man, but Juniper found him to be about as interesting as a potted rubber tree plant. Along with his prestigious college degree, he was a trophy-toting lacrosse defenseman and a self-declared computer genius with a long list of boring accolades. He also liked to play at being a rockstar on the weekends. He listed himself as single but regularly posted pictures with his arms around cheap harlots, none of whom were her granddaughter. Juniper had also identified the two office nitwits he had been arguing with in the lobby, Kendall Childers and Selina Thorne. They were all over his social media, in pictures and posted comments. He had likely bedded both of them at some point, if not at the same time.

There were a few photos of Gigi attached to his social media accounts. A couple of group shots that appeared to be from work functions, but nothing to suggest that they were dating. Juniper searched, but unlike the two other girls, she could not find her granddaughter's name on his "friends" list. She kept scrolling until her vision blurred and her fingers cramped. Needing to rest her weary eyes, she put her head down on the desk, promising herself it would only be for a minute or two.

When Juniper raised her head again, a line of drool stretched from her chin to the ergonomic keyboard. The clock on the computer screen read 9:01. Somehow, she had slept several hours face down on the desk. Rubbing the crick from her neck, she straightened her spine and rolled her shoulders.

"No one my age should subject themselves to such poor self-care." Every inch of her aging body throbbed in retaliation as she kicked her legs awake and waved her arms overhead. "Except when your enemy is about to breach the gates. The big shark is circling! Get your saggy ass in gear."

Ignoring her headache, cramping stomach, parched throat, and sore muscles, she pushed the mouse to unlock the screensaver to pick up where she had left off.

She continued scrolling post after post on Bishop's page until she finally found something concerning. After poring over years of data, she found a single photo posted long before Gigi started working at the financial company. The shot had been captured from a distance as Gigi sat perched on the edge of a park fountain, laughing. Bishop had posted the image with a short caption: *Joyous Perfection!*

The picture had over a thousand likes.

Juniper could not recall if she had ever seen a more gorgeous photo of her granddaughter. But she remembered the first conversation she had with Gigi about the hot guy in charge of the IT department. That was almost three years ago, and it had been their first introduction. Only recently had Gigi shared a juicy bit of office gossip about him having a crush on her.

Funny, according to his social media, that the rumor must have started shortly after his very public breakup with a long-term girlfriend.

Saving a screenshot of the post, she popped over to Gigi's account and began another search. Juniper had a niggling feeling that she had indeed seen the picture before. It took mere minutes to locate the photo. The complete photo. It had been taken when Gigi was on a trip abroad, reconnecting with an old friend.

"Gotcha!"

There was no logical reason for Bishop to have seen the original photo. Much less for him to have altered it and posted it as his own. Though one picture was not much in the way of evidence, it was proof enough that Bishop could have nefarious sexual perversions toward her granddaughter. A picture posted long enough ago that he may have forgotten it was out there to be found. It's a good thing Juniper was relentless in her sleuthing endeavors.

How long had Bishop been trolling after her granddaughter? At least four years. What other information had he collected without her knowledge? Home address? Bank accounts? Credit history? Friends? Previous boyfriends?

Not to mention anything she did at work. Why had he chosen her? Money?

Gigi always had a head for finance. She was good with her money—though maybe not so much with common sense. But an IT guy with a high-paying salary surely made plenty of his own.

Juniper had watched enough murder shows to know cyber stalkers could do serious damage to an unsuspecting victim. And a co-worker with a secret obsession was a far deadlier combination. Unless it was not a physical obsession at all. What if he had conned his way into her bed and gained her trust so he could pin something on her later?

No, wait, that did not make sense. Juniper was confusing herself. This post happened before Gigi started working at Mason, Kemper, and Witt.

Juniper needed coffee. She was not thinking straight anymore. Whatever the reason for his initial pursuit, Bishop had developed real feelings for Gigi. She had seen it with her own eyes. He could not be that good of a con artist. So, what was his endgame?

*Sex slave. Skinsuit.*

Perhaps he was looking for what he considered the perfect woman. Gigi could be that for someone. But what happened when the shine wore off and reality set in? Would he turn on her? Try to control her, beat her if she stepped out of line—

*Wait! What if this is about me?*

Could it be Juniper's secrets that he was after? Oh, and *her* money. She had been born into wealth that significantly increased with the death of her husband. Though frugal, there was no hiding that she was one of the wealthiest philanthropists in the state. And the quickest way to her was through her family. With her daughter locked away—*no, dead*—the only viable option was her gullible granddaughter. Yes, that was it. Gigi might be an unplanned prize, but Juniper had always been his mark.

Even the best con artist had a record. Juniper pulled up the state court judiciary site and began a search on Bishop Mazzeo. Immediately she found what she was looking for. The bruises she saw on Gigi's body last night made a lot more sense now.

Satisfied that she was moving in the right direction, she eased her aching body from the chair and made her way downstairs in search of sustenance, snagging her phone along the way. Despite their feud, Juniper would have to warn Gigi that she was undoubtedly sleeping with the enemy.

# Chapter Twenty-Eight

## Ghost

**B**eads of sweat slid down my back and dripped from my brow. My entire body felt slick, like I had exited a steamy shower without drying off. At night, the thermostat in the bedroom was automatically set to sixty-six degrees. The perfect temperature for sleeping with just enough chill in the air to snuggle beneath a layer of blankets. The oppressive heat that had me wanting to run naked into a snowstorm was the result of too many glasses of wine and the two hundred pounds of male flesh plastered against my side.

Somehow Bishop had managed to encapsulate me with his entire body. His heavy limbs wrapped around me, one hand sprawled across my stomach, the other wedged between my thighs. His thick legs tangled with my own. His grip tightened when I tried to move away to gain some space to cool down. I pushed, pulled, elbowed, and even called out his name. Bishop would not budge. It was not until I kicked his shin that his hold finally relaxed. Half-awake, half-asleep, he let go, but still managed to rub his groin against my hip.

Before he got a chance to latch on again, I slipped out of the bed. Grabbing my robe off the hook on the bathroom door, I quietly made my way downstairs.

I was pouring myself a cool glass of water in the kitchen when I noticed the broom propped up against the wall. Leaning back on the counter, barely holding on to the glass shaking in my hand, I considered finishing the job we failed to complete last night. I ended up walking over and plopping down on the sofa instead. It was already after six in the morning, so there was no reason to return to bed, which meant there would be plenty of time to clean up Grandma June's mess later.

My thoughts returned to the man sleeping upstairs. Bishop had been a great comfort in my time of need, and I was grateful for that, for him. But now I needed space. Time alone to grieve the mother I never knew while also preparing for the fact that I might be the one to take her room at Glen Haven. Would it be hard for Bishop when they locked me away, or would he forget me in a week?

I grabbed the remote and switched on the news broadcast that we never got around to watching.

It was no surprise to see Kendall and Selina preening in front of the camera. Both continuing to interrupt the other in their attempts to steal the spotlight. Boasting about being the ones who had delivered lunch to the board meeting. Overinflating their importance in the strange and deadly events of the day. Even with Mr. Mason's gag order, they could not resist their chance at two minutes of fame. Though it appeared to have been less than a minute before the report moved on to a more productive interview.

The next person to appear on screen was the executive I had seen vomiting outside the conference room. Shelia Brown was the name I could not recall earlier. The interview was being conducted from inside a hospital room. Mrs. Brown's eyes were red and watery, her skin an odd hue of green. She looked as if she might lean over the bed rail and hurl any second.

When the reporter asked her to recount the events of the day, she grabbed a tissue to dab the corner of her mouth and over each eye before proceeding to tell her side of the story.

"The meeting was standard, a bit intense. We had some pressing matters that needed to be sorted out, but still business as usual. It was about an hour after the lunch service that things started to get weird. Mr. Witt wasn't the only one acting strangely. My vision blurred, and I could have sworn someone in the room was whistling the 'Wind of Change' when Mr. Witt's head smacked down on the conference room table. From there, things escalated quickly. For me, it literally felt like my skin had been peeled back and flowers were blooming from my veins."

The reporter leaned in as he asked his next question. "Do you think you were drugged?"

Mrs. Brown's scowl deepened. "Absolutely. This was no accident. We were targeted."

"The lunch that was served came from Dot's Bistro, is that right?" The reporter flashed an overly white smile.

"Yes. And—"

"Were you aware that an employee was recently fired for dealing drugs on the premises?"

A few more pats with the tissue over her face as she appeared to mull over the new information. "I had no idea. Are you saying we were victims of some disgruntled employee bull crap that ended up killing a man?"

"It's one possibility the police are looking into."

"Well, that provides little comfort. Guess I'll have to wait for the results of my tox screening to know for sure."

I had always liked Shelia Brown. She was an unassuming, no-nonsense kind of woman.

The next person to appear on the television screen was Mr. Kemper, with his aging, pocked face. His skin glistened, and the hair around his temples was drenched with sweat. Wide eyes continually shifted up and to the right and then back down to the left. It was hard to tell if he was searching for answers or an escape route.

I heard footsteps on the stairs and hit pause on the remote. A sleepy-eyed Bishop fumbled his way over to the couch. Flopping down next to me, he placed a scorching hand on my knee. "You started it without me." His words stretched to a whine in the most unappealing way. He was not to blame for the spark of irritation.

Still, it took some restraint not to stand up and demand he leave not just the room, but my home.

"I couldn't sleep." I took a long sip of water, placed the glass in the middle of the coffee table—far enough away to maneuver his hand from my knee—and then scooted back into the corner of the L-shaped sofa.

"Anything interesting happen?"

"Drugs are suspected, possibly in the food. Looks like the police are going to have everyone who attended the board meeting tested. Something about an employee at Dot's Bistro getting fired for dealing drugs. I haven't watched the entire thing yet," I said, rubbing the tender spots on my arms, where he had shaken me awake, with my newly scabbed fingertips.

"That's some serious shit."

Bishop inched closer, laying his head on my thigh as a wandering hand snaked around my waist. I was trapped once again. After a volatile mix of stress and alcohol, I was on the verge of combustion. I had to find a way out of these feelings before I ruined everything by blowing up at him over nothing. It was ridiculous that I felt so annoyed. Just a few short hours ago, the only thing I wanted was to have his hands on my body.

What girl would not want to be cuddled and adored by a sexy man who had never been anything but completely wonderful? *A crazy girl, that's who.*

With my heart racing, muscles twitching, and the feeling of tickling insects creeping about beneath my skin, it would not be long before I exploded.

"Here," I said, pushing him up so I could stand and tossing the remote in his lap. "I'm not feeling too great. I'm gonna hop in the shower. You go ahead and watch. Fill me in when I come back down."

"I can do that. Or I can join you in the shower." Bishop lowered his feet to the floor and leaned forward.

There was no way he was getting in the shower with me.

I shoved him back down on the couch. "No, you stay. I'll just be a few minutes." My voice was stern. A quick cheek peck let him know there were no hard feelings. When he stayed seated, I knew he had received the message loud and clear.

The faint murmur of the TV drifted upstairs as I entered the bedroom. I threw off my robe, headed into the bathroom, turned on the shower, and then went to the vanity to brush my hair while the water heated up. I needed a moment of solitude to sort through my riotous emotions. I would ruin it with Bishop if I did not calm my nerves.

Setting the brush aside, I reached inside the vanity drawer and pulled out my mother's old watch. The one Grandma June had given me some time back. A zigzag crack scarred the clear crystal face. I had never bothered to put it on until now. Buckling the thin leather strap around my wrist, I lifted it to my ear. Like everything else in my life, it was broken.

I knew I was falling hard for Bishop. Real, strong feelings were sometimes difficult to navigate. There was a good chance I would self-sabotage the relationship despite not wanting to. The anguish of losing my mother and the repeated betrayals from my grandmother had me fearing where and when the hatted man would make his next appearance.

The bricks were stacked high. I was not sure if I had the strength or dexterity to carry such a heavy load. Regardless, I could not allow myself to give up. I had to see it through, find my truth, and deal with whatever consequences landed at my feet, even if that meant having my toes crushed under the enormous weight.

"You can handle this," I announced to the mirror, noting the dark circles under my eyes, the dull flakiness of my skin, and the growing collection of scrapes, bumps, and bruises. I had not been taking good care of myself. Stress, alcohol, and lack of sleep had taken a toll.

When I stepped into the shower, a blast of scalding hot water had me flattening myself against the back wall until I could ease in and acclimate to the high temperature. The oppressive heat I had been trying to escape with Bishop was now the most soothing feeling in the world. When I added a little lavender-mint soap to my loofah, it was practically heaven.

The door hinges squeaked, and I froze.

I had not thought to lock the bathroom door. Now a dark shadow loomed outside the frosted-glass stall. Unlike Janet Leigh in *Psycho*, I knew the attacker and his intentions. He was not there to maim. Bishop had come with plans for seduction.

Unfortunately, I was not in the mood. That was why, when he sneakily tried to open the shower door, I grabbed the handle and held it shut. "Finished with the news already? I'll be out in one sec." I had to stand at an odd angle to rinse off while keeping a firm hold on the handle. Then the door jerked hard. Feet slipping on the wet tile, I had to let go and grab the marble shelf behind me to keep from falling.

Bishop stood naked, stern-faced, and seemingly unfazed by my attempt to keep him out. Snagging my hands, he pulled me from the shower wall and began what appeared to be a thorough inspection of my wrists and forearms.

What was he inspecting me for? Did he seriously come in here to see if I had harmed myself? At what point in the evening had I given him the impression that I was suicidal?

Most of the damage I had sustained over the last couple of days, bruised back and handprints on my arms, was technically from him.

Bishop tried to slide my mother's broken watch up my arm, but it would not budge.

"Your shower door sticks. Want me to take a look at that for you?" he asked as he unhooked the clasp and removed the watch from my wrist. Then his eyes met mine with startling intensity. "What are you hiding?"

"Nothing. And the door is perfectly fine," I grumbled, snatching my mother's watch from his hand.

Bishop stepped into the shower. "Are you—ouch, this water is scalding!" Bishop hopped closer, pinning me back on the wall as he adjusted the water temperature to suit his delicate needs.

Once the water turned tepid, Bishop eased into the spray and tipped his head back to wet his hair. I slid past him and was about to exit the shower when he pulled me against his chest. It took everything I had not to scream.

"Sorry if I'm intruding." His deep voice had softened with a hint of concern. "I'm worried about you. There's a lot that's happened over the years with my sister. Some of it is still pretty raw. I know you're not even close to being the same, but with everything that's happened, you know... it's just... I'm here for you, Ghost. You might think it's too soon to say, but you should know that I lo—"

"I'm okay." I relaxed against his body, realizing it had taken very little for my rage bubble to pop.

Somehow Bishop mistook my absolvitory words as permission. I might not have been angry anymore, but that did not mean I wanted to have sex. The problem was that I could not find my voice to object. When he started stroking my skin and rubbing himself against me, his lips kissing a line from my ear down the side of my neck, I could have pulled away. I could have told him no. Bishop was a gentleman. If I told him to stop, he would have stopped. Only I did not say it. The word *no* shouted repeatedly inside my head until it grew fingers and tried to pry its way past my closed lips. Even then, I did not utter a sound.

Instead, I remained pliant as Bishop pawed over my body and then positioned me in the shower so he could enter me from behind. Bent at the waist with one hand firmly pressed to the tile wall while the other held a death grip on my mother's watch, I fought a silent battle. As water washed over the back of my head, tears began to fall. Because no matter how skilled a lover he was, at that moment, he was too rough, and I did not want to feel him inside of me. But I was too much of a coward to tell him.

The harder he pumped, the faster my tears fell, until I had to bite down on my tongue to keep from crying out.

"Oh God, joyous perfection!" Bishop grunted, then thrusted twice more before stiffening and releasing an incoherent shout of pleasure.

# Chapter Twenty-Nine

# Ghost

Shortly after the dreadful shower incident that Bishop seemed unaware of, we prepared for the rest of the day by getting dressed. While Bishop sauntered across the bedroom half-naked, taking his time and whistling, I hurried to cover every inch of my body. Once we were back downstairs, Bishop finished sweeping up the glass on the floor, and I was about to start breakfast when a message buzzed his phone. Bishop's fingers moved quickly over the flat surface, his face scrunching as he typed out a response.

"Sorry, no breakfast for me. Kenny wants to talk about the corrupted file he downloaded from the office," he said, pocketing the phone and slinging the backpack he had brought over one shoulder. "Is that okay?"

"Of course," I said. "Did he recover any of the data?"

"His text didn't say, but I have a feeling he did. Probably why he wants to meet in person." Bishop reached across the island, lightly running his fingers up my arm. "Walk me out."

I followed him to the front door as an eerie chill settled between my shoulder blades. Clasping my hands behind my back to hide their shaking, I kissed him goodbye, and he promised to call later.

The very moment Bishop exited my house and flashed his stunning dimpled smile, a deeper sense of dread slipped into the weird void eddying in my stomach. As much as I needed to be alone, I wanted him to stay.

Closing the front door, I flipped the deadbolt and crumbled to the floor. Finally able to break down without a witness, I gave in

160

to the soul-crushing shame with tears, badly wishing I had spoken my truth to Bishop. Voiced my feelings and saved myself from the disgustful stain on my heart that I alone had caused. The one that now surrounded the gaping hole my mother's death had left behind. As much as I wanted to be with Bishop, deep down I knew I could not keep him. I was a wreck. Emotionally challenged, broken, and possibly deranged. Way too much baggage for another person to carry. He had just rid himself of Ava, and now he was unknowingly getting involved with someone in far worse shape.

A pounding headache and blurred vision let me know there was no way of escaping today's turmoil or any of the mayhem-filled tomorrows that I would soon face.

MY TEARS HAD DRIED, but I remained sitting against the front door with my head stuck between my knees. I was trying to ignore the phone that had been vibrating along the island countertop for several seconds. It was not until the phone flipped over the edge and crashed to the floor that I peeled myself off the cold hardwood. Walking over, I snagged the buzzing device before it disappeared under the stove. I thought for sure it would be Grandma June calling to grovel and excuse her way back into my good graces, but it turned out to be an unknown caller.

Switching off the phone, I tossed it back on the counter and headed upstairs. It was time for another shower, and then I would crawl back into bed.

I had reached the sixth step when someone rang the doorbell. Pausing for a second, I debated answering the door and then continued to the top of the stairs. I had entered the bedroom when the doorbell sounded again, followed by a consistent, fast-paced knocking. Realizing there would be no peace until I sent whoever it was away, I went back downstairs prepared with an onslaught of colorful obscenities.

If I had been thinking more clearly, I would have checked to see who was at the door before unlocking it and blindly jerking it open to yell, "Wrong day, wrong house, asshole!"

The hatted man removed his black fedora and held it over his chest like a shield. "Is this a bad time?"

I knew *he* was coming. With my stress levels through the roof and emotions hovering somewhere between agony and mania, how could he not?

A sudden dizzy spell caused me to stumble back a step, reminding me how ill-equipped I was to handle another delusion. "When is it ever a good time to go insane?"

"You're not insane."

"Says the stress-induced hallucination."

"May I come in?"

"Nobody's stopping you. I'm surprised you knocked when you could have just as easily appeared in the middle of my living room."

I closed the door behind him and poked his arm as he walked by. The hatted man felt solid and surprisingly firmer than I had expected. Though how could anyone really know the consistency of an individual's hallucination?

He glanced down at the spot where I had briefly touched his arm, and then seemed to casually survey his surroundings. "I didn't want to startle you."

"How thoughtful," I mumbled as I recalled something I had read recently. Schizophrenics often reported hallucinations as denatured, parts of bodies, or transparent apparitions. Some patients even claimed to have walked right through theirs. Of course, most of them were in treatment and heavily medicated. I, on the other hand, was not. What further damage might be inflicted on my psyche if I was, or was not, able to walk through the hatted man?

I had also read that audial hallucinations tended to precede visual ones. Was it a bad sign that I had seen the hatted man long before hearing him speak?

"It looks as if you've been crying," he said, placing his hat back on his stubby head.

My feet continued to move, carrying me from the foyer to the kitchen and back again. "I've had a rough morning, night... Well, as you know, the last several days have been exceptionally hellacious."

He stepped into my path, placed a gentle hand on my elbow, and guided me to the living room couch. "I came to offer my condolences for the loss of your mother."

At the edge of the couch, I crossed my arms, refusing to sit. "Not necessary. I'd much prefer not to lose my mind right now."

The hatted man remained standing, though his eyes seemed to implore the respite of the cushioned sofa. "Don't you find it just a tad odd that your mother dies so soon after the argument with your grandmother? It should come as no surprise that Juniper White has become close friends with death. It's not a secret that she would do whatever she had to do to ensure you and your mother never met."

*Is he accusing Grandma June of murder?*

"Just think what would have happened to you, if you had eaten your grandmother's crab cakes instead of taking them to your office."

"Huh, she, n-n—" His ludicrous accusation had me floundering for words as my thoughts raced. Grandma June could not have purposely drugged food and delivered it to my doorstep. No way! Not possible! It was a mix-up, a mistake. No one from the boardroom ate those crab cakes. They were still in the breakroom fridge, as far as I knew. "Grandma June is a lot of things, but she's not a murderer. She would never harm me. And she did not kill my mother! How could she? Why would she?"

There was no doubt in my mind that my grandmother loved me and my mother. She would never do anything to *intentionally* hurt either one of us. Or anyone else, for that matter.

"You cannot honestly expect me to believe that my grandmother, the person who raised me and cared for me my entire life, the only person who ever loved me, would want to do me harm. Or that she would walk into a secured facility with dozens of witnesses and murder her own daughter."

The hatted man took a seat and sighed. "And you know that how?"

I threw my hands up. "Because she loves us. And we love her. All her lies, everything she's done. It's only been to protect me. To protect her daughter. She made sure we both had lives worth living! Good, safe lives. We take care of each other. We're family!"

"Matricide, patricide, infanticide are all words used to describe how *family* treats one another."

"Not us." Shaking my head, I closed my eyes. *How can I rid myself of the monster in my head? Make an appointment. Get on some meds.* It was time for me to see a doctor.

"There's a dark, very sinister reason for why you never got to meet your grandfather."

I opened my mouth to dispute, to reiterate that my grandfather had perished in a boating accident, but the hatted man's pursed lips and scornful blue eyes rendered me mute.

Turning away, I swiped at tears that had yet to fall. I did not want to hear any of it. Because if any of this turned out to be true, then I would lose the only family I had ever known. I would be alone with only myself to depend on. And I already knew I was unreliable. If not completely incompetent.

"Why are you doing this to me?"

"You've gotten a small glimpse of the truth. A single letter that had been hidden away. There's so much more. It's time for you to learn the rest."

The urge to flee was building, but there was nowhere to run from myself. I headed over to the kitchen and filled a tumbler with tap water. Keeping my back to the hatted man, I doused the fire burning in my stomach and then immediately refilled the glass.

"How could you know anything? You're just an extension of me, and I know nothing!"

"Ghost, you know more than you realize. Do you know why you freaked out at the mall when I said the name Riggie?"

I had to set the glass down and brace my shaking hands on the counter to keep from spilling the water all over the kitchen floor. "It was the name I'd given my imaginary father as a kid."

"Riggie is not only the name of your *imaginary* father. It is the real name of your very real father, Charles Riggie." There was shuffling behind me. Beyond anything else, I feared the hatted man would touch me, force me to turn around and face him.

When he spoke next, the location of his voice had changed. He sounded distant. "You were young the first time you heard his name, but thankfully your subconscious held on to a piece of it. And I want to give the rest of it back."

Except that was not true. I had named my imaginary father after the little red rig I found one morning playing behind the boat shed when I was young. Trucks were for boys. I had kept the toy hidden under my bed so Grandma June would not take it away. If memory served me, that toy was still at the lake house in my old room. "Nope, you're wrong. I named him after a toy."

"Yes, the red truck *he* left for you."

I nearly choked on a flood of overwhelming emotions. Coughing through guttural noises that continued to emerge unexpectedly, I rallied for control. There was no denying the fact that I had completely lost it. In my insanity, I accused my grandmother of murdering multiple family members. And then, to top it off, I announced the identity of the rapist father I had never known, much less heard of.

My delusion remained silent, likely reveling in the fresh wounds it had inflicted. With no idea what to say or do next, I stared at the hands gripping the countertop. The longer I stood there, the more foreign my fingers appeared. The once slender, elegant digits were now a pair of hooked claws coated in pasty flesh pulled too tight around the knuckles. The internal monster I feared most had finally taken physical form. Screaming in terror, I snatched the glass from the counter, spun around, and threw it across the room. The glass shattered on the far wall, just above where the hatted man had been sitting.

He was gone. The living room was completely void of life.

# Chapter Thirty

# Juniper

"I did not grant permission for an autopsy! As her mother and sole executor, my daughter's wishes will be fulfilled to the letter. And she specifically stated in her will that an autopsy was not to be performed. I demand they cease whatever they've started doing right now!"

*This cannot be happening!*

A gruff sound came from Juniper's attorney before he announced what she already knew. "It is regrettable, and I understand your outrage in the matter, but your daughter died in a state institution. An autopsy is required by law."

She did not know that last part, but she definitely should have.

"What if I sign something saying I won't file a malpractice suit against Glen Haven? Can we stop it then?"

*There has to be a way.*

"Unfortunately, no. I'm sorry, Mrs. White, but it will happen no matter what."

"My daughter did not want to be cut up, mutilated, or studied."

"I would think you'd be pleased. If they find evidence of a doctor's wrongdoing, you won't even have to file the paperwork for a wrongful death lawsuit. You'll have Glen Haven by the balls. All we have to do is name our price."

"I don't want money. I want to bury my daughter."

*I want all of this to go away.*

Juniper ended the call with her moneygrubbing lawyer by slamming the phone on the kitchen counter, knowing full well she had cracked the screen under the forceful blow.

Nothing was going the way it was supposed to. Not with her lawyer. Not at the coroner's office. And not with her granddaughter, who she had still not heard from.

Juniper needed someone on her side. She had to find at least one person to help her escape this mess. The clock was ticking. She did not have much time. In a couple of weeks, maybe more, all the lies she had protected, all the secrets she had buried, would be resurrected and on display for all to see.

# Chapter Thirty-One

## Ghost

I t took a long time for my tears to dry and for my hands to stop shaking. I was holding on by a fingernail and praying that what happened next would not cause it to snap off.

As I made my way across the first floor to the den I used as a home office, I began to wonder if the hatted man had always been with me. A phantom residing somewhere in the deep recesses of my mind, shuffling through my subconscious, compiling data, and picking up important clues that I had missed or ignored over the years. Staying hidden until the time came to make himself visible to protect me from those who meant to do harm. Though it was just as likely that he was a deviant delusion working to gain my trust before unleashing mayhem and setting me on a path of self-destruction.

It really felt like it could go either way. The urge to vomit forced me to pause outside the powder room door.

A muffled hum sounded in my ears that reminded me of being underwater. After a couple of deep breaths, I continued down the hallway, my legs lethargic and burning as if moving through thick sludge. Finally entering the office, I slid into my rolling chair with so much force that I had to grab the edge of the desk to keep from flying into the wall. The control switch for my body had gone haywire. Almost as if someone had a remote control, slowing me down and speeding me up at the most inopportune moments.

Closing my eyes, I took some more calming breaths, hoping the air would help reset my nervous system.

Opening the laptop on my desk, I entered my security PIN and started a web search for Charles Riggie. There were few results. According to the ancestry website that popped up, there were less than a hundred Riggies registered in their database. A complete list of the rarest surnames in the world noted that if you had one of these scarce names in your family tree, you should consider yourself lucky.

I did not feel lucky.

The second link I found was to an old news article. Charles Andrew Riggie, an orderly at Glen Haven, had been fired for misconduct, though no other details were given.

*The name and the dates match! Is this really my father?*

The date confirmed that his firing would have been around the third trimester of my mother's pregnancy. I was surprised that no rape charges appeared to have ever been filed—not by Glen Haven or my grandmother. A deep dive into judiciary websites had come up with nothing. How could they just let him walk away?

Surely Grandma June would not stand for such an injustice. But then I had to remind myself that I did not know my grandmother as well as I thought.

The first image I found of Charles Riggie was from a missing person poster. The picture the family provided was grainy, but I could tell he was handsome. The poster listed Charles as six feet tall with sandy-blond hair and blue eyes with no identifying characteristics, like a scar or tattoo. I enlarged the photo, distorting the image a little more, but I could still see an expressive glint in his eyes. It was impossible to discern whether he exuded mischief or anarchy. Was he a sick man who preyed upon my mother, a defenseless and confused teenager? Or could he be something else entirely?

He was my age, twenty-six years old, when he went missing, four years after he had been fired from his job at Glen Haven. I would have been just over three years old at the time of his disappearance.

Which coincided with the revised story Grandma June told last night. The attack on me as a toddler had been brought on by the pain and confusion my mother had suffered due to his sudden absence from her life. Although he had been fired years before, he must have found a way to remain in contact with her.

Or had my mother manifested that connection for herself?

I was not sure how I felt after seeing his face and learning his name. Knowing that this man was possibly a part of me. I should have felt something, anything. But I could not find a name for the complete lack of emotion. The lost piece I was not searching for had been found. Sort of. He was still a missing person. The relationship he had with my mother was even more of a mystery. Although, now that I knew his name, I might be able to learn more about him and if through him I had any extended family. But how much did I want to know? Should I subject myself to more emotions I could not name or process?

Despite my reservations, my fingers continued to hit more keys, bringing up more information on Charles Andrew Riggie and his next of kin. His mother, Ruth, had passed ten years ago, but his father, Jacob, was still alive and living in the area. There was also mention of an older brother named TJ.

*I might have a grandfather...and an uncle.*

The first thought that went through my head was: *Do they know I exist?* The second thought was: *If they do, are they ashamed of their son and what he did?*

Swiping at something tickling my cheek, my fingers came away wet. I had gotten used to being the White family tragedy, but was I prepared to be the Riggie family embarrassment?

I was sitting at my desk, face in my hands, so I did not have to look at my computer screen anymore when I decided that I had had enough torture for one day. It was time to put it aside for a few hours. Slamming the laptop shut, I rushed into the kitchen, powered up my phone, and sent a text to Mina and Jessa. Two new friends who knew nothing of my tainted past and were oblivious to my disastrous present. And what luck, we had already made plans for tonight to meet at Jimmie's for happy hour, which I had completely forgotten about until now.

*Hey, Mina & Jessa, I've been meaning to reach out... Still on for happy hour? I could really use a drink or 4.*

Determined not to lose any steam, I made something to eat while I waited for a response. I was nibbling on toast and sipping orange juice when my phone alerted me to a new message.

*Mina: Hey Ghost! Been wondering if we'd hear from you! I'm off at 5:00.*

Another immediately followed Mina's text.

*Jessa: In! Jimmie's is out though, band canceled. Pick a place you want to go.*

I texted back that I would meet them downtown for happy hour at The Drunken Duck and received back-to-back thumbs-up emojis.

# Chapter Thirty-Two

# Juniper

J uniper was making a tuna salad sandwich for lunch when an announcement blared on the living room TV. She dropped a spoonful of mayonnaise on the counter and rushed into the next room to catch the rest of the breaking news report. A dark-haired reporter was talking too fast from excitement or time restraints, forcing Juniper to lean closer to the screen. She used to be pretty good at reading lips, but the reporter's wiggling mustache was a distraction. Taking a deep breath, she closed her eyes and focused on the sound of his voice.

"The attendees from the fatal boardroom meeting earlier this week are lucky to be alive. Urine samples taken from individuals who showed signs of intoxication and illness have tested positive for mephedrone and butylone, both illegal and potentially deadly substances. Further blood tests will reveal more about the dangerous psychedelic concoction that was served to the unsuspecting board members at Mason, Kemper, and Witt Financial. Forensic investigators are testing food samples, the leftovers from the boardroom lunch provided by a local bistro, as a possible source of poisoning. Police have officially ruled Carl Wallace Witt's death a homicide, as the combination of those drugs with the heart medication Witt took regularly would have lethal consequences. However, full autopsy results are still pending. The investigation is ongoing. Anyone with information is urged to call the crime hotline on your screen now."

Juniper stood in the center of her living room, stunned and wide-eyed, twitching and rocking as her mind waged an attack on her body. While her weary muscles wanted to give out and collapse in defeat, her problematic brain whizzed through every possible scenario that could have taken place.

*But how? Why?*

She headed back into the kitchen and picked up her phone. The call she placed to Gigi went straight to voicemail. No surprise there.

"Gigi, I know we're not in a good place right now. But I lost a daughter, and you lost a mother. Emotions got the better of me. I love you so much. We need to talk about it. Oh, and I just heard the news of Mr. Witt's unexpected passing. I'm so sorry, deary. We need each other now more than ever. Please call me."

Juniper suddenly found herself standing in front of her pantry, holding the small jar of herbal highs that she kept tucked away in a special compartment in the pantry. Police would investigate the office workers and anyone in the building before and around the time of the incident. Interviews, reports, and such took time. Full lab analyses of the food samples could take weeks. What were the chances that her daughter's autopsy and this other one would be compared?

*Cunning and wise beats them every time.*

Nodding in agreement with herself, she addressed her absentee husband. "I won't go down for this, Henry!" She tapped the top of the jar with manicured fingers. "I'm the Frugal Philanthropist," Juniper sang, quoting a recent newspaper article that praised one of her more significant charitable donations. "Everybody loves me."

*Almost everybody!*

Juniper set the jar aside to finish making her lunch so she could enjoy her sandwich with a tall glass of sweet tea. Then, she planned to send Gigi the message she had already prepared. The text was saved and ready to go with a photo of Bishop's social media post, the image of Gigi he had stolen and posted as his own years before the two ever met, and a snapshot of the online court record for a protective order issued against Bishop from some years back.

Juniper had failed to include the records that immediately followed, where the order had been rescinded by the woman who had filed against him. Juniper could leave no room for doubt. Gigi had to believe Bishop was a stalker and that the woman had lived in fear of him. The second case document meant nothing to Juniper. Deep down in her gut, she knew there had been no misunderstanding between Bishop and the ex-girlfriend. He was a cyber stalking, sex-addicted conspirator. And it was about time someone knocked him on his ass.

Juniper was sitting down to eat when her thin, tightly pressed lips curved into a sinister smile. "No time like the present, right, Henry?" She sent the images off without typing a single word of explanation. There was no point in writing words her granddaughter would never read. It was best to let the facts—the truth—speak for her.

Once Gigi saw the text, there would be no denying Bishop's pervy deviancy.

# Chapter Thirty-Three

## Ghost

Determined to put the recent days of death and deception in my rearview, I turned up my favorite song and forced myself to dance around my bedroom as I got ready for a girl's night. Despite being full of fear and doubt, I knew there was nothing more I could do. My mother was dead, and my grandmother was a liar. So, an evening of distractions was how I planned to escape that inner turmoil.

By four o'clock, I was dressed in black leather pants, a sheer tank top, and a green jacket to hide the newly acquired bruises on my arms and back. My favorite silver heels were waiting for me next to the front door. Sitting at the kitchen island, I stared at my phone, debating the messages I had ignored. The number over the phone icon alerted me to several missed calls, but only a single voicemail had been left, while the number two let me know how many text messages had come in.

Without looking, I knew one had to be from Grandma June, and it was likely that Bishop had reached out after his meetup with Kenny. I was not in the mood to hear from either of them, but with an hour left to go before I had to head out and no more lives left to play on Candy Crush, I decided to pull up my big girl pants and find out what they had to say.

The most recent text, sent about thirty minutes ago, was from Bishop.

*Hey beautiful, what a day! Kenny found some incriminating data on Mr. Sadler. He's at the police station now. Going home 2 take care of a few things. See u later this evening.*

Even though we had not made plans, Bishop assumed we were getting together tonight. For some reason, that angered me more than the fact that my boss might be implicated in a crime. I did not want to send the wrong response, so I switched to my voicemails. An unknown number had called earlier today.

"Good morning, Ms. White. I'm calling to confirm your 5:45 appointment this evening with Mr. Rutledge—"

I deleted the message. That was why Bishop thought we had plans. He was going to accompany me to the lawyer's office. Something else I had completely forgotten about, again. *What else am I forgetting?*

There was no point in meeting with a lawyer anymore. Scrolling through my recent calls, I tapped the unfamiliar number and waited.

My call was answered on the third ring.

"Good afternoon, you've reached the law office of Paul Rutledge. How may I assist you?"

"This is Ghost White returning your call from earlier. Sorry for the late notice, but I have to cancel my 5:45 appointment for today."

"Oh, may I ask why? When we spoke on Sunday, you made it very clear that it was an urgent and time-sensitive matter. We moved a lot around to make room for you this evening."

"I'm sorry, but my—" It felt as if someone had wrapped their hand around my throat and squeezed, trapping my words, forcing me to keep it all inside.

I hung up the phone and poured myself a glass of wine.

After a few citrusy sips of wine, I replied to Bishop's text to keep him from showing up at my house while avoiding the recent text from Grandma June. No good could come from it, and so, I wisely ignored her.

*Wow, Mr. Sadler!? Can't wait to hear what you & Kenny discovered. No lawyer appt. 2-day. Gonna be out, text you when I get home.*

I followed up the text with a heart and smiley face emoji. Then, I downed the rest of my wine, grabbed my purse, and went to the foyer to put on my shoes. Nobody said I could not arrive at The Drunken Duck a little early.

MY FAVORITE BAR, LOCATED in the old warehouse district of town, had a great view of the bay. Décor leaning toward an upscale hotel-style, the place had two oversized bars with a spacious dance floor in between, and plenty of indoor and outdoor seating. They were known for their signature cocktails, with a six-page drink menu. I am sure they served plenty of top-shelf spirits, as well as foreign, craft, and domestic beers, but I never made it past the wine list. Taking an empty seat at the corner of the bar, I ordered my usual, Jermann pinot grigio and a glass of ice water. It would be another thirty minutes before Mina and Jessa arrived. Perched on a stool, I spent that time flipping through social media on my phone. It was also the perfect vantage point to sit and watch other people's lives for a few moments.

I sipped my glass of wine while watching a pair of overzealous businessmen vying for the attention of a leggy brunette. She had turned her eyes my way for the umpteenth time when my phone alerted me to a new text message.

It was Jessa. She was out front and waiting for Mina to park the car. I was in the process of texting her back when one businessman punched the other in the face. As a scuffle ensued, the shock-faced brunette darted over and sat on the empty barstool on my right.

"Hi," she said, holding up an empty tumbler and signaling the bartender for a refill. "Crazy night, huh?"

"It's a little after five," I responded with a shake of my head. Security had arrived to break up the fight. One of the men was escorted out, while the other had pled his case and was allowed to stay. Straightening his tie, he ordered a glass of ice that he held to his cheek and then glanced our way. With his prey still in sight, it would not be long before he pounced again.

I was gathering my phone and glass to move to a table when my phone chimed again. I was about to open the new text when the brunette bumped my arm and placed her hand on mine. "Please don't leave me alone with that imbecile."

"Sorry, I have enough of my own problems," I said, leaving to find a more private spot for me and the girls to hang out. Once I had slipped into an empty booth in the back, I grabbed my phone to let Jessa and Mina know where to find me, only to discover an opened text message from Grandma June.

She had sent an old picture of me at the Trevi Fountain in Rome. Only Marcus had been cropped out of the photo. That picture was taken several years ago, long after Marcus and I had stopped dating. A friendly reunion in Italy that almost ended in us getting married. For a second, I was not sure what I was looking at.

Then I read the caption underneath. "Joyous Perfection!"

But that did not make any sense. Why was my grandmother sending this to me?

A familiar, boisterous laugh had me glancing up. Jessa and Mina were at the bar ordering drinks. Turning back to my phone, the image finally registered. This was a snapshot of a post from Bishop's social media page. Something he should not have, much less have seen, and long before we met.

I clicked on the second image Grandma June had sent and nearly dropped my phone. It was an online record of a restraining order against Bishop Mazzeo for stalking and domestic violence. It did not take a genius to figure out the implication and why she had sent it to me.

I barely noticed Mina and Jessa giggling as they slid into the booth across from me.

*My boyfriend is a stalker.*

*And despite how I treated her, Grandma June is still trying to protect me.*

"Hey, sexy lady," Mina said as she leaned forward, looking down at my phone and then at my face.

Jessa paused, eyeing me with a raised brow. "What's up? Looks like you've seen a ghost," she said, elbowing Mina with a bark of laughter.

Only it was not funny. *How did I end up here?*

This was supposed to be a fun night out.

Instead, another brick had been added to the towering stack. A thousand more pounds weighing me down, pushing me beyond my limits. I could not let them know that I had just snapped under the pressure. How long until the hatted man appeared?

He would probably beckon me to the dance floor while the intro to "Crazy Train" played on the overhead speakers. I silently counted to ten and back down again before addressing my new friends.

"I've had better days, that's for sure."

"Sorry to hear. Want to talk about it?" Mina asked.

"Don't know if you've heard the news, but someone at my office died yesterday. And now police are calling it a homicide." Best to stick to as much of the truth as possible. No need to alarm them with the rest of the disaster that was my life.

Jessa and Mina leaned closer, elbows on the table, hands wrapped tightly around their pints of beer. "Holy shit, you work for Mason, Kemper, and Witt? Were you there when it happened?"

Draining the last remaining drops in my wineglass, I nodded. "Yeah, it's all been pretty horrible. But you know, right now, I'd like to forget rather than rehash."

The last thing I wanted to do was discuss any part of my life with this lovely couple. I refused to darken their doorstep with my Mt. Everest–sized problems.

"We hear ya, sister. Let's get shots." Jessa was out of the booth and halfway to the bar, shouting her order for three lemon drops before I had a chance to respond. Sitting there in stumped silence, Mina reached across the table and took my hand. Her eyes exuded sympathy, though she uttered not one word, and I smiled with sincere appreciation.

They say people come in and out of your life when you need them most. Jessa and Mina were precisely who I—

An undeniable swagger stole my attention. There was no mistaking the man who had just sauntered into the bar.

Bishop had not responded to my text, and yet here he was, striding boldly across the room, sidling up to Jessa as she gathered the shot glasses to bring back to our table. The trapdoor to a pit in my stomach opened when she greeted him with a smile and nodded to where I sat, dumbfounded. He flashed his dazzling dimples and then turned to address the all-too-attentive female bartender.

Jessa was setting our shots on the table when Bishop came up behind her, a full beer in hand. "Evening, ladies," he said, oozing charm. *Or is it something else?*

A shot glass had never been so small. Grabbing the closest one, I raised my glass and toasted the girls, "To a great girls' night." And downed the liquor without acknowledging Bishop, who had started sliding into the booth beside me. I pushed back. Slamming the shot glass on the table, I excused myself to the bathroom, eyeing Jessa and Mina and secretly hoping they would follow.

Bishop relented, but as I moved past him, he grabbed my waist and pulled me into an embrace that was more intense than the occasion called for. Had I not received the text from Grandma June, I might have thought it a remarkable coincidence and probably melted against him to enjoy the moment, even after the shower incident. But knowing what I knew now, I could not squirm out of his arms fast enough. "Gotta pee."

I felt the heat of him behind me as I rushed through the bar and down the service hall to the bathroom. There was no way he knew about my grandmother's text, though after that exchange, he had to be suspicious of my reaction. I heard him call my name as I ducked into the women's restroom.

For the longest time, I stood on the other side of the bathroom door, hands clasped over my mouth stifling a scream as I waited for Bishop to burst through it. Thankfully he did not. Though I did not find much relief in his restraint. Slipping into a stall, I leaned against the side wall and locked the door while continuing to wait for an attack or reinforcements. Neither arrived, leaving me to my own inept devices.

Bishop was out there with friends I barely knew, spinning a web that would endear them to him and poison them against me. Grandma June and I had indulged in enough true crime to understand how it worked. Stalkers were obsessive and controlling. They seduced their victims while at the same time alienating them from friends and family.

I could not allow him to do that to me. *If I don't stand up for myself, no one will.*

The uncertainty was overwhelming, like anything I did would not make a difference. But doing nothing was not an option. I unlocked the stall and headed for the exit—as if I could outrun the anxiety that had grabbed hold of me. By the time I reached the door, my steps were unsteady. My body disconnected from my movements as panic set in. I paused. Closing my eyes, I leaned against the wall, rapped my knuckles on the tile, and started counting.

*Count to ten, and then all the way back down again. I'm fine. I'll be okay...*

Only I was not fine. But I had to be okay enough to get through this moment in one piece. After that, I would find a way to move on to the next.

# Chapter Thirty-Four

## Ghost

Before the door could close behind me, I ran into Bishop. I had expected to find him waiting at the table with Jessa and Mina, but instead, he was standing guard outside the bathroom. He wore a weary expression that marred his otherwise perfect face. Unsure of what to do or say, I waited for him to explain. Bishop always apologized for overstepping boundaries, but knowing what I knew now, this was not something I could forgive. Especially if he was not going to speak. We were standing too close, and the silence stretched too long, forcing me to make the first move.

Taking a deep breath to steel my nerves, I blurted out exactly what was on my mind. "This isn't a coincidence. Did you follow me? What are you doing here?"

Bishop flinched, stepped back, and then casually leaned against the wall. "Didn't realize my presence would be such an imposition. You look gorgeous, by the way."

His dark eyes left a chill as they traveled the length of my body. He gave no denial or explanation, only a form of misdirection that made me even more uncomfortable. I crossed my arms, wanting to rub away the sudden cold. "How did you know I was here?"

"What's wrong with you? Are you okay?" Seemingly aware of my increasing distress, Bishop stepped forward and reached for me.

I pulled away. And like a puppet on a string, he moved with me. "If you can't answer my questions, then you should leave."

Bishop moved, eliminating the short distance between us. Abruptly my hands were out, palms pressed flat against his chest to keep him from pushing me into the vacant bathroom. When he looked at my hands on his chest, his scowl deepened as he moved forward until my back was against the door.

"You want me to go? Just like that, for no reason other than I showed up at the bar where my girlfriend is drinking away her sorrows with a couple she barely knows. You're so worried about my intentions. What about theirs?" he growled, pointing down the dimly lit hallway.

*Why are Mina or Jessa not coming to check on me? How is it that no one in this bar has to pee?*

We were both staring into that space when he sighed. I had one hand behind my back, feeling for the door handle. I intended to slip inside and shut him out when he took my face in his hands.

"Please." His deep voice softened even as he turned my head, forcing me to look at him. "You know how deeply I care about you."

The well-orchestrated emotional display was annoyingly heartbreaking. His usually smoldering eyes glistened in pain as his full, kissable lips pulled down at the corners. No matter how hard I tried, I was not impervious to his charms. There was a small part of me that wanted to take his hurt away, but I could not allow myself to give in. I was not the weak, helpless woman he made me out to be, and I did not need a man to come to my rescue.

Gently stroking my cheeks, he moved his thumbs to caress my bottom lip. Placing his forehead to mine, I thought he might try to steal the kiss I had withheld earlier.

"We've been under severe duress and experienced some extenuating circumstances in a short period of time. I'm looking out for you, making sure you're okay. Please don't be upset. It's not like I'm some creepy stalker guy—"

"Except you are!" I said, jerking my face out of his hands.

Bishop shot back so fast you would have thought he had been struck. "What?"

"Joyous perfection, right?"

"Huh?" Bishop looked confused as he shook his head.

I pushed away from the door, resisting the urge to run, and calmly approached the busy bar. I had reached the end of the hall, able to see the patrons, but not out in the open enough for them to notice when he grabbed my elbow and pulled me back a step. "What are you talking about?"

Glaring, I wrenched my arm free. "The photo you stole, the one that was taken while I was on vacation in Italy. The photo you cropped and posted on your social media account with the caption 'Joyous Perfection!' Ring any bells?"

With brows raised and mouth hanging open, Bishop appeared positively stunned.

"Are you two okay? You've been gone so long we were starting to get worried."

The instant I heard Jessa's voice, my shoulders relaxed. I gave her a smile of thanks and then addressed Bishop, who once again seemed calm and collected. "We're good. Bishop was just leaving."

With a slightly puckered expression, Jessa linked her arm to mine. We headed back to the table. Her head tilted close to my ear when she asked, "What happened to your hands? Looks like you've been fighting with a brick wall."

"Gym. Forgot to put on the boxing gloves." It was a flimsy excuse. One Jessa probably did not believe. But it was all I could come up with on the spot.

Mina stood when we approached, her eyes stretching a bit too wide. I stopped and turned just as Bishop stopped short before he bowled us over.

"Oh my god, Ghost! That was nothing." He did his best to keep his voice low. "It was so nothing that I completely forgot about it. This is not nearly as bad as you think it is. Trust me."

Except I could not trust him. I did not know if I ever had. "Not here, Bishop. Just go." I cringed as soon as the words left my mouth. It sounded too much like begging.

"Do we need to get security?" Mina asked, moving around the table to stand next to her wife.

"No!" Bishop and I replied in unison.

Placing a hand lightly on my elbow to gain my full attention, Bishop continued to plead his case. "Back in the day, I took a photography class. I was behind on an assignment due to a gig I had the night before. I was searching the internet for something I could use. It turns out that we have a couple of mutual friends; I found your photo and thought it was an amazing shot. The lighting was perfect for the project. I copied the photo and accidentally posted it to my personal page instead of the group page for the class. It's why when we met at work, the first thing I said to you was, you look familiar—"

"Are you sure we haven't met before?" I said, finishing his sentence.

Sensing a change in my resolve, Bishop flashed a timid smile. "I swear to you, I am not a stalker. I am not trying to control you or own you or anything like that. But I am protective of the people I love. That will never change."

It was hard to ignore that he had just indirectly told me he loved me. There had only ever been one person in my life who loved me. And despite all that had happened, she was still trying to protect me now.

"Okay, then why was a protective order filed against you?"

His hand dropped from my elbow. "You did a background check?"

"No, but Grandma June did. I got a text from her this afternoon."

Then I remembered what the hatted man said earlier. That my grandmother would stop at nothing to keep me from meeting my mother. Could the same be true for Bishop? Did she now have her sights set on him?

"And she's such a trustworthy source? Did your grandmother also send you the case record that shows the order was rescinded? Here's my phone, look it up." Bishop handed me his unlocked phone.

Jessa leaned in close. "Girl, this is crazy. Let's get out of here."

It did not take me long to find the state judiciary site. Glancing up, I noted Bishop's calm composure, which indicated he knew exactly what I would find.

I felt Mina and Jessa pressing in to read the search results over my shoulder. The order had been rescinded. No other charges had been filed. Not even a traffic violation.

"Doesn't really exonerate him," Mina whispered.

"That happened years ago after an intense relationship turned toxic. I made some mistakes, and so did she. I never stalked her. I can admit that sometimes my temper flares, but I never laid a hand on her or anyone else. That's not who I am. We were young and stupid." With each word, he sounded more sincere and perhaps a bit desperate.

The truth was that Bishop had never been anything but open with me. He was always a perfect gentleman. Too many times, I had been critical, moody, and possibly crazy.

"You do believe me though, right?" Bishop implored with the saddest, most pathetic smile I had ever seen.

The "no" that sounded came from the two birds still hovering over my shoulder. I could not help but laugh.

"Sure, I'll believe you," I said, moving in to give Bishop a hug. Then I whispered in his ear, "Now get out of here. I'm going to enjoy what's left of this girls' night."

Because I was nobody's fool. Not anymore. I needed time to sort through things and come to my own conclusion about him and my grandmother.

Bishop seemed reluctant to let go. Then suddenly, he was arm's length away with his hands resting on my shoulders. Clearing his throat, he dropped his hands and turned to Jessa and Mina. "Okay. I'm leaving. But first, I'm buying you girls a round for the interruption."

"I want the best scotch they have," Jessa demanded.

"I think champagne is in order," Mina chimed in next, nudging me with a smirk.

"Another glass of pinot grigio for me."

Graciously, Bishop went to the bar to place the order while the girls and I settled back into our booth. "Ghost, you gotta fill us in. What was all that about?"

I waited until we had our drinks and Bishop had left the bar before diving into the details of the boyfriend-bashing text I had received from my grandmother and the ensuing drama that they had witnessed.

# Chapter Thirty-Five

# Juniper

Juniper had not been sitting around waiting for her granddaughter to respond in person to the message she sent earlier. There was much to do. But she had hoped that Gigi would say *something*. She had gone through a lot of trouble to uncover the disturbing truth about Bishop Mazzeo. And good manners dictated a response. A simple "thank you for letting me know my boyfriend is a psycho piece of shit" would have sufficed. But alas, the "Grandmother of the Year" award would not be presented to Juniper White today.

Not because she did not deserve it. Juniper knew she was more than worthy of the title.

The doorbell rang as Juniper stood in front of the entryway mirror, applying her signature red lipstick. Aiming to look pristine, she went about fluffing her hair and straightening the collar of her blouse before answering the door. Just because she was grieving did not mean she had to look like a wreck.

A single heartfelt call to Daniel Garrett meant she was about to be descended upon by a group of sympathetic friends and neighbors. It was exactly what she needed to escape her troubles and legal concerns, if only for a spell.

It had been Juniper's experience that the police did not like to work too hard, and rarely did they have any sort of imagination. Many innocent lives were wasting away in jail because of it. The men in blue viewed the world primarily in black and white. Anyone who went the extra mile or dared to think outside the box was eventually squashed into submission by corruption, politics, and outdated bureaucracy. It was one of the many reasons Juniper created a colorful world inside a home of black and gray. The White family would always remain one step ahead of Johnny Lawman.

"I can do this, Henry. Easy peasy lemon squeezy. Isn't that what you always used to say?"

Juniper's late husband did not answer. Dead men do not speak. But that did not stop her from pausing with a sharpened ear in case he chose that moment to break his silence.

The second ring of the doorbell twisted her bold, bright lips into a smile.

Juniper opened the front door to find Daniel holding a simple bouquet of daisies and fidgeting with his favorite green tie. It was a sweet gesture from a gentle old man who was too kind for his own good.

"Oh, Dan, thank you for coming," Juniper said, accepting the small bundle when her dear friend offered it. "I'm going to go put these in some water."

"How are you holding up?" Daniel asked as he closed the front door and followed Juniper through the house.

"I'm not sure. I cried for a while and then raged through the house."

Daniel paused as he passed by the living room, seemingly taking notice of the broken vase and dark stain on the carpet.

"Apologies for the mess." Juniper sucked in a breath and fluttered her hands about. Several delicate white petals fell to the floor between them.

"To be honest, I don't know what to do with all these emotions." Juniper did not expect tears to fall in his presence and abruptly turned away.

"Of course, it's understandable. Where's Gigi?" Daniel asked, placing a gentle hand on her shoulder.

Juniper appreciated his use of her granddaughter's nickname and turned around to embrace him. Daniel rubbed her back and held her close while she cried.

Juniper had not allowed herself to cry in front of another soul in many years. Thankfully, Daniel Garrett was as discreet as he was gracious. When folks began to arrive with condolences and casseroles, he ushered Juniper up to her room so she could collect herself. As she climbed the staircase, she heard him greet people, offer drinks, and direct them where to place bereavement gifts. Though she appreciated the effort, he was doing someone else's job.

*Gigi should be here.*

The tears Daniel saw earlier were not for the loss of a daughter, but rather for the absence of a granddaughter. Instead of supporting and comforting her grieving grandmother, Gigi was off somewhere doing God only knows what with Bishop. Had her granddaughter even bothered to read her text? How long would she remain oblivious to the danger she was in?

Juniper finished freshening up her makeup and headed back downstairs, where she found a lively group of friends and neighbors gathered in her dining room. The length of her rosewood table was littered with a collection of half-empty glasses, bottles of spirits, a pitcher of water, and a large tray of cheese and crackers.

Daniel had made himself at home, providing everything her visitors needed to feel welcomed. Juniper had to admit he had done a much better job than she would have.

Mrs. Duncan from over on Kilmer Street was the first to notice Juniper lingering at the bottom of the staircase. With a slight gasp, she rushed over with a plastic grocery bag already in hand. "Oh my, I'm so sorry to hear about Meredith. How are you holding up?"

"I'm not sure." Juniper tried to smile and failed.

"Well, we're all here for you, whatever you need," Mrs. Duncan said, reaching out to pat Juniper's arm. Then, Mrs. Duncan seemed to remember she was holding a bag. Her other hand shot out. "And this is for you."

Juniper was a tad reluctant, but once she looked inside the bag, she clutched the precious gift to her chest. And she nearly started crying again.

"I know it's your favorite. Came across the last box at the market today."

It was a bald-faced lie. Both of them knew the dirty chocolate herbal tea had been out of stock in every store in a fifty-mile radius, but still the corners of Juniper's mouth lifted. Not quite a smile, but close enough.

By 8:30 p.m., Juniper had had her fill of company. She had started dropping hints, saying it was getting late, that she was tired, and then that she was flat-out exhausted. When those clues were not picked up on, she went about clearing dishes and removing empty and full bottles of wine from the table. She even snatched a freshly poured glass of wine out of the hands of her neighbor from two houses over. It was time for everyone to go.

Juniper placed plastic wrap over a dish of spinach dip when the cell phone on the counter rang. A specific ring—an annoying theme song from some show Juniper had never seen. The one Gigi had personally downloaded when she had shown her grandmother all the tricks and gadgets her new cell phone had to offer.

Juniper's hand shook as she reached for the phone. She hit Accept and raised the phone to her ear.

"Hi, Grandma. It's me." Gigi's voice sounded as weary as Juniper felt.

"I know, deary. How are you doing?" Juniper replied, trying her best to stay calm even though her heart was practically beating out of her chest.

"Okay, I guess... You?"

"About the same. Did you get my text?"

There was a pause, then a shuffling noise before Gigi responded. "I did."

"I'm so sorry, but you know it's always best to find these things out early."

Another long pause. Juniper was afraid Gigi had hung up when another timid response sounded.

"It is."

"We have a lot to discuss and plans to make. When are you coming home, dear?" *Please say you're coming home. I need you.*

"Soon, Grandma...soon."

"Gigi, I—"

Her granddaughter ended the call before Juniper could finish her sentence.

# Chapter Thirty-Six

# Ghost

After a quick phone call to my grandmother that made me sound weak and pathetic, I escorted Jessa and Mina out of The Drunken Duck to wait for a driver from the rideshare app to arrive. Neither one of them was in any condition to drive after a never-ending string of shots that I had refused after downing the first one. My usual coping mechanisms for stress were unhealthy and dangerous. I had to find another way to curb my appetite for oblivion and self-destruction. The sudden awareness came out of nowhere. It was like someone had reached over and plucked a dunce cap off the top of my head. At that moment, my mind's eye conjured an image of the hatted man holding a tall pointy hat.

While Mina and Jessa made out like a couple of teenagers on a nearby bench, I looked for the now infamous post on Bishop's social media page.

Grandma June could not be trusted. I had to see *it* for myself.

I scrolled through his feed until I found the stolen, cropped picture with a long string of comments. Some of them were very flattering. However, Bishop's responses never mentioned a mistaken post or a photography class assignment. Not only had he taken credit for the photo, but he also credited himself for the smile on my face.

A smile that was intended for someone else. The same smile that had upset a few of his female followers, based on several snarky comments attached to his post.

I searched deeper, trying to find anything that would back up Bishop's claim of a mis-post or anything about a photography class. I came up empty. However, I did discover something else. A picture of Selina and Kendall partying with Ava Parker at Mad Cow Cantina popped up on my feed. A bar that just happened to be only a few miles away.

Ava's half-assed warnings and lackluster threats were not going to cut it. The time had come to discover exactly what I was getting myself into with Bishop. It's not the most pressing matter, but it might be the easiest one to resolve.

My grandmother was never going to tell me the truth, and I had lost the chance to get the answers I needed from my mother. I could not afford to make the same mistake again.

"Want to ride with us?" Mina asked as a small SUV with a lighted dashboard sign stopped at the curb. There was a hint of mischief in her inebriated gaze as she fixed her sights on Jessa's butt, who already had the door open and was crawling headfirst into the back seat.

"No thanks, I'm good. Get home safe." I held the door for Mina as she stumbled around and then plopped down on the seat next to Jessa. They nodded in unison and blew sloppy kisses. I closed the car door as Jessa leaned over and kissed Mina, boldly slipping her hand down the front of her pants.

Standing on the sidewalk, I stared longingly at the phone in my hand as the SUV pulled away. Bishop and I could have unfinished business that resulted in something hot and steamy. Much like what Jessa and Mina were doing in the backseat of that stranger's car.

A flash of red forced me to look up. It was the taillights of the SUV braking before turning left out of the parking lot. I took it as a warning sign and dropped my phone back into my purse.

Walking across the parking lot to my car, I scolded myself for even thinking of calling Bishop.

I never knew my mother. I did not know my grandmother as well as I thought I did, and I barely knew Bishop. So, I was desperate to find the truth about at least one person in my life. Because as soon as I got my shit together, then surely the hatted man would disappear.

THE MAD COW CANTINA, popular among the rowdy twenty-something crowd, was a gaudy country bar with sticky floors, fried food, cheap beer, and thunderous live music. Despite being in the appropriate age demographic, it was not the place for me. But I would suffer it all with a smile if it led to some answers.

A sea of denim and cowboy hats parted as I approached the bar. I was dressed for the runway, not a hoedown. If I had had more time, I would have gone home and changed. But there was not much I could do about it now. When I reached the U-shaped bar, I ordered a vodka tonic. Casually, I sipped my watered-down drink as I scanned the crowd in search of three familiar faces.

I was about to remove myself from the presence of the overly aggressive flirt next to me when I spotted Selina. Her hot-pink cowboy hat was easy to follow as she pushed into a thick line of people gathered around the dance floor. A choreographed group dance had just started. As the song blared, I caught a glimpse of Kendall and Ava as they stepped, spun, and swayed to the music. I had never been line dancing before, especially not in four-inch spiked heels, but that did not stop me from grabbing the hand of the man beside me and pulling him onto the dance floor.

"Didn't think you were into me," the guy said as I guided him over to where Kendall and Ava would have a clear shot of us together.

I flashed a shy smile and placed my hand on his hard bicep. "I don't know the steps. Can you show me?" I was not shy or interested, but I had to give Ava a reason to approach. Catching me out with a strange man was a juicy tidbit the gossiping trio would not be able to resist.

The dance moves were simple, but I still turned the wrong way twice and stepped on more toes than I dared to count. Thankfully the guy was a good sport about my lack of experience. He laughed and placed an arm around my waist to help guide me in the right direction. An intimate move that was sure to get the trio salivating.

An explosion of claps, stomps and howls sounded as the rambunctious song came to an end, followed by a slight pause as the DJ cued up the next song.

"Thanks for the dance. That was fun," I said, pulling away from the guy holding on a bit too tight.

He leaned in as the new song played. "My name's Steve." His lips brushed my cheek. "What's yours, pretty lady?"

"Sorry, but I gotta go," I said, ducking through the line of arm-linked couples who were now swiftly moving around the perimeter of the dance floor.

I had just made it to a recently vacated high-top table in a far corner of the bar when I felt the presence of someone behind me standing too close.

"Trouble in paradise already?"

I breathed a sigh of relief when I turned around to see Ava posturing with both hands on her hips. Her eyes were focused, her stature steady. She did not appear *drunk* or *emotionally troubled*. But of course, Bishop had been the one to apply those labels.

"You might say that."

With a flick of her long, red ponytail, Ava hopped up on a barstool. "I tried to warn you. But hey, you got out before it got bad."

I looked around and did not see any sign of Kendall or Selina. I moved to the empty bar stool across from Ava and sat down.

"Did it get bad for you?" she asked.

It was hard to gauge the sincerity of a near stranger, but at that moment, Ava sounded genuinely concerned.

I gave a slight nod. Not because things were *bad* with Bishop. I was more confused than anything else. But I had to know why she felt the need to warn me off on multiple occasions. The niggling feeling in my gut told me she might not be a jilted lover. Maybe that was only what Bishop wanted me to believe. Just like his claim that the stolen photo was an accident. Perhaps he was just as good at telling stories as Grandma June?

"What happened between you two?"

Ava glanced down as she fingered a puddle of condensation on the scarred table. "Not sure I should tell you since you're the reason he threatened me."

*Ouch!* I had been the one to tell him about the bathroom incident and again when she approached me on that awful day in the office. Hard to believe it had only happened yesterday.

"Threatened how?"

Ava's head snapped up.

"I mean, you're talking to me now. Aren't you scared he'll make good on his threat?"

"I don't think it matters if you're not together anymore," she said, blotting her wet fingertips on a discarded napkin. "How did he end things with you?"

"He didn't."

"What?" Ava hopped off her barstool. Her startled expression appeared to be a mixture of betrayal and fear.

"It was me." *Well, actually Grandma June. And technically, we're not over yet. Hell, we've barely gotten started.*

In an attempt to appear casual, I glanced around the bar. "Did you know he had a protective order filed against him for domestic violence?"

"Really? When? Who?" Now Ava was digging for details.

"First, tell me what happened with you and Bishop?" I pressed, determined to get what I came for.

"It's always great in the beginning, as I'm sure you know. He asked me out. We had a string of great dates. And amazing *sex*." Her emphasis on the word sex had me leaning more toward her being a jealous ex. "Then I felt him getting distant, distracted. So, when Selina and Kendall told me about the rumor going around your office, I called him out on it. Bishop freaked! Like an off-the-charts reaction. Everything was different after that."

"So that's when you broke up?"

"We still hung out. But he treated me differently. It's like I had transformed into a meaningless piece of meat overnight. He used me. It was awful, but I took it. I thought I deserved the punishment for questioning him and once I had suffered enough, we'd go back to the way it was before. I know it was stupid. I'm stupid."

"You're not stupid, Ava." *But I might be.* Because a small part of me was still hanging on, hoping beyond all hope that Bishop would not be *that* guy with me.

I was already in the middle of an existential crisis when we started dating. Then my mother died, and I discovered Grandma June's deceit and the name of my missing father. So, maybe I just did not want to lose one more thing. Or I refused to let go of what little bit of happiness I had found with Bishop.

"Oh, but I am. I've done many dumb things when it comes to him, and I probably would do it again if given the chance. And Bishop's never going to let me forget that."

"What does he have on you?"

"There you are!" Selina shouted as she and Kendall rushed over to our table.

At first, I thought they were talking to Ava, but then Kendall dropped a hand on my shoulder. "Bishop's here."

"What did you do?" Ava asked, wide-eyed and already standing on her tiptoes, trying to catch a glimpse of Bishop. "If he catches me talking to Ghost..."

The smirk on Kendall's face said it all.

"What will he do?" I asked when Ava pointed me toward a side door exit.

"He'll release the video."

"What video?"

Ava had backed up, about to head in the opposite direction. "Duh, it's a sex tape."

Immediately, I wanted to know if it was a tape of them having sex together. Or had she sent a private moment for his eyes only? What would it mean if he had been the one to take the video of her?

Before I could gather enough of my thoughts to ask these questions, Selina stepped in front of me, making sure that I did not follow Ava through the crowd.

"Kendall posted a picture of you dancing with that guy," she said, nodding to the side door Ava had pointed to earlier.

*Oh no!*

# Chapter Thirty-Seven

# Ghost

Leaving through the side door was a smart move. I did not want to be the reason Ava suffered public humiliation. Bishop had always been a gentleman, and releasing a sex tape seemed grossly out of character. But then again, how well did I really know him?

*How well do I know anyone?*

It wasn't like I could confront him on the video or the supposed threat. If I did, he would know I had talked to Ava.

I was almost to the car when I was hit with a terrible thought. What if whatever wrath Kendall's post incited in Bishop fell back on Ava?

Bishop might not have known that we were talking, but he did know we were at the same bar and that I had been in the arms of another man. It would not take a genius to put two and two together.

Even though the last thing I wanted was another confrontation with Bishop, it was wrong to leave Ava behind to deal with him on her own.

Taking a deep breath, I turned around—and nearly screamed as I stumbled back to get away from the hatted man.

"Surprised to see you out tonight, Ghost." His tone was accusatory, with a menacing air. But I refused to show fear in the face of the imaginary.

"And why is that?" I said, attempting to sidestep him and his ill-fitting suit as my delusion leaned closer.

"Because your grandfather and mother were murdered. Your father's missing. And you have much to do regarding both."

"Yeah, I have a lot on my plate right now."

"Time is running out," he gritted through barely moving lips.

*For who?*

"Two people die on the same day. The only connection between them is your grandmother and you." The hatted man adjusted the fedora that had slid to the side and then pointed a stiff finger at my chest. "There's more going on than you realize. Open your eyes."

"Wait, two people?"

"Carl Witt and Meredith White died on the same day."

"Oh right, back to that." The hatted man's push to link Grandma June to Mr. Witt's death was a real stretch, since Dot's Bistro provided the boardroom lunch. "It has to be a coincidence. My grandmother has never even met Mr. Witt. The crab cakes weren't served to the board members. They're still sitting in the office refrigerator."

"Juniper White delivered a meal to your door that you then brought to work, which killed a man, and then she took the same meal with her when she visited her daughter—your mother. It is *not* a coincidence."

A door banged somewhere behind me, followed by the echoes of footsteps chewing up pavement. I turned to see Bishop storming out of the bar.

When I turned back around, the hatted man was swiftly weaving through the rows of cars, heading for the other side of the parking lot. I waited until the black fedora disappeared behind a big dually truck and then focused my attention on the man stomping up to me.

Dressed in drawstring sweatpants and a loose V-neck tee shirt, it was obvious that Bishop had not been planning to come back out tonight.

That meant he was only here because of Kendall's post on social media.

"What the hell, Ghost? What's going on?" Bishop stopped just short of running into me. His breath was hot on my forehead, his normally handsome features marred by fury.

"Stalker much?"

Bishop took a step back. "That's not fair."

"Doesn't look like it from this side." Despite his earlier defense of everything being a series of misunderstandings, the fact was he followed me twice.

"I never got to tell you why I showed up at The Drunken Duck. So, let me fill you in so it's all crystal clear." His serious tone and stern look had me crossing my arms, crushing them into my chest. He was almost as overbearing as Grandma June.

"Besides having original plans to go with you to your lawyer—"

I opened my mouth to remind him of the terrible event when he lifted his hand. A signal for me to allow him to finish.

"Unfortunately, that was no longer necessary. I came by your house today because I know what Kenny uncovered and took to the police."

When Bishop paused, seemingly for dramatic effect, I asked, "What did Kenny find?"

"Mr. Sadler has done some terrible things, and as his assistant, you had your hands on the account and the numbers he was cooking. Sadler was embezzling."

I'm sure my face registered shock. My eyes were moving about as I tried to recall each time I had worked with him on that account.

"Ghost, it looks to be hundreds of thousands of dollars, maybe more. You understand what that could mean for you, right? That's why I came to see you. I wanted you to know before the police called you to make a statement. Then I saw you leaving your house, dressed like a million-dollar movie star, and followed. I was concerned that you were going to meet Sadler."

Unlocking my arms, I stepped back and threw my hands up. "Oh my god, I had nothing to do with it. How could you think I'd be a willing participant in something like that?"

He closed the distance, reached out, but then seemed to think better of it and dropped his arms to his sides. "I wasn't sure, I didn't think... I sat in my car for a long time in front of the bar. I was about to drive away when I saw Jessa and Mina in the parking lot, and then I knew it wasn't as I had feared. I was so relieved that I came inside, hoping you'd be happy to see me too."

"I'm not happy about any of this," I said, shaking my head, already feeling the pressure of the added weight of his news on every muscle and bone in my body.

"Of course not. But is it all that different from you believing that I was an abusive stalker? Nothing that happened tonight happened the way it should have."

There was no arguing with Bishop's reaction or his reasoning. We did not know each other that well. Which was why we had both been quick to think the worst of one another.

"You may have a point, sort of." I was not about to let him off the hook. There was still no reason for him to have shown up here when he could have just sent a text or called.

"Yeah, well, I'm not bulletproof. The picture Kendall posted online got to me. I came to find out if that stuff from your grandmother was the final nail in the coffin for *us*."

My grandmother's text was far from the worst thing I had heard about Bishop, if what Ava told me tonight turned out to be true. Then again, it could be another one of her attempts to scare me away from Bishop.

"Nothing happened *here*. I stopped in to have one drink. Tried my hand at line dancing, which I'm pretty bad at, and now I'm going home." I gave a slight shoulder shrug, thinking it might defuse some of the tension, but then I noticed Bishop's hands were now clenched into two large fists.

"Are you kidding me with that? What happened to Mina and Jessa?"

"They went home drunk." I did not think it wise to tell him that they did not come here with me.

"And the guy in Kendall's picture, who's he? Was it an attempt to get back at me?" He was practically yelling. "I never thought you'd stoop to their level. Hell, I didn't even think you liked them."

"You're right, I don't particularly care for Selina or Kendall. But I didn't come here with them. And the guy is just someone who wanted to dance."

Bishop's lips turned in, and his jaw shifted back and forth several times as if he were holding something back.

"This is not about you." Except it really was. Only not in the way he assumed.

Bishop shook out his hands. "Don't give me that! You were ready to call it quits after a couple of mean girl stunts and a few choice words from my ex."

"At least now you know how it feels to be on the receiving end." *Oops, that did make it sound like a bit of payback.*

Bishop blew out a breath as he rubbed the back of his neck. "If the tables were turned and you saw a picture of me out with my arms around some girl, you would be standing exactly where I am now...wondering what the *fuck* is going on."

He had me there. Though I never would have shown up at the bar to confront him. I also did not have the time or energy to fill him in on *everything* that was going on with me.

"Look, it's been a long night, and I really don't feel like fighting," I said, pulling my key fob from my jacket pocket. "You're just gonna have to *trust* me that nothing happened and that I never wanted anything to happen with that guy. It was just a dance."

I had reached my car when I heard Bishop's reply. "I guess I'll have to," he said, rather unconvincingly.

Then I felt a tug on my jacket.

After opening my car door, I turned to face Bishop. The anger in his hazel eyes had softened.

"Can I ask one more question before you go?"

I was done with him and this conversation. "Sure."

"Who was that guy you were talking to?" Bishop had taken my right hand in his, lightly rubbing the pad of his thumb over my skin.

"I think he said his name was Steve."

"Not the guy in the bar. The man you were talking to out here in the parking lot."

My heart stopped and then leapt into my throat, beating erratically.

Suddenly Bishop had taken hold of my arms. And that was the only reason I was still on my feet. "Are you okay?" he said, looking more concerned by the second.

"What did you see?" A strained cackle followed my words. I glanced over my shoulder and, when I saw no one else, realized the horrifying sound had come from me.

"I saw you...talking...to an older...man." Bishop's words had slowed. An obvious reaction to what had to be the growing look of horror on my face. "Black. Hat," he continued, carefully pronouncing each word as specks of darkness invaded my vision.

"Oversized. Pinstriped—"

# Chapter Thirty-Eight

## Juniper

One by one, Juniper's visitors filed out of the house. As she stood by the door, she thanked everyone for coming and willed them to move along a little faster. The hour had grown late. Gigi's earlier phone call had left Juniper wanting nothing more than to close her eyes and never open them again. Each passing hour that her granddaughter did not appear, the heaviness in Juniper's heart increased until it felt like the weighted muscle was tearing in half.

When friends and neighbors first arrived, after settling in with food and drink, they offered their condolences for Juniper's daughter's death. But they soon followed up by asking why her only granddaughter was absent. It was a time for family, after all, and so family should be in attendance.

Juniper thought she had answered their questions logically, citing the recent workplace tragedy as Gigi's reason for not being there. Then the sideways glances and murmuring started, and Juniper quickly informed everyone that Gigi would be there *soon*.

That was the moment Juniper's heart cracked open. She had actually looked down at her feet to see if the bloody contents from her chest had splashed all over the floor.

"Do you want me to stay until she gets here?" Daniel said, coming up behind her, pulling Juniper from her painful recollection.

"Thank you for the offer," Juniper replied. Daniel Garrett had been drying the crystal wineglasses in the kitchen while Juniper made sure her guests had left the premises. The man was a godsend.

But she did not need a babysitter. And she did not need a witness to her emotional demise should her granddaughter not appear.

"Gigi just sent me a text. She'll be here soon," Juniper said, though she had received no such message.

"Okay then, well, please call me if you need anything."

"I promise I will."

"Soon?"

Juniper felt her shoulders creeping up to her ears and nodded. *Soon* was such an awful word. It meant so much and so little at the same time.

"Good night, and pass along my deepest sympathies to Gigi," Daniel said, placing a kiss on Juniper's forehead before stepping out into the night.

The door closed with a heavy thud, as if marking the exact moment when the house became as cold and empty as Juniper's heart.

Eyeing the light switch on the wall, Juniper leaned against the closed door and debated if she should turn off the porch lights.

Something as simple as a light could not alter the decision Gigi had made. Her granddaughter was the only one who knew if or when she would arrive. A part of Juniper wanted the house to be as dark and uninviting on the inside as it was on the outside. Then again, could a darkened doorstep and an unlit interior give Gigi pause? Would that be enough for her granddaughter to turn around and leave?

Juniper would not take that risk.

"Soon. Soon, soon, soon," Juniper mumbled as she moved away from the door without touching the light switch and vowed to remove the word *soon* from her vocabulary.

"But what does it mean, Henry?" Juniper said, as she often bent her dead husband's ear during her most troubled times. "It could be minutes, hours, or days. Gigi never said. She just hung up."

Juniper headed back to the kitchen in need of a favorite and long sought-after comfort—a steaming cup of dirty chocolate herbal tea. The one that had been withheld out of jealousy or malice. Did not really matter which. All Juniper knew was that Mrs. Duncan had been hoarding the tea for months.

She was not one for revenge, but now she could not wait for next week's book club meeting. Because Juniper had every intention of revealing Mrs. Duncan for the greedy, conniving little shit she had proven herself to be.

Juniper entered her freshly tidied kitchen in anticipation before realizing she did not remember where the bag of tea had ended up. She recalled carrying it around for a bit, but then what?

Odds were she had put it somewhere safe to keep greedy hands and mouths from helping themselves. Now, if she could only remember where that safe place was.

First, she checked the pantry, carefully inspecting each perfectly organized shelf in the spick-and-span custom-designed food closet. She found neither the local grocery bag nor the box of herbal tea. So, she began looking throughout the rest of the kitchen, growing more anxious as she opened every cabinet and searched every drawer. She even checked inside the oven, the refrigerator, the dishwasher, and the microwave, and still, she could not locate her precious chocolate tea.

The longer Juniper searched, the more frantic she became, until it finally dawned on her—Mrs. Duncan had taken it back. She had gifted Juniper a highly coveted prize in her very public time of need with the sole purpose of receiving recognition. Which Mrs. Duncan had gotten plenty of. Everyone had praised and applauded the thoughtful generosity of her neighbor.

The old hag, with her gnarled-up fingers. She must have snatched the bag, tucked it into her coat, and snuck away the first chance she got.

Rage and hatred began to fill the recently emptied chambers of Juniper's heart. Now, she had no intention of waiting until book club to confront Mrs. Duncan. An atrocity such as the one she had committed demanded a swift and resolute response. She went back to the pantry and rummaged around until she came across a dented can of Old Bay.

"And to think, before she left, Mrs. Duncan had accepted my invitation to join me for a cup of chocolate tea tomorrow! Henry, did she really plan to arrive with that kind of charade in place? Did she think I'd be too distraught to figure it out?"

Juniper paused when she thought she heard a rustling noise overhead. Tilting her ear toward the ceiling, she waited. Not another sound was heard.

"She has no idea who she's messing with."

Storming to the front door and snagging a coat and her keys along the way, Juniper exited the house prepared to issue her brand of justice.

Reaching the end of the stone path where her cherry-red Challenger was parked, she paused to consider driving to Mrs. Duncan's house. But after a short debate, Juniper decided the crisp night air would do her some good and began her walk to Kilmer Street.

# Chapter Thirty-Nine

# Ghost

Acomforting warmth encased me as a fragrance of linen and spice flooded my nostrils. I breathed in the familiar smell with a deep appreciation. Through the haze clouding my mind, strange voices grew louder. Serious, angry words were spoken, but I could not determine what they were saying. I could feel solid ground under my feet, but it was two strong arms that held me upright. I straightened my legs to get a better footing, then lifted my head, but it felt like it weighed a hundred pounds, and I flopped sloppily back to where it had been resting against Bishop's chest.

"Wha—di—you—her—"

"Call the—"

"This is—what the hell—"

"I didn't do anything. She passed out!"

The words were getting clearer with each voice that spoke. And then reality flooded in. I had passed out after hearing that Bishop had *seen* the hatted man. And if he could be seen, then he was not a hallucination.

The hatted man was real! He had been following me for weeks, purposely trying to deceive me. The only upside to this horrifying scenario was that my mind was intact. Rash and naïve, as Grandma June always said, but at least I was sane.

That knowledge gave me better control of my facilities. I managed to push myself away from Bishop and then looked at the gaping faces around me.

"I'm okay," I said, straightening my jacket and smoothing my hair.

Bishop and I were still beside my open car door, where he must have caught me before I fell flat on my face in the parking lot. Ava, Selina, Kendall, and that guy Steve were all gathered around. Each face formed an expression of suspicion or displeasure.

Ava took a step forward. "Are you sure you're, okay?" While her voice sounded strong, her eyes kept darting over to Bishop, which let me know she did not believe anything out here was *okay*.

"Yes, I'm fine. Sorry for the scare," I said, dropping through the open car door and into the driver's seat of my car.

*He's real!* The hatted man had been stalking me, telling me disturbing things about my family—he tried to make me believe I was crazy. *I have to get out of here. I have to find out why.*

"Hey, Kendall, Selina, by chance did either of you take a container of crab cakes out of the breakroom fridge yesterday?"

"Why, were they yours?" Kendall said as a tight grin formed on her lips. I could practically see a pair of red horns pushing up through her moppy blonde hair. Selina nudged her with a sharp elbow, and the two started bickering. It was enough for me to know that they were the ones who had delivered Grandma June's crab cakes to the boardroom meeting. This meant the terrible thing the very real hatted man had been implying was true.

A cold shiver traveled the length of my spine as I swung my legs into the car. I was about to reach for the door handle when Bishop grabbed hold of it, keeping it open.

"Wait, you can't drive," he said, pushing his body into the opening to block everyone else out.

I grabbed the handle and pulled at the door, but Bishop held firm. "Ghost, I just watched all the blood drain from your face. It was scary as fuck. You're in no shape to drive. Let me take you home."

*I'm not going home.*

"Everything all right over there?" a voice boomed.

When Bishop released his hold on the car door and turned to see who had spoken, I saw a man in a uniform. A cop was walking our way. I took the opportunity to shut and lock my car door.

Starting the engine, I rolled down the window. "Everything's fine, Officer."

Bishop moved aside as the officer marched right up to my car door. "Have you been drinking, miss?"

"No, sir. Just need to get home...my mother died."

A small gasp sounded behind the officer, drawing his attention away for a second. When his gaze returned, it was a bit softer. "Sorry for your loss. Are you sure you're okay to drive?"

"Yes, sir. I am."

The officer leaned in with a look of intent, searched my eyes, and sniffed. A second later, he patted the car door and backed away.

"Get home safe," he said, then he addressed the others, telling them to go about their business.

With a creased brow and firm scowl, I thought for sure Bishop would argue. He did not look like he was going to let this go. But then the officer placed a hand on his shoulder and told him it was time to leave. As Bishop stood unmoving, the knuckles on the cop's hand began to whiten. It was a silent, unyielding request.

After a few tense seconds, I was on the road, heading for the lake house. It was a tough pill to swallow, but now I was certain that Grandma June had tried to poison me, and Mr. Witt died as a result.

I had gotten as far as the first intersection when my phone started ringing. It was Bishop. I let his call go to voicemail and pressed the gas pedal. His number appeared again and again and again on my car's dashboard touchscreen. Until I finally reached into my purse, fumbled around for my phone, and turned the damn thing off.

Bishop was the least of my concerns.

# Chapter Forty

## Juniper

Juniper arrived at the yellow house on Kilmer Street just after eleven p.m. It was a large lake property, comprised of several acres, at the bottom of a dead-end road. What was once a sweet little bungalow now sprawled across a good portion of that acreage. Decades of additions had been added on, each by different owners with opposing tastes in style, architecture, and decor. The seventy-year-old, one-story summer cottage had been transformed into a lengthy, misshapen monstrosity. Long ago, it was labeled an eyesore by the recently upscale, renovated community.

And deep down inside, Juniper White loved every nonconformist inch of it.

"I should buy it when it goes on the market," Juniper muttered into the night as she walked across the lawn and around to the back of the house, careful to stick close to the side to avoid triggering the poorly placed motion-detecting security lights.

"No, no, you're right. That will never do. Of course, my other plans," she said, continuing her quest for revenge.

Juniper checked each window as she passed, taking note of the unlit interior. At this late hour, Mrs. Duncan was most likely in bed. Lucky her. There would be no sleep for Juniper tonight. No rest. At least not until she saw her granddaughter. Only once they had spoken and cleared the air would she be able to relax. In the meantime, she would relieve her frustrations with a surprise visit to a prickly old lady.

"Yes, it's necessary," Juniper whispered when she reached the second, creaky porch step.

Crossing rough planks on the landing, Juniper reached behind a round green planter and retrieved a hidden key. As elderly neighbors and friends, they all knew where to find the spare key and who to call in case of an emergency.

"Well, you're too young, you've never had it, so you wouldn't understand." Juniper shook her head, slid the metal key into the deadbolt, and turned it. There was a slight click, and then the back door popped open.

Juniper illuminated the dark entrance with the light on her smartphone and quietly entered a cluttered mudroom. The harsh smell of florals assaulted her nose. Juniper sniffled through the tickle of a sneeze as she passed the laundry room. A narrow hallway to the left would lead her to the recently remodeled kitchen, one that suspiciously looked a lot like her kitchen at home.

*Some people have no originality.*

The doorway on the right led to an office space attached to a guestroom with a full bath nestled in between. Beyond that was a zigzag maze of rooms and alcoves consisting of a dining room, family/living room, library, den, play area for the grandkids, multiple bathrooms, and five more bedrooms. The primary bedroom, where Mrs. Duncan laid her head at night, was the farthest room from where Juniper now stood.

"What would be the point in that?" Juniper whispered as her fingertips swiped over the edge of a nearby tabletop and then rubbed the dusty residue against her thumb. "Much like you, Mrs. Duncan needs to be taught a lesson."

The idea of taking back what belonged to her and leaving without a trace was stupid, too peaceful and too easy a solution. Watching Mrs. Duncan as she frantically searched for the highly coveted chocolate tea might have been fun, but Juniper had important stuff to do. She could not afford to stick around like a fly on Mrs. Duncan's wall.

A hint of a smile crossed Juniper's red-painted lips. Death would be an exorbitantly high price to pay for a twenty-dollar box of organic tea. But this was not just about the tea now.

Mrs. Duncan had orchestrated a devious plan to trick Juniper while she was mourning the loss of a child. An evil deed such as that should not go unpunished. The only dilemma now was how much suffering to inflict.

Juniper turned left down the narrow hallway and walked into the kitchen. The first thing she noticed when she switched on a light, besides a large amount of disorder, was a familiar plastic bag on the counter next to the refrigerator. A quick inspection of the contents only confirmed what Juniper already knew.

*I'm never wrong.*

Leaving the bag and tea where it lay, Juniper stealthily made her way through the dark, still house. The only sound was the padding of Juniper's soft-soled shoes on the carpet. But as she neared the closed door of Mrs. Duncan's bedroom, she heard voices. A deep baritone that would have broken her heart if there had been anything left to break.

Daniel Garrett was in that room. With Mrs. Duncan.

Juniper pressed her ear to the thin, prefabricated door, straining to hear the low rumblings of conversation. But the voices remained unclear. Could Daniel Garrett truly be on the other side with Mrs. Duncan?

The visual that crept into Juniper's mind had her squeezing her eyes shut and shaking her head. The two of them together was not something she wanted to see, much less imagine.

For as long as Juniper could remember, Daniel had been pining over her. Though she rarely let her guard down, there was a night several months ago, after some laughs and strong cocktails at a seniors' happy hour downtown, when he had driven Juniper home. That night, they shared more than a few passionate kisses. Poor Daniel had been angling for a repeat performance ever since.

Maybe she should have taken Daniel up on his offer tonight. Would it have been so terrible for him to have stayed?

It was not like Gigi was rushing home to comfort her.

# Chapter Forty-One

# Ghost

I had arrived at Grandma June's house in record time. Though I was reluctant to get out of the car and walk up the stone path. A pair of round yellow headlights had been behind me since Exit 17. Their beams never wavered from my rearview mirror. At first, I brushed it off as paranoia, until I took a couple of random turns and then looped back to the main road. The dim headlights remained, keeping a safe distance but still tracking my every move. It was clear then that I was being followed.

I considered driving to a police or fire station, except it would have taken me twenty minutes out of my way—not that anyone should risk safety to save time. Instead, I sped up, barely touching the brakes on the curvy backroads, until the headlights disappeared from my rearview mirror. Their absence did not make me feel any less afraid. Whoever it was could still be out there.

What if it was the hatted man?

Never in my life had I felt the shock that hit me when Bishop told me he saw a man in a black fedora, wearing a pinstriped suit, walking away from me in the parking lot. He was a living, breathing human being who had been following me for days. He had infiltrated my home and place of work. He had even sat next to me in the strict confines of my car. The whole time I had believed him to be a fabrication. When I insisted that he was not real, he had responded with, "I'm as real as you want me to be."

Why had he encouraged the idea that he was a hallucination? He wore the same ridiculous outfit for days. From the beginning, he had wanted me to believe he was an illusion. That *I* was delusional. For what purpose? What had he hoped to gain? Why would he want me to think I was going insane?

*I'm not crazy!*

The fact that I was not losing my mind should have been more of a comfort than it was to me. Because whatever was actually going on was enough to push anyone over the edge. And maybe that had been the hatted man's intentions all along.

On the drive over, my thoughts had evolved into a category five tornado, scattering the days and events into disarray, though not entirely irretrievable.

Sitting in my car outside Grandma June's, my mind started to clear. I first realized that the hatted man had not been tailing me. The vehicle following me was much larger than the green Honda I saw him drive. The headlights were higher, more like a truck or small SUV.

Then I recalled that the hatted man also had a name—Terrence Riggie—or at least it was the one he had given me that day in the mall. Charles Riggie! They had to be related, which meant the hatted man must be my family, too.

After a deep, calming breath, I reached into my purse to grab my phone. I immediately dropped it when something thumped against my car.

I jerked to see a creased piece of paper pressed against my driver's side window. The familiar black cursive script belonged to Grandma June, but the large hand holding it there did not.

*When I speak your name,*
*It brings screams to my ears,*
*But now I watch without shame,*
*As death for you is so near.*

I read the note twice before its meaning finally sank in. My grandmother often refused to say her daughter's name, but I had never once heard her speak my name aloud.

It was like an ice pick had plunged into my racing heart. But soon the sharp pain of acceptance was swept away in a flood of other emotions—fear, sadness, anger.

Grandma June wanted me dead. Which would have made zero sense had I not discovered that she had been lying to me for most of my life. Or that she had tried to poison me with her crab cakes.

Only when the note was removed did I recognize the person standing outside my car window. Now, the headlights behind me made sense. Bishop was driving his Jeep and must have followed me from the bar. But then confusion crept in as I wondered how Bishop came into possession of the poem and how long he had been holding on to it.

Bishop stepped back from the car, dropped to his haunches so we were face-to-face, and started talking loud enough for me to hear him through the tempered glass.

"I found this on the floor at your house this morning while cleaning up the broken glass. I didn't know what it was; I just stuck it in my pocket before I started sweeping...not even sure why. I didn't remember that I had it until later when I was changing clothes and cleaning out my pockets. Well, I read it and didn't think it was your handwriting. I would have shown you earlier, but you passed out and then took off. I'm really worried. I believe your grandmother wrote this. The way she cringes anytime she hears your name—"

I threw open the car door, unable to stomach another word from him, and stepped out. Bishop had to scramble back to avoid being hit by the door. As he got to his feet, our eyes locked. We stared at one another for what felt like forever, neither seeming to know what to do or say next.

Our uneasy standoff ended when Bishop suddenly held out Grandma June's note.

My hand trembled as I reached for the scrap of wrinkled paper. Bishop was reluctant to let go, but eventually he surrendered my grandmother's twisted note. I fisted her threatening words in the palm of my hand, crushing her hatred of my name into a tight little ball, and then threw it on the ground.

Bishop flashed a timid smile and moved a step closer. "I know I shouldn't be here, and you probably don't want me to get involved in whatever this is, but please don't ask me to leave."

Behind him, an unexpected bolt of lightning brightened the night sky over the old Victorian house as the first drops of rain spotted the dry ground. When the wind blew, I caught his signature scent and closed my eyes to breathe it in.

"Are you sure?" I said, opening my eyes.

Bishop had taken another step forward. We were mere inches apart.

"Ghost, I'm here for you. I will not walk away and leave you to face this on your own."

Bishop was right. I could not enter my grandmother's house alone. The supposed sex tape and threats he made toward Ava would have to be put on hold for now.

"I'm glad you're here, and I'm so sorry for that." I moved back and swept my hands up in the air. As if a single gesture could reveal everything that was wrong. "This is a whole lot all at once."

*And he doesn't even know the half of it.*

Bishop turned around to look at the big house looming over us. "And where is here?"

I watched his eyes widen as he scanned the expanse of the gothic Victorian. Even in its weathered state, the pitched roofs, wraparound porches, cylindrical turrets, and roof tower never failed to impress. Though the gray-and-black exterior was always meant to deter.

"This is Grandma June's house." My grandmother had fully embraced the notion of living in a haunted house. Even the Addams Family would be hard-pressed to compete with this place.

"Wow, you grew up here?"

"Yeah, I didn't have many friends growing up."

Bishop glanced down at the crumbled ball of paper near our feet and then moved to stand next to me. "Are you sure this is a good idea?"

I shook my head. "I have to talk to her. There's more going on than you know, but there's no time to explain. So, either come in and stand quietly by my side, or go home and I'll call you later."

"I already told you. I'm not leaving."

A clap of thunder rumbled overhead. As I raised my face to the falling rain, I felt the brush of Bishop's hand before he slipped his pinky finger around mine. I squeezed it tight, knowing the ominous weather outside was nothing compared to the storm we would face once we walked through my grandmother's front door.

# Chapter Forty-Two

# Juniper

It was unfortunate that Mrs. Duncan was not alone in her bedroom and instead was doing God only knows what with Daniel Garrett. Juniper backed away from the closed door, needing to rethink her approach. She had to keep her wits about her. It would no longer be a one-on-one confrontation or her word over Mrs. Duncan's. Juniper could not allow riotous emotions to rule the night.

While quietly navigating the mazelike home in the dark, Juniper pondered her limited options. Give up and leave. Throw open the bedroom door and combat them both. Or come up with a better plan. Juniper had to be smart. Smarter than everyone else.

When she came upon a worn loveseat near a curtainless window, she plopped down to calm her thoughts. Suddenly, the darkness was interrupted by a flash of light from outside. And a rumbling that did not quite sound like thunder. Leaning closer to the window, Juniper watched as some poor lost soul in an old green car attempted to make a U-turn in the middle of Kilmer. The better option would have been to back up instead of getting stuck in the deep rut along the narrow street.

Juniper wondered if they were lost or if the dark house at the end of the road discouraged them from visiting. It reminded her of her home and how she had made sure to leave the porch light on for Gigi. A lighted entry invited you into safety. It welcomed guests to come in from the cold... Juniper jumped from her spot on the loveseat and began feeling around for light switches.

First, she turned on a tableside lamp in the living room, then moved to the front door and flicked the wall switch. As she entered the kitchen, she snagged the grocery bag of tea from the counter and exited the same way she had entered. After tucking the hide-a-key back into its spot under the planter, Juniper rubbed her eyes until they were red and teary. Then, she made her way around the house to the lighted front steps as the first drops of rain fell.

*Ding. Dong.*

Juniper looked at her watch, waited a full minute, and then rang the doorbell again.

*Ding. Dong.*

Another minute passed as Juniper shifted her weight from one foot to the other. It was not like they had to open the door. It was late. And her appearance at this hour was certainly unexpected. If not downright strange. But the rain was falling faster. They had to let her inside.

Juniper wailed as she stepped up to bang on the solid oak door.

A few seconds later, a clamoring on the other side let Juniper know that Mrs. Duncan was finally there. Juniper would not be denied entry now.

"Mrs. Duncan," Juniper cried out. "So sorry to bother you at this late hour, but I saw your lights on... May I come in?"

As the door cracked open, Juniper held up the bag in her hand. "I brought our favorite tea."

The contorted look on Mrs. Duncan's face brought a smile to Juniper's lips.

Before answering the door, Juniper knew Mrs. Duncan had to be wondering why the lights in her house were on and must have been trying to recall if she had indeed turned them off before going to bed. Now that the door was open, Mrs. Duncan's beady eyes locked on the grocery store bag. Juniper could almost see the puzzle pieces flipping about inside Mrs. Duncan's head as she tried to figure out how the tea had gone from the spot on her kitchen counter to Juniper's outstretched hand.

It was a mystery Mrs. Duncan would never solve.

"Juniper, it's close to midnight. Is everything okay?" The way Mrs. Duncan craned her neck and raised her voice, Juniper knew she was alerting her company to the identity of the late-night visitor.

Was Daniel Garrett brave enough to face Juniper, or would he be a coward and slip out the back?

"I'm sorry, Mrs. Duncan. Gigi and I had a terrible fight. I'm so distraught. I was feeling like I didn't have a friend in the world when I saw the tea you brought. And then I remembered our earlier conversation." Juniper sniffled. "I just knew I couldn't drink it without you. I know it sounds weird and maybe a touch pathetic. And I understand if—"

Daniel Garrett came into view. His clothes were slightly rumpled, but he looked no worse for wear. "Don't be silly, Juniper. It's raining. Come on in." Daniel had issued the invitation Mrs. Duncan was reluctant to give.

Feigning surprise, Juniper fluttered a hand over her heart. "Oh my, I've interrupted something, haven't I?"

Mrs. Duncan nodded while Daniel stepped over the threshold to escort Juniper inside. "Oh, it's nothing. Just a powwow between a couple of night owls."

Daniel led Juniper through the house to the kitchen. Reaching into a side drawer, he handed her a small dish towel. Clearly, he felt at home in Mrs. Duncan's place. Which meant this was not the first time they had spent the night together.

While Juniper patted droplets of rain from her skin and hair, Mrs. Duncan trudged into the kitchen, surveying every countertop in search of something that was no longer there. A loud clanking was heard as Mrs. Duncan went about gathering cups from a nearby cabinet.

Instead of sitting in the chair Daniel had pulled out, Juniper grabbed the kettle off the stove and went to the sink. "You two sit. I will make the tea."

Juniper filled the kettle with water, brought it back to the stove, and turned the gas burner on high. Mrs. Duncan and Daniel were having a barely disguised argument behind her. Juniper kept her back to the hushed voices as she prepped each cup with a tea bag. Waiting for the water to boil, Juniper made sure no one saw her pull a small can from her jacket pocket. Because they were involved in a low-key but heated discussion, they did not see her sprinkle the powder into two of the three cups, nor did they notice when she returned the dented can back to her pocket.

"So, what happened with Gigi?" Daniel finally asked.

Juniper turned as Mrs. Duncan sat in the chair that he had pulled out for her. "I believe Gigi's gotten into some bad trouble with a new boyfriend."

"Is it serious?" Mrs. Duncan asked as Daniel dropped into the seat next to her.

"Afraid so."

Juniper jumped when the kettle whistle blew. Then she anxiously poured the hot water into two cups and delivered them to the table before retrieving the third cup of tea for herself.

Only when she was seated at the table, with everyone repetitively dipping their tea bags, did Juniper go into more detail.

"I'm scared for my granddaughter. Last night, I stopped by her house to let her know that her mother had passed away." Juniper physically shook her head in an attempt to rid herself of the naked images of Gigi and Bishop. "It was late, and of course, she wasn't expecting me."

Juniper closed her eyes tight, pushed back from the table, stood up, and then paced the kitchen floor. "Gigi had handprints on her body, scrapes and scabs on her hands, and a horrible bruise on her back."

Mrs. Duncan gasped. Daniel Garrett muttered something about having a shotgun.

Juniper returned to her seat at the table. "She didn't even seem to care that her mother had died. She was just so mad that I had seen what he'd done to her. She demanded that I return her house key and then threw me out!"

Mrs. Duncan had taken a sip of tea and nearly spit it out across the table upon hearing that someone had the audacity to force Juniper White from their home.

Juniper went on to tell them how Bishop had been stalking Gigi on social media for years and somehow tricked her into a relationship that she could not easily get out of because they worked together and how, as a worried parent, she had done a little investigating and found that Bishop Mazzeo had a violent past. Documented cases of domestic violence. She even elaborated on how Bishop was the reason Gigi failed to show up this evening. That he had simply and violently not allowed her to come. Not to mention the suspicious death that had occurred at Gigi's office.

"Oh, my Lord, you have to do something," Mrs. Duncan said, her hands shaking so hard she had to put her cup of tea down. "What are you going to do, Juniper?"

"Well, I'm going to take care of it. Just like I always do." Juniper watched as Mrs. Duncan and Daniel took their final sips of chocolate tea.

"Juniper, you need to call the police," Mrs. Duncan announced as if that would solve the problem.

Daniel Garrett stood up from the table. "Or we can go there right now and get her." Looking a tad flushed, he eased back down into his chair.

"I appreciate your support. I sincerely do. But after our blowup on the phone, I don't want to agitate the situation any further. Things could escalate and get out of hand. I'll go over there tomorrow morning when I know she's alone, and then that man will never lay a hand on my sweet granddaughter again."

"Are you sure? A lot can happen in a day," Mrs. Duncan asked, her head bobbing forward as if she were fighting off sleep.

"Yes, I'm sure."

"Okay, but we're coming with you tomorrow." Daniel pulled at the collar of his wrinkled shirt. Closed his eyes and took a deep breath. "No way should you go alone, in case the guy shows up."

Several silent, awkward minutes passed until Juniper pointed a finger at Mrs. Duncan and then over to Daniel. "So, how long has *this* been going on?"

"Umm—we uh—" Beads of sweat had gathered around Daniel's temple. He dotted at them with his fingertips and slid his hand over his upper lip. By now he likely could not feel either one.

"T-two months-s." Mrs. Duncan sounded like she was sucking on a couple of marbles. Juniper watched as saliva spilled from her mouth, leaving a glistening track down her chin.

"That's wonderful. I'm so happy for you both," Juniper said, as her glazy-eyed companions slumped back in their chairs.

# Chapter Forty-Three

## Ghost

For the first time, I rang my grandmother's doorbell. My body was shaking while we waited on the porch. When she did not appear, I pulled out my key and unlocked the front door.

"Grandma June?" I announced with some hesitation before fully entering my childhood home. "I hope you're decent. I brought company."

No answer.

Bishop stayed in the foyer as I moved deeper into the house.

"Grandma June, are you here?"

My grandmother's beloved Challenger was parked by the stone path in its usual spot, so I knew she had not driven anywhere. I was about to check my phone for messages when I remembered it was still in my car, having tumbled under the seat when Bishop scared me by slamming Grandma June's threatening note against my car's driver-side window.

I was having a hard time imagining that she wanted me dead. Or that she had killed anyone, much less her own daughter. I knew these things were possible, even probable at this point, but I still did not want to believe it.

A chill tickled the back of my neck as soon as I stepped into the living room.

The wall-mounted TV hung slightly askew. Shattered pieces of multicolored pottery littered the floor. A deep dent marred the far plaster wall, with a spiderweb of cracks spreading out from the center. Something had spilled and dried to a crust on the hardwood floor near Grandma June's favorite chair. The room was wrecked.

*What in the hell happened?*

I knew Grandma June's friends and some neighbors had stopped by earlier in the evening to pay their respects. But they were not the type of folks to trash someone's property, especially not my grandmother's house. Had there been a disagreement? Or something far worse?

The teasing chill deepened and settled around my shoulders before moving down my spine as I stared into the dark, curved stairwell.

"What happened in here?"

I nearly jumped out of my skin at Bishop's deep voice. My nervous reaction had him reaching out to take my hand.

"I was thinking the same thing," I said, turning my gaze back to the shadowy staircase.

"Are you sure you want to be here?" he asked, glancing over at the nearest exit.

Given the state of the living room, I should have been more concerned about my grandmother's well-being, but I was not. Grandma June was tougher than anyone. My main concern was getting answers—discovering the truth.

"No, but I have to be. I need to know what my grandmother has done. Not only to her daughter but possibly to my grandfather." *And my missing father.*

Bishop's fingers tightened around my hand. "What did she do?"

"I think she killed them."

Since I had allowed Bishop to stay, it was time to divulge more information. While walking room to room in search of more damage and Grandma June, I filled him in on some of the things that had happened, starting with the appearance of the hatted man and how he always wore the same ridiculous suit, showing up at odd hours and unpredictable places to convince me that I was delusional. I explained about finding my mother's letter and the conversation in my car with Terrence Riggie, along with the questions he had raised about my grandmother and the implications he made about my family history. How this strange man had given me the name of my rapist father, who I later discovered was reported "missing" not long after my mother attacked me as a toddler. A story he had heard that awful night when Grandma June barged into my house to announce my mother's untimely death.

Had she killed her daughter just hours before? Was I the next intended victim in my grandmother's murder spree?

"I wish you would have told me this sooner."

"I couldn't have. It's all too crazy. Up until an hour ago, I thought I was insane."

Bishop squeezed my hand. "That's why I said *wish*."

When we found nothing else out of place on the first floor, we headed upstairs.

In the office, the desktop computer was powered on. A screensaver showed a red ball bouncing from one corner to the next. Bishop's social media page appeared when I slid the mouse across the desk. He leaned in behind me to get a closer look and then released my hand. When the heat of him vanished, the eerie chill returned.

Next to the keyboard was a notepad with a list of names. There was no mistaking my grandmother's slanted script. I recognized the names she had written down. Bishop Mazzeo had been underlined so many times that the paper had ripped. Next to the name Zelda Watson, my mother's nurse at Glen Haven, Grandma June had doodled a smiley face with devil horns. I was unsure what to make of the page other than it had the possible makings of a hit list.

Bishop returned to my side and nudged my elbow. I ripped the paper from the pad, crushed it into another tight ball, and let it drop to the floor.

"Why do you think your grandmother was playing detective, looking into my history?"

"My guess is she wanted you out of the picture." I waited to gauge Bishop's reaction, which was merely a raised brow.

*Where in the hell did my grandmother go? What else has she been up to?*

We left the office to continue our search. The rest of the bedrooms and bathrooms on the second floor were perfectly intact. Not a thing looked to be out of place. Before heading to my grandmother's bedroom, I checked to make sure the deadbolt on the door leading up to the third-floor attic space was engaged. As a child, that part of the house had been the source of many nightmares. I once believed the unfinished storage space was a tortuous maze of deadly creatures lying in wait. But even as an adult, the thought of going up there filled me with unfounded dread.

We entered my grandmother's spacious bedroom and found it neat and tidy, as usual. Only the presence of a large suitcase appeared out of the ordinary. It had been pulled out from underneath the bed and left with a key inserted into one of the two locks. The second lock was a combination code. Leaving the numbers on the dial where they were, I took a chance and turned the key.

*Click.*

I lifted the suitcase lid.

"Oh my God! There's so many." Even before I touched the contents, I knew exactly what I had discovered.

Bishop sat on the edge of the bed as I knelt on the floor next to the open suitcase filled to the brim with letters. One by one, I pulled sheets of paper and envelopes from the case that contained decades of correspondence from my mother.

No longer did I care that my grandmother was nowhere to be found or that a man who had tried to pass himself off as imaginary was digging up dirt on my family. In that moment, it was me and my mother. Only the letters mattered. I should have received them years ago, and I would not wait another second to read her words.

From the worn and wrinkled pages, it was obvious my grandmother had handled the letters often. They were well cared for...preserved, and perhaps even loved. The letters were painstakingly categorized by date and subject matter, as I noticed the crayon drawings were in a section all to themselves. After viewing the first image, a gray-colored baby hanging from a red rope with blacked-out eye sockets, I decided to skip that row entirely.

"What is all of this?" I had almost forgotten that Bishop was there.

"Letters from my mom. Years and years of letters that Grandma June kept hidden from me," I said, knuckling a stray tear before reaching back into the case.

"Why don't I give you a minute? I'll go down to the kitchen and make us a coffee or something."

"Okay."

I heard the squeak of mattress springs, felt the pressure of Bishop's hand on my shoulder, and then he was gone.

BY THE FIFTEENTH LETTER, I was trembling and unable to control the steady flow of tears. Bishop, having returned earlier with two cups of tea, moved down to the floor next to me and placed his arm around my shoulders, but thankfully he had not said a word. Before now, I had only read one of my mother's letters. The absorption of that content had been difficult. These were so much worse. It was impossible to wrap my head around the reason my mother had written almost daily to a daughter that she believed to be dead. In some letters, she wrote of the love and the emptiness she felt at my absence. In others, I was the monster she had failed to destroy.

It made sense that Grandma June had kept them from me. It did not make it right, but I understood her reasoning a little more.

# Chapter Forty-Four

## Juniper

In front of her captive audience, Juniper was a star as she explained the truth of things to people who were once longtime friends and neighbors. She wanted them to gain some perspective. Mrs. Duncan and Daniel Garrett needed to know that their careless, selfish behavior had forced her hand.

"It's always something, you know. I try and I try to be the best person I can be, but there's always someone somewhere willing to go through a lot of trouble to muck it up. My husband never understood. Not until I had to make him understand. But by then, it was too late. The damage was already done."

Juniper circled the kitchen table, eyeing the drowsy pair. She watched as their heads bobbed to the side and then dipped slightly forward. At times, when their heads lolled to an odd angle, she would pinch Mrs. Duncan on the neck and tap Daniel Garrett on his shoulder. Juniper received no more than muffled groans in response.

"Nothing happened the way it should have. Arguing with my beloved Gigi started everything going in the wrong direction. I've been distraught for days. It's been impossible for me to think clearly. And that's led to mistakes." Juniper threw her hands up in frustration.

No way would these two get it. She looked at their long faces and knew they were judging her, blaming her, wishing her to fail.

"Except this here." Juniper pointed a stiff finger and then waved it around the table. "This is your mistake. Not mine!"

Juniper leaned in close to Mrs. Duncan, slapping her palms down on the table. "Did you think I wouldn't notice the missing tea? Even a moron would have figured it out. Is that what you take me for? Do you think I'm an idiot?"

There was a slight flutter from one of Mrs. Duncan's eyelids, followed by a twitch of her upper lip. Juniper reared back from the table and then crossed her arms over her chest. "Sorry, Mrs. Duncan, but no apology will suffice."

A soft moan pulled Juniper's attention away from Mrs. Duncan. Daniel Garrett's eyes were slightly open, and his right hand lifted a couple of inches. Almost as if he was trying to signal Juniper for something.

"Oh, my sweet Daniel, no excuses, please. Did you happen to tell your girlfriend about the night we spent together? Or how you've been angling for a repeat performance ever since? Yeah, I didn't think so."

Juniper went over to the same drawer where Daniel Garrett had retrieved a dish towel from earlier and pulled out two clean towels. "Now that that's out in the open, it should be painfully obvious that your punishment is well deserved. You cannot go around messing with other people's lives and expect there not to be consequences."

Juniper returned to the kitchen table and folded the terry cloths into neat, flat squares, placing one in front of Mrs. Duncan and the other in front of Daniel Garrett. Then she removed the empty teacups and set them in the kitchen sink. She considered washing and putting the cups back in the cabinet but realized it was unnecessary.

Her daughter's autopsy report would reveal the truth any day now. There was no getting out of this one. "One body, two bodies, three bodies or four... Does it really make a difference?"

After grabbing the bag of chocolate herbal tea from the countertop, Juniper went back to the table to find the two sorry sods twitching and moaning in what appeared to be an attempt at making a final plea.

"Oh, no need for those sad, pathetic faces. I'll be back to check on you."

Before leaving and locking up Mrs. Duncan's house, Juniper carefully placed their heads, facedown, on the dish towels. If they had the strength to turn their heads to the side, they would likely make it until morning.

If not... Well then, who cared.

# Chapter Forty-Five

## Ghost

"**I**'m exhausted." It took every ounce of energy I had to not put my head down on the kitchen table and go to sleep. Bishop had finally talked me into taking a break and coming downstairs. The hour was late or early, depending on how you gauged the clock, yet he was bursting with energy as he cleaned up a nonexistent mess.

He nudged the cup of tea that sat untouched in front of me before taking another healthy sip of his own. He was already working on his second cup. "And rightfully so, you've been tormented, lied to, and on top of that, you lost your mom yesterday."

Had it only been twenty-four hours since my grandmother showed up to deliver *that* news? It felt like a lifetime ago. Though I no longer needed the answers my mother took to her grave, I did need answers from my grandmother. Not about the letters that she had hidden from me. But rather the events surrounding my mother's death, my grandfather's boat accident, and my missing father. If Grandma June was truly responsible, I had to find out the whys and hows of it all.

I pushed the teacup aside. Despite my efforts to locate and discover the truth behind my grandmother and the hatted man, the search would have to wait until I had a few hours of sleep. I was in no shape to drive. And Bishop had started doing some wiggly dance in front of the stove. Which probably meant he was punchy due to exhaustion. I decided it would be best to stay here and catch a few z's behind the locked door of my old bedroom.

"Let's go to bed," I announced, getting up.

"Woo hoo, I thought you'd never ask." Bishop popped up in front of me. Startled by his sudden appearance, I turned and nearly fell over the chair I had just vacated. Bishop wrapped his arms around me. Pressing his chest firmly against my back, he buried his nose in my hair. "You smell like rainbows."

His fingers felt like the softest feathers as he brushed sweeping strokes over my collarbone. Then Bishop slid my jacket off my shoulders. I looked down at his fingers while they inspected the flowing silk tank top I wore underneath. When he dipped them between my breasts, he giggled. "Your skin tickles."

"*My* skin tickles?"

"It's electric." I felt his tongue on my neck, tentative at first, and then lapping like a hungry dog. "Mm, and you taste like the sugary pop rocks I used to eat as a kid."

We were both tired and stressed, but something was very off with his behavior. I pulled away from his covetous hands and turned around to face him. Bishop had a strange, almost detached look on his face. When he leaned closer, muttering something about beauty and love, I noticed his eyes—glassy, pupils the size of pinpricks.

"What are you on?" He had not been with me all night. He could have taken just about anything while I was upstairs reading my mother's letters.

"Huh?" Bishop looked around the room while scratching at the top of his head.

"I'm tired and don't have time for this," I said, steering him out of the kitchen, through the dining room, and over to the curved staircase, where he promptly sat on the floor.

"What did you take, and when did you take it?" I added.

Bishop looked up, flashed one of his perfect dimpled smiles, and then reached for my hands. Suddenly, we were locked in an awkward game of tug-of-war at the bottom of the stairs. While I tried to pull him up, he was attempting to pull me down to the floor.

"Stop it!"

Bishop froze. It was as if my words had turned him to stone. For several seconds he did not so much as blink. And then he erupted into a flurry of motion. Jumping to his feet with hands waving about, he shouted, "Nothing's wrong with me. What's wrong with you?"

"I'm trying to get you upstairs in bed."

"Oh, yeah."

Despite his agreeable response, getting Bishop to my old bedroom took a herculean effort. He giggled half the time, stumbled some of the time, and did his best to distract me the rest of the time. I continued to ask him what he had taken, but he stuck to his claim of being high on his love for me. I did not believe him. But there was no point in arguing. Once I got him to abandon his hands-on inspection of every shiny object in my old bedroom, he flopped across the queen-sized mattress and closed his eyes.

I sat, listening to his breaths until they slowed and deepened, showing all the signs of sleep, and then I left the room.

The physical effort to get Bishop upstairs and into bed had produced enough adrenaline to wake me up. I needed to get my phone from my car, search online for Terrence Riggie, and message my grandmother to find out exactly where she had gone.

Outside, a roll of thunder grew faint as the rainstorm moved westward. The drizzle that remained had me briskly rubbing my hands over my naked arms—I'd forgotten my jacket, still lying on the kitchen floor. I was halfway down the stone path when I heard the crisp crack of a twig. Immediately, I scanned the woods for movement. But this time, no hatted man was darting into the brush. Probably just a deer or a fox. Still, I hurried down the rest of the way to my car and grabbed the door handle...

"Shit!" The key fob was still in the pocket of my jacket.

More cracking and swishing sounds emerged from the nearby tree line. Whatever it was, it was large and cumbersome. After reading so many letters about demons, death, and torture, my imagination had conjured vivid images of grisly ghouls out on a hunt.

A surge of irrational fear had me running back up the stone path. Once I was safely inside the house, I closed and locked the front door behind me.

I needed sleep more than anything else.

After snagging my jacket off the kitchen floor, I headed back upstairs to slip into bed with Bishop. But as I reached the top of the stairs, flipping my high heels from my aching feet, the light in my grandmother's bedroom beckoned me. The large suitcase remained open with several of my mother's letters strewn about on the floor. The last thing I needed was for Grandma June to come home and find the open suitcase. I did not want her to know that I had seen them.

I stepped inside her bedroom to put everything back the way I had found it.

Kneeling, I replaced the pages as best I could back where I thought they belonged. I was about to close the lid when I noticed an envelope slightly different from the rest. The thick envelope was brown instead of white. And it was addressed to Mrs. Juniper White. The return address was not from Glen Haven Psychiatric Hospital but rather a city address—one belonging to Charles Riggie.

My father.

# Chapter Forty-Six

## Juniper

Juniper arrived at the sprawling lake house at quarter past three in the morning. The devil's hour. A fitting time considering something was amok inside. The first—and second—story windows were ablaze with light, adding warmth where there should be none. More of an invitation to the outside world than she had left. And one that the Gothic Victorian was not permitted to offer. She had made sure of that. Cheery and bright did not suit her taste. Not after her husband's accident and having sent her daughter away to a psychiatric hospital. Juniper could not bear to reside in a home that did not reflect how she felt on the inside. The first chance she got, she transformed the beautiful historic home her late husband loved into the unwelcoming dwelling that stood before her today. She took a moment to appreciate the air of majesty that remained despite its grim outer shell. The house reminded her so much of herself.

Juniper breathed a sigh of relief when she saw a familiar car parked next to her red Challenger. Thank the gods, Gigi had returned home. But then she noticed a strange Jeep parked a little farther down, its nose buried deep in the bushes that lined the narrow drive. Who else was inside with her granddaughter?

Walking down to the Jeep, Juniper found the door unlocked and looked inside for any indication of the owner's identity. Popping the little metal glove box, she read an unexpected name on the vehicle registration card.

*What the Hades is Bishop Mazzeo doing here?*

"I thought we nipped that in the bud, Henry. Guess I'm going to have to strong arm the bastard—shh kid, and don't interrupt, this is none of your concern."

Juniper marched across the lawn to the boat shed. There was no time for mistakes. This time everything had to go according to plan. Though at the moment, she was not exactly sure what that plan entailed. All she knew was that she and Gigi had to get away. It was time to start over somewhere new.

Entering the shed, Juniper located the weatherproof go-bag she kept stashed behind the rakes, shovels, and other lawn equipment. A swift inspection of the contents—passports, offshore bank records, a few personal keepsakes, and several wads of cash—confirmed that she had the means to escape her past and present. The second item she retrieved from beneath a loose floorboard was a spiked bottle of Scotch whisky, a special concoction brewed for quick inebriation, followed by a nearly permanent incapacitation. There had only been one person on her mind when she had created the mix. Juniper always hoped there would never come a day when she would need to use it. But if it came down to it, if she had no other option left, she would smile and make a toast to all the dastardly deeds she had done.

The last and final item, she collected from a lockbox she had tucked away behind a pile of tangled fishing tackle. She loaded the Smith & Wesson revolver and announced her passing thoughts to the empty shed. "Alas, Henry, if only I had more time to do it right, I would carve the proper initials into each of these bullets. There'd be no mistaking my intentions then."

After placing the bag in the trunk of her car, she dropped the gun in her coat pocket. It clanged against the small, dented tin of Old Bay as she strolled up to the porch with the bottle of whisky tucked under her arm. The lock was still engaged when she tried to turn the doorknob. Her palms were damp as she retrieved her keys and unlocked the front door.

The house was eerily quiet. As she made her way through the first floor, she found nothing disturbed, except for that which she had already disturbed. The living room was still a mess. So far, other than the lights, there was no sign that Gigi and Bishop had been here.

Something did not feel right. The stillness in the air. Nothing touched other than the light switches. Then, finally, she found two teacups on the kitchen table. The practically full one was cool to the touch. It looked like someone had taken a sip or two and then abandoned the drink. Juniper smiled. That one must have been Gigi's. Her granddaughter hated tea. So, why had she prepared it and served it to Bishop? The second cup had a bit of gritty residue at the bottom.

Juniper lifted the empty cup to her nose and sniffed. A smile emerged on Juniper's face. Gigi had unknowingly served Bishop one of her homemade tea bags.

After placing the whisky bottle on the table, she checked the trash can and found three discarded tea bags. The truffle tea might be mild, but it could do a number on an unsuspecting guest. Finally, she had some good news.

Odds were the two of them were passed out somewhere, with at least one of them drowning in a puddle of their drool. Confident Juniper would be the one to surprise them and not the other way around, she made her way upstairs.

Every light in every room had been turned on and left on, with no respect for the cost of electricity. Easing silently from the hallway into the main bedroom, Juniper discovered her granddaughter sitting in front of an open suitcase with a piece of paper clutched in her hands.

"I warned you, Gigi. It's not for the faint of heart."

Startled, her granddaughter jumped to her feet. Perhaps a little too fast for someone who had ingested even a partial cup of truffle tea. Gigi was a terrible sight to behold, with her messy hair, puffy eyes, and red blotchy face. If not for the vicious snarl she had flashed, Juniper would have thrown her arms around the ruined child.

"How *could* you? Why *would* you?" It appeared that Gigi had decades of suppressed rage coursing through her veins.

So, her granddaughter had found what Juniper had hoped to always keep secret. It was very unfortunate for them both. Damn her sappy sentiment. She knew she should have burned those letters years ago.

"I did what I had to do. No matter how difficult the task, I did what needed to be done to protect you. To protect us."

"No!" Gigi shook her head. "If what *my father* said is true, you did it all for you!"

Her granddaughter's eyes were full of so much hatred that Juniper widened her stance, preparing for a physical attack.

"It's always been about you. Not me. You never gave a shit about me or Meredith—"

"Shut up!" Juniper fingered the pistol deep in her coat pocket. "If you don't, I'll make you regret it."

"Is that what happened? Your *daughter* wasn't going along with the plan, so you had her locked up." Gigi's words were strong, but her hands were visibly shaking. "Is that why you tried to poison me with your crab cakes? I wasn't going along with your plan?"

"Deary, you have no idea what you're talking about. I wasn't trying to poison you. I merely added a little something to help you relax. Why did you take them to your office? We wouldn't be here right now if you had just eaten my delicious cakes. And as for that letter in your hand, it was written by a rapist. His words do not exonerate his crimes. Nor do they convict me of mine. Charles Riggie was not a well man. He had as many delusions, as your mother did. But it turned out so much worse for him. He was never diagnosed. He didn't get the help he needed. I tried with him, just like I tried with your mother. As you know, stubbornness is a deep-rooted gene in the White family. Oh, how I wish I could have plucked it from the two of you."

When Juniper stepped over the threshold, Gigi dropped the letter and scrambled across the bed. The width of a king-sized bed did not appear to create enough distance for her granddaughter to feel safe. Wide-eyed and fidgeting, Gigi looked like she was ready to bolt out of the room.

The question Juniper repeatedly asked herself—as she tucked the old letters safely back into their proper place—was: would she allow her granddaughter to run?

# Chapter Forty-Seven

## Ghost

In the span of twenty minutes, my world was officially shattered by a horrifying truth—my grandmother was a killer. Not only had Grandma June murdered her husband, but she also silenced her own daughter, my mother, through mind-altering drugs that she had continued to administer regularly until they finally killed her.

The first Charles Riggie letter I found was a single typed page, pleading to spend time with his infant daughter and vehemently explaining that there had never been any rape. Though the relationship was improper given his position at Glen Haven, I was not the result of a vicious assault. Comfort, compassion, and even a bit of joy had preceded my birth. It was not a mistake. In his words, I was their little miracle.

Apparently, his initial pleas fell upon deaf ears because the next letter written in thick bold print was a threat. He knew my grandfather was murdered. And that my mother had witnessed every bloody second of the attack. Although he failed to mention specific details.

The demand was clear. He would be a part of my life, or the truth behind Henry White's boating accident would be revealed. He briefly explained that in a moment of clarity, my mother had confided in him. Unlike everyone else, Charles believed Meredith. And he knew where to find the evidence to prove what my grandmother had done.

Of course, Grandma June made sure that information never saw the light of day.

Whatever happened to Charles Riggie, I knew it was not good. Juniper certainly never allowed her daughter to have any kind of peace. Even locked up hundreds of miles away, she had found a way to make my poor mother suffer until the very end. It was time to make my grandmother pay. However, I was unsure how I would accomplish that with my grandmother obviously teetering so close to the edge. Even as she went about tidying up the suitcase of letters, she eyed me like a viper ready to strike. I believed her when she said she would make me *regret it*. Terrified of what she was truly capable of and what she would do next, I knew I had to get beyond her reach. Running out of the house would have been an option if it was not for Bishop. He was asleep in my old room, completely defenseless and unaware of the danger we were in.

Under no circumstances would I lose another person to Grandma June.

That might have been the toughest thing to wrap my head around. The fact that there had been people out there who had wanted me, loved me. And my grandmother had taken it upon herself to steal them away.

"What's going through that pretty, pea-sized brain of yours?" Grandma June said, closing the lid and shoving the suitcase back under her bed. "Do you think you have enough grit to be a hero? Wouldn't it be better—no, *easier*—to put your head back in the sand and let me take care of everything? I promise I can make all of this go away. Like nothing bad ever happened."

"I'm no hero." But my thoughts were spiraling through all the malicious deeds Terrence Riggie had accused her of. Acts of violence that I now knew without a doubt were true and real. After reading my father's letters, I had a good idea that the man Charles referred to as TJ was actually Terrence Riggie.

"Grandma June, does the name Terrence Riggie mean anything to you?"

There was little more than a twitch in her still posture as her frozen features slowly contorted downward. A frown pulled at the corners of her mouth. Her eyes narrowed to a pair of black slits below furrowed brows. "Terrence? Where did you get that name?"

"He told me his name." The surge of triumph I felt at her startled reaction was noteworthy, but brief.

Many identifiable emotions flickered across Grandma June's face before she barked out a laugh and then perched her hip on the side of the bed. "How did that idiot find you? What has he told you?"

"Not much. He had me believing that he was a figment of my imagination. For a while, I thought I was turning into my mother. Why would he do that?"

"I don't know, but you've always been too naïve." When she turned to face me, I pressed myself flat against the wall.

"Gigi," she said, "I am not going to hurt you. I promise. Things are complicated. I've not made the best choices in the past, but I've always meant to do the best I could for you. Terrence was a cop back in the day before he did something stupid and lost his job. Said the wrong thing and broke too many rules. Crawled away with his tail between his legs to live out the rest of his pathetic days in squalor. Not a pretty history there. He's had it out for me ever since his brother disappeared."

She paused with a pointed look. "Or maybe it was even before that. It's been so long. Your *uncle* has been after my money for years. It's always been about money for him. He tried it before. And it did not end well for him. Don't bother messing about creating more fantasies about your father. Charles was a sick man acting on his own delusions, which would have caused great harm to you and your mother."

What Grandma June meant to say was that he would have caused *her* harm. Charles knew exactly what she had done and how to prove it. Too bad that crucial information had not been revealed in the letters he had written. But that did not mean I could not find it. My grandmother had kept his letters all these years—very incriminating letters. So, there had to be some sort of evidence somewhere. If I could get my grandmother talking, maybe a clue would slip out.

"What happened? Do you know where my father is?"

"Hmm...I sure wish I didn't know."

Grandma June straightened her coat and moved toward the door. "If we're going to do this, I need a drink. Come downstairs, and I'll tell you everything you want to know over a glass of Scotch whisky."

I did not believe she would tell me the whole truth, but getting her downstairs was a good idea. The farther away from Bishop she was, the better. For now, I would put on a brave face and go along with whatever Grandma June said.

"You're right. Let's go downstairs."

I followed Grandma June out of the primary bedroom and into the hallway. She had reached the top of the stairs when I paused outside my old bedroom. My need to check on Bishop pulled me toward the door. What if he was in there dying like all the rest?

"I'm cold, gonna grab a sweatshirt. Be down in a sec."

Slipping inside, I rushed over to the bed, where thankfully Bishop appeared to be sleeping. I pressed my hand to his warm forehead and listened to his deep, steady breaths. He looked so peaceful in his slumber.

"This is going to be a problem, Gigi."

"No!" I spun around, throwing my arms wide. It was a poor attempt to block her view of the man in my bed. "He is not a problem. He's been out for hours. Never saw anything. He doesn't know about my father's letters. Let's go downstairs and talk."

Grandma June leaned into the doorframe, her head craning to get a better look at the bed behind me. "So, he's the one who drank my truffle tea."

*Truffle tea!* Was nothing in my grandmother's house safe?

At least now Bishop's strange behavior made sense. He was on some psychedelic trip. Living in this house all these years, how had I not accidentally dosed myself?

Now that I thought about it, maybe I had. There had been several occasions when I had lost *time*. Days blurred, memories dark and spotty. Miraculously, Grandma June had always been there to fill those voids with her stories. I wondered if it had been the same for my mother.

"Yeah, I guess he did."

An unnatural stillness fell over my grandmother. The transformation occurred in a second and without a single movement. There were no words to explain it. The expression on her face had not changed, yet I no longer recognized the person standing in the doorway. Then her right hand jerked erratically about in her coat pocket, making a weird clanking sound. I pressed back against the bed, fearing she was about to pull a weapon. Then, I breathed a sigh of relief when her hand came up empty.

She motioned for me to follow her downstairs. "Come on, let's go."

I hesitated because I was terrified over what would happen next and because Bishop's pinky finger had squeezed mine. Glancing back, I knew he was awake, feigning sleep. But there was no way of knowing if his mental state had improved.

*How long do the effects of truffle tea last?*

"Don't forget your sweatshirt," Grandma June called out as she descended the stairs. "Wouldn't want you to catch your death."

Ignoring the strange snickering that echoed through the house, I snagged an old high school sweatshirt from the dresser's top drawer, slid it on, and said a silent prayer that Bishop and I would make it out of the lake house alive.

# Chapter Forty-Eight

# Juniper

The mental image of her lifeless granddaughter bleeding on the floor of her old bedroom was the very thing that had stilled Juniper's hand. It would have been over by now if she had just pulled the revolver from her pocket, aimed, and fired. A few shots, and her problems would be solved. Well, maybe not all of them. There was still the matter of Terrence Riggie. Though that hardly seemed important now that Juniper realized she would have to kill Gigi and her asinine boyfriend. Once she got her granddaughter to drink the whisky, she would return to the bedroom upstairs and discharge her weapon, twice. The first shot would be aimed at Bishop's private parts, because she needed to erase *that* image from her brain. The second shot would be at point-blank range to one of those blasted dimples. He would not be so pretty after she got done with him. Then she would grab some clothes, maybe a few more personal items, and set the house ablaze.

Juniper would be long gone by the time authorities arrived. Let them sort through the mess. By all the gods and devils, she had been cleaning up for them long enough.

"It's all coming down in a blaze of glory, Henry."

"What's that, Grandma?"

Juniper had forgotten her granddaughter was behind her. "Oh, nothing, dear."

Plucking the whisky bottle from the kitchen table, she grabbed two crystal tumblers from the cabinet and then walked back to the dining room, where she positioned herself in a seat at the head of the table. As much as she hated to admit it, she knew she had been slipping. A near miss incident here, a barely explainable thing there. She could not avoid the fact that her aging mind was deteriorating. The multiple volumes of the stories she had memorized over the years were getting harder and harder to recall. Nothing was as easy as it used to be or should be. So, now it was time for the stories to end.

In the wicked schemes of Juniper White, what difference would a few more bad deeds make? Once these physical lives concluded, she could walk to freedom. There was a sense of peace in knowing she would never have to say goodbye. Death was not the end.

*The dead don't leave you, but some do refuse to speak.*

Gigi slid into the last chair on the left, a strategic spot that placed her within a few steps of the staircase and closer to the front door.

*"You don't want to do this, Junie."*

Juniper gasped. Then, she spun around in her seat as she tried to locate the disembodied voice that once belonged to her late husband. She saw a wide-eyed Gigi stand up and step back from the dining room table. There was no sign of Henry, but he was talking.

*"She doesn't need your help anymore."*

Juniper heard his voice. She could still hear him.

*"Let her go."*

It was the first time he had spoken since the day he died.

"She'll always need me, Henry!" Juniper cried as she uncorked the whisky and filled one of the crystal tumblers to the rim. "She's not strong enough, so I have to be strong for her."

"Grandma June, who are you talking to?"

Juniper shook her head to clear a sudden clanking in her head.

*"She deserves to be happy, just like you and me. Come home, Junie. It's time."*

How could her husband be so forgiving? She would not forgive him if she had been the one murdered. It was *not* her pragmatic nature and take-charge actions that had disrupted their marriage and broken their fragile daughter. But she would be the one to send their only grandchild back to the grave.

When Juniper looked up and saw Gigi's terror-stricken face, she knew something was off. With her trembling lips and darting eyes, she looked like a poorly trained ventriloquist. Only one problem: where was the dummy?

"Of course, it's you! It's always been you, hasn't it?" Juniper shoved back in her chair and raised the whisky-filled glass as she stood up. "He's been silent since the day of his death. Now all of a sudden, I'm forgiven. I've tried everything with him and not a peep. Tell me how you did it?"

"What? Who are you talking about?" Gigi backed up another step, edging out of the dining room, where she could either dart up the stairs to her slumbering boyfriend or escape through the front door.

*"It's not her, Junie. It's me. The time has come to give up the ghost."*

Juniper scrunched her face and released her agitation in a high-pitched squeal. She had to decide: whisky, or gun?

*"Or neither."*

A dark shadow appeared on the wall in the stairwell behind her stunned and frightened granddaughter.

Henry had come back to her! He had truly returned with forgiveness in his heart.

"Henry deary, is that you?" Juniper recoiled from the unexpected quiver in her voice.

The shadow paused and then seemed to shift in its spot on the stairs. Henry did not answer. Would he leave again if she did not do as he asked? Juniper wanted nothing more than to see his handsome face, but he refused to descend to the bottom where she could get a good look at him.

*"Make a toast to our undying love, and then we'll see each other again."*

"Gigi, have a drink with me. One last toast to your dear ole Grandma, and then you and Bishop are free to go."

*"No, Junie!"*

Setting her full glass aside, Juniper splashed a bit of whisky in the second glass and sent it sliding down the tabletop. The glass came to a stop in the middle of the rosewood table. "Come on, Gigi, for old times' sake. One toast to all the good times we've had. I still love you. And no matter what happens, I'll never stop loving you."

When her granddaughter continued to stand near the base of the staircase—not moving or speaking—Juniper reached inside her coat pocket and pulled out the gun.

# Chapter Forty-Nine

## Ghost

Fear, or something far worse, held me where I stood, anchored my feet to a spot near the base of the staircase with an arctic grip. My body shook as I focused on the gun in Grandma June's hand and the index finger that slowly wrapped around the trigger.

"Gigi! Pick up the glass and drink with me."

My grandmother had lost her mind. She had stepped over the edge to swim in a turbulent sea of unhinged mania. A psychopath determined to kill me if I did not comply with her demands. I only wished I had noticed it sooner instead of always accepting her for who she was. I never thought to question her erratic behavior. Now, I realized there had been plenty of signs. Mood swings, incoherent mumbling, tics, and odd phrasings. Things that I thought were simply a part of what made her *my* Grandma June. All of those unusual things overlooked and excused away.

I had grown up with it. Strange and bizarre was part of my everyday life.

Coming to terms with the fact that my grandmother would shoot me if I did not have a drink with her was not nearly as difficult as it should have been. In the past, she had been my loving protector. In the present, I had no doubts about her becoming my executioner. And yet I remained frozen. Afraid to even flinch. Terrified that the slightest movement, even the one she had ordered me to make, would result in my immediate death.

A horrifying scenario had begun playing in a loop inside of my head.

*I obey her command and step forward, only to see a flash before feeling the sting of a bullet as it passes through my flesh. After a hiccup of time, my grandmother closes her eyes and smiles. A smile of satisfaction. The one she brandishes whenever she gets her way. Then I crumble to the floor, and everything fades to black. Once I'm gone, she climbs the stairs to do the same to Bishop.*

Even if I somehow avoided the imagined sequence of events and reached the table unscathed to drink a toast with her, what was stopping her from shooting me afterward?

*Nothing!* No one was going to stop her. I would be an even bigger fool to trust the drink she offered. Given Grandma June's tendencies, the whisky was not just whisky and would likely kill me.

No matter what I did or did not do, the end result would remain the same. I was going to die. I only had to decide how I wanted to go. Which would be the least painful?

I found neither option appealing but knew from the *Jeopardy* music blaring in my head that I had to choose before my grandmother made yet another decision on my behalf.

Grandma June's shoulder ticked upward twice, and then she shook her head so hard that I thought it might topple off her shoulders.

"You will have to, Henry. I won't beg. You're just going to have to live with the decision. You don't understand. It has to happen this way." The torment she suffered continued to move down her body, causing erratic quaking in her arms and legs. Then as quickly as it began, it stopped. Her limbs were so still it looked as if rigor mortis had suddenly set in.

"Gigi, stop dawdling now, we haven't got all night," Grandma June announced as she came alive to wiggle the gun about in the air. "Henry, you'll have to come down as well. No need to stay up there sulking," she added with a huff.

The way she continued the two separate conversations was disturbing. One with me and the other with the husband she had murdered decades ago.

Grandma June reached down to retrieve the nearly full glass of whisky she had discarded earlier, both hands now wielding deadly weapons. "Darling, I need to see your handsome face. It's the only way for me to know if your words are sincere."

She waited quietly for my dead grandfather to appear. It was not possible for her to conjure him, other than in her mind's eye, but I still did not want to risk it and said the first thing that popped into my head.

"He can't. Not with me here. He doesn't want me to see the way he looks. He says it's an awful sight. That it'll scare me."

Her eyes fixed on the empty staircase behind me. "Nonsense, Henry! Gigi's a big girl. She can handle it."

A creak sounded on the stairs. Someone or something had moved. Or maybe it was my imagination. I did not have the courage to turn around and look. "No, I don't want to see him that way."

"We don't always get what we want. Do you think I wanted this?" Grandma June threw her hands up, splashing whisky on herself and all over the table. "I wanted a happy life with my granddaughter, but you ruined it. Just like Henry ruined it for me and my daughter."

There was more creaking and another sound, like something heavy scoring wood. Then I caught a glimpse of a shadow. Someone was standing on the upper landing, though not visible with the slight curve in the stairwell. For a moment, I imagined a decayed corpse descending the stairs, but then I realized there was only one person it could be.

My main focus turned to Bishop. He would not fall victim to Grandma June like the others. After a deep breath, I stumbled to the dining room table and grabbed the glass of whisky. Thankful that it was the least full. Maybe there was a chance I would survive. Though the cruel smile distorting my grandmother's face told me otherwise.

"Your granddaughter's manned up. Now it's your turn, Henry. Come down. Meet your only grandchild before it's too late." With her head tilted and eyes still glued to the stairs, she waited, seemingly listening for a response I would never hear.

She stood stock-still for so long that I had almost set my glass down. Then I heard a faint bump followed by mumbling voices. It only lasted a second. I could not tell if it was Bishop who made the noise or if I had imagined the muffled exchange. When nothing else happened, Grandma June shrugged. A quick rise and fall of her shoulders before targeting me with her dead-eyed stare.

"Okay, stubborn old fool, have it your way." With the gun aimed at my chest, Grandma June began inching down the edge of the rosewood table, sloshing more whisky along the way. Her twisted grin stretched wider, making her inhuman appearance even more monstrous.

I was shaking so badly that I had to hold on to the glass with both hands to keep from dropping it. Never had I been so scared—not just for myself but also for Bishop and, surprisingly, even a little for my grandmother.

The end of most things tends to be difficult. Recognizing that I was about to meet my end was absolutely terrifying.

# Chapter Fifty

## Juniper

"**D**o we toast? Or do you want to confess your crimes first?" Gigi's tumbling words held no bravado, but at least she had managed to push them through her shivering lips. "That's why we came down here, so you could tell me what happened to my father."

Juniper took in the sight of the wreck of a girl in front of her and sighed. There was no need to go into a detailed confession. It did not appear as if Gigi could handle any of the gory particulars anyway. With the amount of shaking and silent tears, Juniper was surprised the weakling was still standing upright. Juniper had chosen to protect and shelter Gigi from the worst the world had to offer. Now she saw just how wrong that had been. She should have ruled with a ruthless hand, beaten logic and true understanding into her granddaughter on a daily basis. That would have kept everything in proper order. Juniper would not be here now if she had instilled fear and obedience from the start.

Hindsight was a bitch.

In life, you often look back and see what you should have done differently. Maybe things would have been better if she had dispatched her daughter when she had gotten rid of her husband. But then she would have missed out on all those wonderful years with Gigi.

"Ah yes, well, it's been a long night. I'm tired and don't feel much like sharing."

As it turned out, hindsight was not a bitch, but rather a smear of shit that Juniper could easily wipe off the bottom of her shoe.

"All you need to know is that Charles Riggie deserved what he got. He never should have threatened me the way he did. Telling me he was going to ransack my home. Rip up my floorboards in search of evidence to prove something that needn't be proven. A boat accident is the only thing anyone will ever know about Henry's death. And my husband is okay with that. The stains of that day reside on his hands, not mine. The same goes for your father. Now, if you'd like to place a wreath of flowers for the insignificant man who donated sperm for your existence, then feel free to hang it on the boat shed, because that's where I buried his good-for-nothing bones."

There was a faint growl, followed by a tapping sound. As if someone was rapping on a nearby windowpane. Juniper took her eyes off her granddaughter long enough to catch a glimpse of movement. A dark shadow inching its way along the outside porch.

*How did that little bastard escape the grave?*

She should have dug a deeper hole.

Henry was right. The time had come for her to move on. It was time to quiet the voices, vanquish the shadows and put an end to the drama.

"Raise your glass, dear. It's time to make our toast."

Gigi stared into the glass of whisky, then unexpectedly tipped it over and poured the contents out. A splash of amber hit the tip of her bare toes before puddling in a gap on the scuffed hardwood floor. "I don't want to drink with you, Grandma June. Nothing you've said or done is worthy of a toast."

Juniper guffawed. If her granddaughter wanted to do things the hard way, then so be it. Juniper had no qualms about splattering brain matter all over her dining room wall. Whatever disgusting deeds she performed tonight were erasable. Like chalk on a blackboard. The liquor Gigi had spilled only added fuel to the soon-to-be fire.

Juniper sucked in her lips and then rolled them between her teeth. "Aren't you an ungrateful bampot. I am worth so much more than a toast. More commendable than any man alive, and I'm certainly more worthy than you."

A loud commotion echoed in the stairwell. Then a bumbling fool came into view, tripped, and nearly broke through the banister as he crashed to the bottom of the stairs. Bishop was still feeling the effects of the truffle tea with his failed attempt to rescue Gigi.

Or perhaps Henry had given him a push.

Juniper aimed the revolver at Bishop. He was in the process of pulling himself to his feet with the aid of a wobbly railing when he saw the weapon and floundered back to the floor. If she had to guess, Bishop had never looked down the barrel of a gun. She was so glad to be the one making the introduction.

"Are you planning to shoot both of us? Or just me?" Bishop yelled.

They were indoors and only a few feet apart. There was no need to shout. Unless he was trying to inform Henry of the gun. Just because Henry talked after his death did not mean he could see everything about to transpire. She could not recall if she had purchased the weapon before or after he had died. He was well aware of her tendencies to spike drinks. She had done that enough over the years for him to commit it to memory. Dead or alive, you did not forget the day your wife served you up a special cocktail after your first fight. They did not argue much after that. Henry knew to keep civility at all times and let Juniper have her way. Or else he would end up paying for it later. Eventually, it cost him his life. But that was neither here nor there. Or was it? Where was Henry? He had not voiced a plea in several minutes.

"Henry, are you still there? Are you able to watch this? If you don't want it to happen, then you'll have to be the one to stop me!"

Juniper adjusted her grip on the gun and closed her left eye—

An explosion against the side of her head whited out her vision as pain blasted from one side of her face to the other. Had she squeezed the trigger? Did the gun backfire?

Before she fully realized what had happened, she felt another powerful blow to the back of her head, propelling her forward. She pulled the trigger again and then hit the ground face first.

# Chapter Fifty-One

# Ghost

When Grandma June turned her gun on Bishop, my stomach sank into itself. An explosion of thunder crashed into my head and made my ears ring. Some distant piece of me wanted to believe the storm from earlier had returned and it was not a gunshot I had heard.

I could not recall the exact moment I made the decision or if there had been a single thought in my head as I smashed the empty glass in my hand onto the side of Grandma June's head. The remaining drops of whisky dotted her pale skin. When she staggered but did not fall, my arm came up and swung again. The second blow landed near the base of the skull, causing a crack to splinter through the base of the heavy crystal tumbler. My grandmother dropped to the floor, but not before firing another round.

When I looked at Bishop, he was cradling his arm as red darkened his shirt. Blood seeped around knuckles so white they looked like bone.

*Oh my God, he's been shot!*

I had to get to him. He needed my help.

A deafening boom echoed through the house as I tripped over my grandmother's body while trying to get to Bishop. I started to crawl, but something grabbed hold of my leg and pulled. It kept me from reaching him.

A sharp crack of splintering wood was soon followed by loud shouts. Some sort of chaos had forced its way into the house, but the only thing that registered clearly was my grandmother's gnarled fingers around my ankle. She would never let me go.

Grandma June mumbled with a slight wobble of her head, as if she was attempting to lift it. She released my ankle, and I jerked my leg away. When she reached for me again, her arm shook violently from the effort. Then I noticed the blood—her blood. It was soaking through her hair, turning gray to rust. The edges of an expanding puddle were now visible beneath her cheek.

I looked behind me to where Bishop was bleeding at the bottom of the staircase, his face pale, his eyes closed. *What if he doesn't make it?* Was I about to lose *everyone* I had ever loved?

A scraping noise pulled my attention away from Bishop. My grandmother's hand was fluttering about at her side, searching for—the gun! It was still there on the floor next to her. Only a palm's length away. I scooted back, wondering if she had the power to lift it and if I had any strength left to run.

As soon as her fingers touched the metal barrel, a shadow emerged on the floor between us. I felt the presence of another. When I looked over my shoulder, I saw the hatted man. He had a gun, too. And it was pointed directly at Grandma June.

His expression was grim as he dipped his head and said, "I'm very sorry for this."

Another thunderous bang and a flash of light followed, as the smell of burnt sulfur filled the air. A prolonged ringing in my ears was followed by other sounds. I clamped my hands over my ears and curled into a tight ball.

# Chapter Fifty-Two

## Terrence

A rush of overwhelming joy dropped Terrence Riggie to his knees. His relentless pursuit of this woman, who had used wealth and privilege to get whatever she wanted and showed no remorse for those she crushed along the way, had finally come to an end.

Pulling in a deep breath, Terrence tucked his firearm back into his concealed holster. Rarely did a pissant like himself get the chance to take down a giant like Juniper White. He had tried over the years to expose her crimes, only to have his efforts thwarted, twisted, and then used against him. She had always managed to stay one step ahead, until he finally swallowed his pride and stooped to her level.

*Manipulation and money rule the world. Honor and truth be damned.*

Terrence's success did not stop him from feeling bad for the young woman balled up on the floor and for the part he had played in her misery. He watched each vertebra poke to the surface as Ghost's spine bowed in an attempt to make herself as small as humanly possible.

"I'm so sorry. I had... I mean—I proved it. My brother—I couldn't let her get away with it." Terrence extended his hand with the desire to offer comfort. A small kindness that she would likely recoil from. His fingers hovered an inch above her shoulder before he retracted them. He deserved her hatred but did not care to see it firsthand. In the same way, Ghost did not wish to see her grandmother shot in the head.

"It all started the day your grandfather died. Your grandmother's account of events did not coincide with the physical evidence. Only the higher-ups didn't want to drag a wealthy, upstanding citizen through the mud, even though they knew she was hiding something. Most believed her to be a mother protecting her daughter—a noble cause. Besides, no one wanted to prosecute an unstable girl for murder when ruling her father's death as accidental tied the case up with a tidy bow. I never agreed. The honorable thing would have been to dive deeper and get to the truth, but I wasn't given the chance. When I pressed the issue, Juniper White snapped her powerful fingers and got me demoted from detective to sergeant.

"Decades later, when my brother turned up missing after going toe-to-toe with her over custody of you, I knew she had done something to him. I couldn't prove it. No body, no crime. I was thrown off the force after I tried too hard to get to the truth. There's been no justice for Henry or Charles...until now."

Terrence hung his head and stood up. He hoped that the day would come when Ghost could forgive him for the trauma he had caused and for his final act of revenge against her psychopath of a grandmother. He did not feel an ounce of guilt for killing Juniper White. She got what she deserved. But he did feel sorrow for his innocent niece, who was forced to bear witness to the brutal death of someone she loved.

Clearing the lump in his throat, Terrence continued, "Ghost, there are other lives that she's ended. Your grandmother did something to the crab cakes she left at your house and then went on to personally deliver a second batch to your mother at Glen Haven. Your mother died before Juniper had even left the premises."

Terrence had been keeping tabs on Ghost and Juniper for weeks. It was how he knew the crab cakes Ghost brought to her office had inadvertently caused the death of the CEO. All he had to do now was wait for the lab results. In a few days, the drug tests would link Carl Witt's murder to the death of Juniper's daughter, Meredith.

"Plus, the attempted murder of the neighbors down the street. I was lucky to have gotten turned around on that dead-end street, or I wouldn't have noticed Juniper sitting in the window of that dark house. My gut told me something wasn't right there, so I went back. I arrived just in time to help those poor people, but that delay nearly cost you and Bishop your lives. Again, I am sorry."

A sigh followed by a tiny cough confirmed that Ghost was conscious and listening. She was still curled up on the floor, but her hands no longer covered her ears.

"Which part are you sorry for?" Her voice sounded ragged as she unfurled and sat up. When Ghost looked at Terrence, he saw the hurt swimming in her eyes.

"I'm sorry for the pain I've caused," Terrence said, turning away.

He was headed for the front door when he was cut off by two uniformed officers and an EMT wheeling in a gurney. Another paramedic was tending to Bishop, who was propped up at the bottom of the stairs, shirtless, with a large bandage over his shoulder.

"Are you also sorry for deceiving me? How about spying, stalking, and the invasion of privacy? Are you sorry for any of that?" Ghost called out.

Terrence heard the patter of bare feet on the hardwood floor behind him. Everyone in the house was now looking his way.

"For weeks, you ran around in the same goddamned suit!" she yelled. "I thought I was going insane! Do you regret that, too?"

Ghost's slender fingers wrapped around his elbow and pulled with such force he nearly yelped. "Was it worth it? Taking my grandmother down, splattering her brains all over her dining room wall. Did it make you feel good?"

Terrence was reluctant to turn around. Ghost was in a state of grief and unable to process the facts he had given, but then she shoved him hard enough that he had to take a few steps to keep himself from falling. When he finally turned around, he was stricken by the sight of her tears, wild hair, and trembling limbs. She was a beautiful woman, completely destroyed. But no matter what she said to him now, Terrence knew he had done the right thing. Maybe one day she would recognize it.

"My mother's dead! Both of my parents were killed because of *you*! I wouldn't have asked to meet her if you hadn't shown up! My mother would still be alive. This is all your fault! You weren't seeking justice for my grandfather or your brother. You just wanted to be right! Your need—no—your *greed* to prove a point cost people their lives. I know *now* that Grandma June was not a good person, but don't you dare think even for a second that you're any better than her!"

When Ghost raised a hand to strike him, he grabbed her arm and held it tight. Physically, she was nearly a younger image of Juniper White, but at that moment, with her furrowed brow and that fierce look of determination, she was all Riggie.

"I don't begrudge you your anger. The measures I used were unconventional and drastic. And I do regret the lives that were lost. But how many more would have died by *her* hands when things didn't go *her* way? Juniper was a psychopath and a serial killer. I had to put a stop to her. You might never forgive me. But never forget that *you* are alive because of me. *Bishop* is alive because of me. You really should be thanking me."

"Oh yes, I'm sure the day will come when I'll thank you for destroying my life," Ghost announced before jerking her arm out of his grasp. She refused to back down, even when it was apparent she had lost. Terrence fought back tears as memories of his brother flooded his thoughts. Ghost was so much like her father. Terrence only wished he had seen it sooner.

"Hey, TJ, we've got stuff to do here... You need to surrender your weapon."

Somehow, Officer Malcolm Watson had come to stand between Terrence and his niece without Terrence even noticing, which seemed impossible given Malcolm's size. The man was bigger than most NFL linebackers.

"Ms. White, you've been through a lot this evening. But I want you to know everything will be handled by the letter of the law from here on out."

Malcolm punctuated his statement by giving Terrence a stern side eye. He then placed his mitt-sized hand on Ghost's shoulder. "I thought you would like to know that Mr. Mazzeo is doing okay. They're loading him up for transport now. Would you like to ride with him to the hospital? I can have an officer meet you there to take your statement."

Ghost never took her eyes off Terrence, but she did give Malcolm a slight nod. The only sign that she was paying attention.

"Ms. White, your name is on the deed to this house, correct?"

Ghost nodded but did not blink.

"Is it okay if we conduct a search of the property? Things would go much faster if I had your permission to do this now."

"Sure, you have my permission. Do whatever needs to be done." Ghost closed her eyes and walked past her uncle and out the front door, without a word or a second glance.

Terrence removed his revolver from its holster and presented it to Officer Watson for processing. Malcolm was a long-time friend and confidant and the only cop in the state Terrence still trusted. Malcolm was the only reason the cavalry came when Terrence placed the emergency call from the house on Kilmer Street.

The witch hunt he had been ridiculed for had finally come to an end.

# Chapter Fifty-Three

## Ghost

Hospitals always turned my stomach, not due to the smell, though the combination of bodily fluids and bleach was unpleasant. I hated hospitals for the reminder of death. The inside of an ER was evidence of human frailty, a chaotic display of how quickly a life could be stolen. After coming so close to my own death, and having seen both Bishop and my grandmother shot, it was the last place I wanted to be. But for the last ten hours, I had been sitting in an uncomfortable chair next to a mostly unconscious man while listening to the beeps and blips of the machines monitoring his life. A life that was nearly lost. Whenever I closed my eyes in search of a moment of peace, a barrage of images flooded my mind: the tumbler smashing against Grandma June's skull, Bishop on the floor holding his bleeding shoulder, Terrence Riggie pulling the trigger, my grandmother's head exploding.

There was no way to escape it—not that I would find sleep with the steady stream of intrusions. Some were necessary, like the nurses and doctors checking vitals and updating charts. Others, such as officers and detectives, were draining and basically useless. Two different men came in at separate times to rattle off a list of identical questions. My responses were precisely the same, though neither of them was informed enough to answer any questions for me.

I wanted to know about their search at the lake house. Had the body of my father been discovered? Did they find the evidence to link my grandmother to my grandfather's death, the evidence Charles Riggie had claimed was hidden somewhere in the house?

What else would they uncover in Grandma June's gigantic house of horrors?

I was staring at a blank white wall, trying to make my mind just as empty, when the screech of a door and an earthy aroma aroused my senses. Heavy footsteps approached, and then I felt warmth next to my face. A dark-skinned hand was holding a steaming cup under my nose. Graciously I accepted the coffee and drank deeply despite my aversion to hot liquids. It tasted rich and a bit like dirt, but what did that matter? I needed the caffeine.

"How's he doing?" Officer Watson asked as he slurped from his cup.

"It wasn't as bad as it looked. Doctor says he'll be discharged tomorrow."

A bullet grazing the shoulder was far better than a bullet through the heart. If I had not hit Grandma June when I did...I might have stopped my grandmother from killing Bishop, but he had been the one to place the 911 call and then left his phone on speaker on the stairs. The most damning parts of my conversation with Grandma June were recorded. How long until her admissions of guilt was spewed all over the airwaves?

"That's good news." Officer Watson pressed his meaty hand down on my shoulder. "How are you holding up?" he asked with a reassuring pat.

I eyed the time on his large-faced watch. It was late afternoon, and I had not slept or eaten since yesterday or maybe the day before. "Dunno, I'm exhausted."

"Understandably. Why don't I drive you home? We have a few things to discuss, and then you can get some much-needed rest."

Bishop's eyelids fluttered as his legs jerked beneath the thin hospital blanket. The sound of our voices was breaking through his drug-induced slumber. Before the second dose of morphine hit his system, he had begged me not to leave. He even tried pulling me up on the bed to lie next to him. Bishop did not want to be left alone, but what good would I be to him if I could barely stand?

"Okay, just give us a minute."

With a stiff nod and another swig of coffee, Officer Watson exited the room.

"Wait, you're leaving?" Bishop sounded like he was talking through a mouthful of sand.

I got up and poured him a glass of water from the pitcher on the bedside table. When he had finished drinking, he reached out with his good arm.

I took his hand and clutched it to my chest.

"Your parents will be here soon. I need a shower and some sleep." I also did not want to be in the room when his family arrived. My brief conversation on the phone with them had an underlying current of blame. I could not fault them. Bishop and I were barely a couple, and my grandmother tried to murder him. My actions may have saved his life, which might earn me good favor down the road, but it would not be any time soon.

Bishop flexed his fingers as he grabbed a hold of my sweatshirt and pulled me closer. "It's not a good idea. We almost died. She would have killed us both—"

"But she didn't."

"Yeah, because of—you."

The hitch of emotion in his voice had me swiping at an unexpected tear. I perched my hip on the side of the narrow bed and gently leaned against his uninjured shoulder. "Because of us."

I might have been the one to knock my grandmother down, but Bishop was the reason help had arrived so quickly. "She's gone. There's nothing left to worry about."

He wrapped an arm around me and held on as tight as he could, then planted a firm kiss on the top of my head. "You know that's not true," he said.

When I pulled away, there was an exorbitant amount of worry in his sleepy eyes.

"My sister will stay with you, just for the night," he said. "You shouldn't be alone right now." When he started to reach for his phone, I stopped him.

"No. I won't be able to sleep with a stranger in my house."

"She wouldn't be a stranger for long," he said, inching his hand closer to mine.

"I've got this."

"We came so close to losing each other. I won't lose you, Ghost. Not today, not ever. I love you too damn much," he said, sliding his pinky finger around mine.

"I love you, too." I squeezed his finger before letting go. "See you in the morning."

OFFICER WATSON ESCORTED me to a side entrance of the hospital, where his police cruiser was parked illegally against the curb. As we approached the exit, he reached around me to open the door. Raindrops from an earlier shower still clung to the outside glass, glistening under the rays of light breaking through the clouds. I was ready to feel the warmth of that sun on my skin. Only when I stepped outside it was a cruel blast of arctic air that greeted me.

I was heading for the back of the vehicle when Officer Watson signaled that I should sit up front and then opened the passenger-side door.

"I didn't think it was allowed," I said, bending over to remove a manila folder on the seat.

"You're not under arrest, Ms. White. Besides, there's no partition in this vehicle." Officer Watson waved the folder away when I tried to hand it to him. "That's for you."

"Please call me Ghost," I said before pulling the shoulder strap over and fastening the seatbelt across my lap.

Once in the driver's seat, Officer Watson started the car, turned the heat on high, buckled his seatbelt, and checked his mirrors. I kept my eyes on the grimy windshield as he pulled away from the curb, all the while sliding my fingers back and forth along the thick edge of the folder. I did not stop until a streak of blood marred the smooth, flat surface.

"So, what's in the folder?" I did not think it would be wise to open it until I knew what was inside.

"Something my wife insisted on."

*Wife?*

Officer Watson must have glanced over and seen the questioning look on my face because he quickly continued. "A couple of things you should know. First, my wife is Zelda Watson. She's been a nurse at Glen Haven for many years and wanted you to have the last of your mother's letters."

Watson was such a common surname. I never gave it a second thought. I was not in the mindset where I could have made the connection anyway.

I eased the folder open to take a peek. Just enough to see a piece of folded blue construction paper with hand-drawn red hearts. It was addressed to My Dead Baby Girl. I shut the folder and pressed hard on my lap to keep it from reopening.

"Meredith was always her favorite patient. Zelda would like to sit down with you and tell you about their time together, when you're ready."

There was no way of knowing if I would ever be ready to hear someone else's stories about my mother. I listened to my grandmother's for so long, and look where that got us?

"Tell her I said thank you." It was a polite thing to say.

After adjusting his grip on the steering wheel, Officer Watson's knuckles whitened. The firm line that settled in his square jaw surely meant he was about to say something else that I did not want to hear.

"Last night, you were very vocal about TJ's pursuit and interference. Most of the time, he's a standup guy, but his heart tends to rule his head. Who can blame him? He's been searching for his brother for more than twenty years." Officer Watson glanced over and raised one caterpillar-sized eyebrow.

According to Grandma June, money had been Terrence Riggie's motivator. What if it still was? What if he and Malcolm were in on it together?

"The DA will contact you to see if you want to press charges. It's considered unethical for a private investigator to stalk, harass, or infringe on someone's privacy, as it's been known to cause significant psychological distress."

Funny, I thought those were the very things that PIs were known for—stalking, harassing, or, in Terrence's case, ruining people's lives by making them think they were crazy.

"TJ's investigator's license will be suspended, possibly revoked, which is quite a harsh punishment. However, if you press charges, one of your remaining family members could do jail time. Your Uncle TJ wants to see you and explain more. It might help you understand why he did what he did."

I would never be able to call him *Uncle TJ*. He would forever and always be Terrence, the hatted man, to me.

A buzzing insect zipped by my head as it swooped through the car's interior. I swatted at it but did not make contact.

"I wrote his number down inside the folder. I hope you'll give him a call," Officer Watson said as he slowed and then turned left onto my street.

I had liked Zelda Watson from the instant I met her at Glen Haven. She came across as genuine and sincere. I could not say the same for her husband, Malcolm. Last night at the lake house, it was obvious that he and Terrence were familiar with one another. They had to be good friends, because why else would we be having this conversation?

Terrence could be the long-lost uncle with good intentions. Seeking justice for his family was a commendable act. Terrence Riggie and Grandma June had agreed on one thing: my grandmother had ruined his life. And now, because of Terrence and what he did, I was about to inherit a fortune—the same fortune, I was told, he tried to acquire once before.

I took another swipe at the annoying buzzing insect as Officer Watson pulled into my driveway. When he parked, I unlatched my seatbelt and exited the car.

"I'll give it some thought. Oh, and thanks for the ride," I said, closing the car door.

# Chapter Fifty-Four

# Ghost

**B**uzzing jolted me awake. For the last week, that annoying insect from Officer Watson's car had somehow taken up residence inside my house. It liked to buzz by my head in the early mornings and late at night, as if coming by to say hello and goodnight. But the noise was constant this time, as if the bug had perched upon my shoulder. I looked at my nightstand to see the time and quickly realized the buzzing was not from the flying insect but rather from an old-fashioned alarm clock.

*How is it already 7:00 a.m.?*

It felt as if I had just laid my head on the pillow.

I slapped the off button and rolled on my side, hoping to catch a few more minutes of sleep, when a warm hand moved against my lower stomach and inched slowly up to tease my breast. Nuzzling into my neck, Bishop placed delicate kisses from my ear to my shoulder and over the old scars on my back.

He had been with me every minute of every day since *it* happened. Part of me wanted to embrace our new love for each other. Our shared trauma forged a strong bond. Bishop had an iron grasp on it—on us. It was clear that he would never let go. At the same time, my grip slipped a little more each day despite having genuine feelings for him.

I grabbed his wandering hand. "Stop."

He stilled a moment, but then his hand and lips continued.

"Bishop, stop!" I pushed him off and got out of bed.

*Buzzz...* I glanced around the room, still not seeing that damn bug.

"What's wrong?"

I heard no anger in his voice, but there was a flicker of darkness in his narrowed gaze.

"I can't do this. Not—I need to get ready." Just when I had found my voice, I caved to domestic civility and took the coward's way out. He had to understand. Today was my grandmother's funeral.

Running a hand through his bedraggled hair, the darkness I saw earlier in his eyes vanished. "It's okay, Ghost. I understand." He slipped from the bed and walked over. Our nudity left me feeling vulnerable, while he appeared all-powerful, even with a bandaged shoulder.

"Actually, I don't understand," he added. "How can I? I've never lost anyone, not the way you have."

*Buzzz... Goddamn that bug!*

I went to grab my robe from the hook on the bathroom door when Bishop blocked me. His eyes roamed, taking in the sight of my naked body and landing everywhere except my face.

"I don't know what I'd do or how I'd react to losing any family member like that. It's awful. You have no one left."

Bishop's words were more condescending than comforting. He portrayed me as weak and pathetic. And maybe I was both of those things—in his eyes. I reached around and plucked my robe from the hook on the bathroom door.

Licking his lips, he finally looked me in the face. "But I want to remedy that."

I had one arm in the robe when Bishop took hold of the terry cloth and used it to pull me against his chest. His heart was racing. So was mine.

He kissed my forehead. "I know it's soon...but almost losing you was a sharp kick in the nuts. You're the one, Ghost. I want you with me always. You lost one family, but you're gaining another. I hope very soon, everyone will call you Mrs. Mazzeo."

The moment he said it, I felt sick. He had terrible timing, and it was the worst semi-proposal I had ever heard. Succumbing to the rush of nausea, I broke free and fled to the bathroom. Closing the door, I flipped the lock and vomited bile into the toilet.

WHEN I CAME OUT OF the bathroom forty-five minutes later, showered and presentable for the day, Bishop was gone. A sleek black dress had been laid out on the bed with a note.

*Always thinking of you. I went home to change.*

*My family is coming to pay their respects. I can't wait for you to meet them.*

*Forever, Bishop*

He had invited his family! And they were coming to the funeral. My grandmother tried to kill him.

I picked up the dress, stunned by the sheer audacity. Soft and sleek, with an expensive price tag. Other than the color, the dress was not suitable for funeral attire. It screamed of first impressions. Was Bishop dressing me up to impress his family? Or was it a last "fuck you" to Grandma June?

It struck me as odd. Then again, my ability to ascertain someone's true intent was on the fritz. Perhaps it was normal, common courtesy for everyone to pay their respects to a former pillar of the community. Grandma June had done some good with her money over the years. And what was wrong with my boyfriend providing a bit of pretty armor on the day his girlfriend would be viciously scrutinized?

Tearing off the price tag, I slipped the dress on. It was a perfect fit.

I had one errand to run before heading to the church: a single favor for the man who had changed my life forever, though not all of it in a good way.

It took me less than a day to reconsider my feelings for Terrence. Once my anger subsided, I became much more reasonable and accepting of his explanations. The day Bishop was released from the hospital, I got together with him and nurse Zelda—two birds, one stone—at a local diner, where we sat and talked for hours.

Terrence told me about the actions that had led to his brother's death, how Terrence had been so hell-bent on revenge that he had coaxed his little brother into using his position at Glen Haven to get close to Meredith, the daughter of his greatest adversary. Terrence claimed that if he had known that Charles would fall in love with the young woman, he would never have gotten his brother involved. It was not until the end of our meeting that Terrence finally admitted that he was the reason my father and I never got the chance to meet. His pursuit and feud with Grandma June had turned her against the entire Riggie family.

Terrence said the truth he had refused to accept then was now an enormous regret that he would carry to his grave.

His story was sad, but my heartstrings had toughened. I was not sure I truly believed him. Still, I owed him my life. If not for Terrence Riggie, it was unlikely that Bishop or I would be alive today. Then again, if he had not appeared determined to discover the truth about Henry White's death and his brother's disappearance, none of it would have happened in the first place.

Terrence had gotten the answers he was looking for while I still searched for mine.

# Chapter Fifty-Five

# Ghost

The hectic days of lawyer meetings, police interviews, and press conferences had been winding down just in time for an overpublicized funeral. Headlines like "The Rise and Fall of the Frugal Philanthropist" had my phone ringing off the hook. Each hour, another stranger came knocking at my door. Officials did their best to keep the press and other vultures at bay, but people were relentless. Everyone wanted to talk about what happened. Everyone but me.

I arrived at the lake house with an hour to spare. To my delight, no cars had followed me, and there were no sleazy reporters hidden in bushes ready to ambush. *They'll all be waiting for me at the church.* I parked next to my grandmother's cherry-red Challenger and got out. The sole purpose for coming was to retrieve that vehicle. When Terrence's old Honda broke down yesterday, I offered to loan him the car until it was repaired.

Actually, I planned on giving Grandma June's car to him. I had no use for it.

This was my first time back since *that* night. My eyes were drawn to the partially dismantled boatshed and the tall mounds of dirt next to two holes in the earth. My father had been there the whole time. As a child, I'd played by his gravesite. I shared my first kiss while standing over his corpse. But his was not the only body police found that day. Another skeleton was buried nearby, just on the other side of the shed, beneath my grandmother's rose garden. Personal items found with the body identified him as Bradley Evans, the boy who tormented me one school year and then later disappeared. For a while, I thought my stunt with the cellar had scared him bad enough that he ran away. But now, I knew my grandmother must have seen what happened and took it upon herself to eliminate the problem. *Poor Brad.*

I caught myself moving toward the empty graves and quickly redirected to the stone path that led up to the house. Remnants of yellow tape still clung to both sides of the front door, flapping gently in the cool autumn breeze.

The first thing I noticed when I stepped inside the house was the smell—an odd mixture of smoke residue, a hint of rust, and something else I could not quite place. I chose not to think about it and made my way upstairs. The creepy Victorian and all its contents now belonged to me, though I had no clue what to do with any of it.

*Bed-and-Breakfast? Haunted Ghost Tours?*

The house was too big for one person. Bishop believed we would marry soon. And if I had to bet, with him coming from a tight-knit family, he would have plans to father children. I was not even sure I wanted kids, for obvious reasons. But we had not been dating long enough to discuss such matters.

Walking into my old room, I sat down on the disheveled bed. Bishop was the last person to sleep in it before crawling out to make an urgent call to the police. I dropped to the floor and lifted the bed skirt. Hidden near the head of the bed was the little metal truck my father had left for me to find. I wondered if that had been the same day my grandmother killed him.

I brushed off a sudden chill, stretched my arm, and slid halfway under the bed to retrieve the toy. Covered in dust and cold to the touch, it had been years since I held it. Sitting back on the bed, I removed my mother's homemade card from my purse to hold a piece of my parents in each hand. I set the truck aside to brush a smudge of dust from my dress and then unfolded the blue card with red, crayoned hearts. My mother had drawn a large rectangle with a smaller square in the center. Inside the square was a skirted stick figure. At first glance, it appeared to depict a woman resting in her grave.

Then I read the words my mother had written underneath: *Every night the demon lies her head upon buried secrets.*

My initial thoughts went to the suitcase of letters my grandmother had stored under her bed, but then I recalled what Grandma June said about my father: *"He wanted to rip up the floorboards."*

THE KING-SIZED OAK poster bed in Grandma June's room was too heavy to move by myself. I nearly ripped my dress, dragging the empty suitcase out of the way. The police had notified me that each disturbing letter my mother wrote would be returned. But for whatever reason, they left the giant suitcase behind. Not that any of that mattered. Right now, I had to satisfy a niggling feeling in the back of my brain. A little tickle that told me to look deeper. Using the light on my phone, I examined the floorboards under the bed and discovered unnatural gaps in several seams.

To keep from destroying my new dress, I slipped it off and pulled a blanket from the bed to help me slide underneath. Thankfully, the bed was high enough for me to pluck the loose boards up and remove the towel-wrapped bundle hidden beneath the floor. Carefully, I pulled the edge of the towel away. It was a broken oar with a large crack in the wood. Old stains—likely blood—had soaked through and turned areas of the paddle black. Thin wisps of brown hair were still visible in the dried, matted substance.

I thought about calling the police for a proper chain of custody until I remembered an official court case would not occur. This was one man's mission to reveal the truth and prove himself right. I snapped a picture of the hiding spot and then one of the broken oar.

After slipping back into the dress, I texted Terrence and Malcolm the pictures.

*I believe this might be what you're looking for. I'll bring it with me.*

As I headed out of my grandmother's bedroom, I noticed the lock on the attic door was gone. The police had stopped their thorough search of the place once they got that door open. The attic contained some horrors my adolescent mind had conjured over the years. Grandma June was using it as a trophy room. Malcolm sent a list of what they had found up there, possible evidence that may help close more than one cold case, but I had yet to sit down and read it.

I locked up the lake house and headed down the stone path. When I popped the trunk of my grandmother's car to place the toy truck and the broken oar inside, I found a bulging tactical bag filled most of the space. I was hesitant to open the bag at first. But the odds that my grandmother made a bomb and stashed it in her car were pretty low. She preferred to get up close and personal. She was the type of killer who wanted to watch the light go out in her victim's eyes.

*Yeah, there's no chance this will blow up, but that doesn't mean it's not full of human skulls.*

I had the bag opened halfway when the zipper got stuck on a wad of cash. After a bit of finagling, I unzipped it all the way. This was a bug-out bag. Only it was not in case of a natural disaster. The bag contained everything Grandma June needed to disappear. And she had packed it for the both of us. Passports. Money. Offshore bank records. A list of supplies to purchase and the name and address of a boat captain in Florida. By the looks of it, she knew that amount of cash would not make it through airport security, so she had planned to charter a boat to the Caribbean.

How did she get my passport? Why pack it if she was going to kill me?

# Chapter Fifty-Six

# Ghost

I pulled my grandmother's car into the bustling parking lot of the community church and immediately wanted to turn around. Though no official funeral announcements were made, I knew the pews would be packed with unfamiliar faces. It was no real surprise, given who my grandmother was and the way she had died. Not to mention the growing list of crimes now coming to light. Thankfully, the church had "reserved" several spaces for family, or else I never would have found an empty spot.

Local news stations had vans parked on and around the church grounds. A handful of reporters stood by, anxiously waiting to jump on any attendee willing to speak with them. A common nuisance I had learned to ignore. Over the last few days, there had also been an abundance of people with their hands out asking for donations and charitable contributions. Some had the next big investment opportunity I had to be a fool not to put my newfound wealth into. My inbox was inundated with unsolicited links to FundMe pages. Each pleading their case as to why they deserved a piece of my grandmother's fortune. It was overwhelming.

Another car parked next to mine in the last remaining space. Zelda Watson and her husband, Malcolm, had given Terrence a ride. They reminded me of circus clowns in a tiny car as they quickly piled out of theirs and then surrounded my car to shield me from curious onlookers.

Fear kept me from stepping out as static filled my head. Two words broke through the noise when I tried to rationalize the feeling: "unprepared and inept." The stern voice that spoke those words sounded a lot like Grandma June.

A rap at the window and a glance around alerted me that I was out of time. The encroaching masses were about to converge on the car. I grabbed the tightly wrapped bundle from the passenger seat and jumped out of the vehicle. With Malcolm on my left, Terrence on the right, and Zelda following close behind, we darted for the side door Bishop now held open.

Once we crossed the threshold into what looked to be the church's daycare center, my grandmother's pastor came around and barred the door, even as knocking sounded from the other side. Worry seemed to drip from his pores, no doubt caused by the mob descending upon his house of worship.

"We will start the service in ten minutes. The first two pews have been kept open for you. Please come out when you hear the organ music and not before," Pastor Denton said, dabbing the sweat on his forehead.

As soon as the pastor exited the room, there was an explosion of voices. Multiple conversations erupted at once. I pushed aside the uproar to focus on four new faces huddled near a corner bookshelf.

Bishop's family was already here.

An older, impeccably dressed couple stood stiffly by their adult children. The *too-perfect* family appeared to have been perusing the children's books before my arrival. Now, all eyes were on me. Bishop and his brother had inherited their father's striking features and imposing stature, whereas his mother and sister were gentler in appearance. Both were fair, though they shared little resemblance.

Bishop lingered off to the side, steadily watching me as I watched them. His broad smile grew, deepening his left dimple, and then his father gave a subtle nod in our direction. As if reacting to a signal, Bishop took a step to close the short distance between us just as Terrence and Malcolm swept in front of him.

Terrence removed the wrapped evidence from my trembling arms. "Where did you find it?" he asked as he lifted the edges of the towel to examine the broken paddle. "Did you touch the wood?"

"It was under her bed, hidden beneath the floorboards. I only handled it through the towel. Hopefully, it will lead you to that final answer."

How Henry White really died.

Holding a piece of deadly history, still caked in what could be my grandfather's blood—and perhaps my father's, too—should have been the reason for my increasing unease. But the restlessness winding its way through my nervous system had more to do with the bold family shooing everyone aside.

Deep in the pit of my stomach, distrust brewed while Bishop began his introductions.

"Ghost, this is my father, Roberto, and my mother, Nora," Bishop announced as his father's hand clasped over mine and pulled me into an unwelcomed embrace.

"My condolences for your loss," Mr. Mazzeo gritted into my ear.

I felt another's light touch on my shoulder, and Roberto Mazzeo turned me to face his wife. Nora placed a kiss on each of my cheeks. Her pale, painted lips barely grazed my skin.

"It's very nice to *finally* meet you, though not under these unfortunate and tragic circumstances." Nora Mazzeo's voice cracked. "Thank you for saving our son."

His parents' tight but pleasant smiles looked well-rehearsed. Nora leaned into her husband as his thick arm snaked around her thin waist. I felt Bishop's arm mimic their movements as he held on to me. When I looked up, Bishop smiled with an expression so possessive it turned my blood to ice. Then, his mother whispered words that set my paranoia ablaze. "Truly a vision of joyous perfection."

Partially stunned by the words I was not meant to hear, I almost missed Bishop's introduction of his younger brother, Navid. That was until his brother took hold of my hand to offer his sympathies as his tongue slowly rolled over his bottom lip. Bishop playfully elbowed his brother while I jerked my hand away, rubbing the itch that Navid's touch left behind.

Another heartfelt "sorry for your loss" followed from Bishop's sister. Florina wrapped me in a quick hug before confirming that my fears were not imagined. "You are so much prettier than your picture."

Grandma June was right! She had been right about Terrence's financial troubles. And she had been right about Bishop.

*"When am I ever wrong, deary?"*

No one noticed my sudden alarm or that I had not verbally responded to a single introduction that had been made. The Mazzeo family was standing in a straight line, shoulder to shoulder, staring at me. Trapped by their fixed gaze, my feet grew hot. I wrung my hands, anxious to move out of their line of sight, but was unsure how and where to excuse myself.

Then big, toothy smiles emerged. First, on Bishop's father, a grin cracked wide until his bottom lip split. Bishop's mother was next to smile, followed by his brother and sister. Their smiles were so broad that the delicate skin around the corners of their mouths tore. I could feel a scream bubbling in my throat as those four vicious mouths leaped from their faces. They floated and danced around the room before finally gathering in the corner just behind the Mazzeo family's mouthless, unmoving bodies. The mouths continued to drift upward until they touched the ceiling. From there, they pressed their serrated lips together and began to make an all too familiar buzzing sound. When I finally got the nerve to look away from the mouths now wide open with laughter, I saw Zelda and her husband Malcolm exchanging pleasantries with the Mazzeos.

*When did the mouths return to their faces? How did no one else see this?*

I was scanning the room again for the detached wayward mouths when I saw Bishop and Terrence patting each other on the back. They, too, were smiling. Though their mouths looked more humorous, even goofy. I had missed whatever inside joke they shared.

*It's a trick! And they're all in on it!*

The sound of organ music hushed everyone in the room. It was time.

As everyone filed out one by one, I hung back, feeling characteristically like an outsider at my grandmother's funeral. Through the open door, I could see the packed church, not an empty seat except for the two rows that were about to be filled by Bishop's *family*.

Bishop held the door, silently imploring me to step into the chapel. Only my feet refused to budge. A single thought raced through my head: *I don't want to be here.*

*I don't have to be here.*

A tickle at the base of my skull fluttered around my ears to deliver a message from beyond the grave.

*"Deary, thanks to me, you have everything you need. Now go."*

Holding up a finger to the waiting pastor, Bishop closed the door. "Ghost, are you okay?" His hands were all over me. "Do you need more time?" The dark, hazel eyes that trailed his greedy hands were even more intrusive.

When I did not respond, he pulled me to his chest, smothering me in the scent of linen and spice. "It's going to be okay. I love you. My family adores you. We're going to be so incredibly happy."

I wanted to believe him, but I did not—not for a second. No matter how strong my feelings were for Bishop, I knew I could not be with him. I would not end up as another cautionary tale by jumping from one dysfunctional relationship to another. My grandmother had controlled—owned—me my entire life. I would not allow Bishop to do the same.

When the organ music stopped, Bishop pulled away. "You got this," he said, reaching for the doorknob.

"You go ahead. I still need a minute."

"Are you sure? I can wait with you."

"I'm sure. I'll see you out there," I said, popping up to my toes to kiss him goodbye.

"Goddamn it, Ghost. You look amazing in that dress."

Once Bishop left, I darted across the room, unbarred the side door, rushed to my grandmother's Challenger, and slid into the driver's seat. I had just freed myself from the clutches of one master manipulator. I would not risk falling into the strong arms of another.

It was possible Bishop was not that guy. But I had to listen to my gut and the voice in my head telling me to get out of there. I was not in the right headspace to debate anything right now.

I only knew for certain that I was the only one I could trust.

The car started with a low rumble, announcing my departure. I backed out of the parking space and drove past rows of parked cars. A man with a heavy black camera stood beside a local news van near the exit. He turned the camera lens, capturing the moment I sped away from the church.

Reaching the highway, I pointed the car south. My grandmother had seen to it that I had everything I would ever need.

"Thank you, Grandma June."

*"You're welcome, Gigi."*

When I checked the rearview mirror to see if anyone was following me, I saw Grandma June perched on the backseat. The same head I saw spattered across the dining room wall of the lake house was fully intact as she sipped one of her infamous herbal brews from a cracked, rose-painted teacup.

~ THE END ~

# Acknowledgments

A MONSTROUS THANK YOU to everyone who played a pivotal role in unleashing this story upon the world! The Writerly Whatnots—Desiree Smith-Daughety, Ellen Smith, and Missy Hodges—are my fierce critics and invaluable sources of feedback. To Andrea Hurst—Developmental Editor—who helped me transform *A Girl Named Ghost* from women's fiction into a psychological thriller that will hopefully haunt readers' minds for years to come. Sarah Hansen of Okay Creations deserves a special mention for her stunning cover design, carved with precision and care. Not forgetting the gracious innkeepers Chris and Sharon at Georges on York in Taneytown for hosting my writers' retreats and providing the cozy haven where a significant portion of this book was written. Last but not least, my eternal gratitude goes out to my husband, Greg, for his unyielding love, patience, and unwavering support. I also want to thank my dear friends and family for always standing by me. Your presence is a constant source of strength and inspiration.

S. R. Webster A Girl Named Ghost

# About the Author

S. R. Webster has previously published works under the name Sandra R. Campbell, including paranormal thrillers *Butterfly Harvest*, *Dark Migration*, and *The Dead Days Journal*. Several of her short stories have appeared in Suspense magazine and various horror anthologies. Notably, Chilling Entertainment produced her short story *Abandoned* for the Simply Scary podcast.

After a brief hiatus, S. R. Webster is back, ready to unleash a new wave of monsters and genre-bending mayhem. A *Girl Named Ghost* is her first psychological thriller. She is a member of the Horror Writers Association and the director of an M.W.A. critique group.

Read more at srwebsterauthor.com.